M.J. FLEMING

My Only Sunshine

She escaped, but is she free?

First edition

ISBN: 9781093703634

Cover art by Erica Goldberg
Editing by Carl Smith

This book was professionally typeset on Reedsy.
Find out more at reedsy.com

This book wouldn't have happened without my husband's encouragement. Thank you for believing that I could do this, even when I did not.

Please leave a review on Amazon, as an independent author I rely on my readers' reviews and word of mouth.

Thank you for taking the time to follow Taylor on her journey.

Contents

I

Part One

Chapter 1

I t was just before sunrise. Taylor watched as light crept up her bedroom walls forcing the shadows back, into their corners. Jet lag begged her to go to sleep, but her mind, as per usual, refused. The anxiety of her life gnawed at the corner of her brain.

After hours of tossing and turning, she admitted defeat and swung her legs over the bed, hoping a run would calm her mind. Suitcases littered the floor, making her best guess which one her sneakers were in, she started digging. Minutes later, amidst a sea of dirty clothes, the 17-year old emerged victorious. The kitchen was dark as she came down the stairs. Rather than turn on the lights, she turned the corner and sat on the bench next to her front door to tighten her laces. Her running stick leaned against the wall to the right; she hadn't had it in California and was happy to feel the weight of it in her hand once more. She flipped open the key pad to the alarm system and punched in the six-digit code temporarily disarming the system so she could get outside before it re-armed itself.

The crisp New England air made her suck in her breath with shock. Slowly she watched it puff out of her lungs, giving herself a minute to adjust. Sometime in late August the morning air would begin to turn noticeably colder; it was a subtle change, fall was coming. She loved the solitude of this time of day. She ran with no ear buds, no phone, nothing to distract her. Running stick in hand she adjusted the can of mace that was strapped to her upper left arm and came down the driveway in long strides, stretching her calf muscles.

At 5'2" Taylor wasn't tall, but her legs were long for her frame and her body well-toned. She ran as often as she could, careful though, to never run on the same days or at the same times. It wasn't curiosity that killed the cat, it was predictability. Starting off at a slow jog, she stretched her neck and shoulders letting her short blond hair brush her skin. Slowly her rhythm built, using the stick in her hand to focus she took a few deep breaths. Her feet were happy to be on their own streets.

The birds chirped incessantly and the squirrels darted back and forth from yard to tree as Taylor approached and passed. She decided to head into the new development that was just behind her house. There were three streets which all circled into one another and the houses for the most part all looked identical; if a stranger to the area, once you got in it could be hard to figure out how to get out. It was however, a perfect three-mile loop if you ran it correctly and her best friend lived back there.

Taylor's feet pounded the streets. In her mind she kept track of the few houses whose lights were on. One car, a silver Audi, passed her, heading for the exit to the development. The man driving was wearing a suit and talking on his cell phone. Up ahead she could see Layla's black Range Rover in her driveway. The house was one of the larger ones in the development and was dark. While, Taylor loved the early morning hours, Layla slept as late as she could whenever possible.

Pushing on, she took a left after Layla's house and ran up a hill, making a serpentine route through the rest of the development before heading back towards home.

The road that led into the development was framed by two houses: one looked new with a perfectly manicured lawn, the other was hers. Set on a large yard the antique colonial was a dull white with no shutters and a wraparound porch that looked as though it would fall apart at any moment. The windows were old and would stick on hot days. It was the only home Taylor had ever known and she loved it. She ran until she reached the driveway before finally stopping. Her breath came out as puffs of smoke. She walked past the front door and continued up the driveway to the back entrance, just off the kitchen.

* * *

His eyes followed her every movement as she rounded the corner from the development back towards her house. He watched her chest heave as she finally came to rest at the base of the driveway. She looked well, he thought. Her time away had obviously agreed with her. Her skin had tanned and her hair was shorter than it had been when she left just over a month ago. He had missed her. From across the street he couldn't see her open the back door, but he knew the house like the back of his hand.

He closed his eyes and imagined her opening the door, enter into the breezeway and kick off her shoes before placing her running stick in the corner and tossing the can of mace into a basket above the coat rack. Saw her head into the kitchen and flip the lights on before going to the fridge for some water. He opened his eyes. The kitchen light shone through the living-room windows which faced the street.

He smiled and sunk deep into the shadows of the morning.

Chapter 2

Taylor took her glass of water and headed towards the stairs. She glanced habitually at the doors, confirming they were locked and the alarm armed. An hour later, freshly showered and dressed in a pair of shorts and tank top, Taylor made a full pot of coffee and sat at the kitchen island waiting for her mother to come home.

An old Jeep Grand Cherokee made a deafening squealing noise as it pulled into the driveway. Moments later Sarah threw her canvas tote bag on the floor by the bench and kicked off her shoes.

"Hey babe."

"Hey Mom," Taylor called back.

"Tell me there's coffee." Sarah's dark brown hair was tied back in a pony tail. The grey at her temples made her look older than she was. Fatigue bled through her mannerisms but her eyes remained bright as she watched her daughter.

Taylor pushed a large mug down the island towards her mother.

"How was the hospital?"

"It was a long night," Sarah said in between sips. "You look cute. What's your plan for the day?"

"I've got to get unpacked and I was going to try and do a few things around the house while you slept. Then hopefully hang out with Layla. I called her yesterday and told her to come down here when she gets up."

"Great," Sarah picked up her coffee and swung herself to the opposite side of the island to start unloading the dishwasher.

Taylor refilled her mug to the very top, kissed her mother on the cheek and headed upstairs to her bedroom.

"I missed you, you know," Sarah called after her.

Taylor's head swung around, "I know, I missed you, too."

Taylor listened to the familiar clink of dishes as she went up the stairs two by two. Her bedroom was at the back of the house with two windows that overlooked the fenced-in yard. Her green walls once covered in posters and pictures of friends were now largely unadorned. Her desk, covered in books and journals, took up the largest area. The cork board above it was covered with papers from last year and college pamphlets. Her bedspread was all white with purple pillows and a purple throw blanket on top. Directly above the bed on the ceiling she had painted the word "breathe."

Two large over-packed suitcases stared at her from the floor. She tackled the one she had dug her running shoes out of first. Tossing clothes in the hamper and personal items up on her dresser, traces of pine and dirt still lingered on everything and made her wish she could go back.

Taylor had two friends in the entire world. One who lived minutes from her home and one, Kristen Greggor, who lived on the other side of the country. Kristen was the type of rich that made the Kardashians look middle class. Her parents owned a retreat in the woods that they went to every year for the month of August, and each time Taylor was invited to join them. Retreat was 'rich' for resort. It was in fact an enormous house with five bedrooms and seven bathrooms. It had two fireplaces, a game room, and its own movie theater, all overlooking a lake. The boat house had everything you could imagine: boats, jet skis and canoes, plus another bathroom, fireplace and two more bedrooms. Kristen and Taylor mostly stayed in the boathouse, coming into the main house only for food or to have movie nights. More importantly, though, it was the only place Taylor didn't jump at every shadow, wince at every noise. Its seclusion offered a sense of peace and calm that she never felt the other forty-eight weeks a year.

Slowly she got through both suitcases, storing away trinkets and notes. Her room had been clean when she left. It was starting to look more like its general state of disaster.

"Haven't even been home for twenty-four hours yet," she sighed, surveying the mess.

Taylor lost track of time, her mind drifting between the last few weeks and the few days left of summer break. The door bell pulled her back to the present. Glancing at the clock, 10 a.m. she smiled, it must be Layla.

She grabbed her now full laundry basket and headed downstairs, dropping the basket at the bottom. Careful to make sure she saw who it was before they saw her, she rounded the corner into the kitchen, and looked out the window before she walked into the entryway. Standing on her porch was an attractive girl her own age with perfectly styled hair and a Swarovski crystal-crusted phone case which bounced as her fingers flew across the surface. Taylor unlocked the dead bolt and punched in the code to the alarm before she opened the door. The phone quickly disappeared and Layla wrapped her friend in the biggest of all bear hugs.

Taylor laughed, "You're squishing me."

Layla giggled, "I missed you."

"I missed you, too; get in here so I can reset this thing before it scares the crap out of the neighbors ... again." Layla stepped in over the threshold and Taylor quickly closed and dead bolted the door before resetting the alarm.

"Hi, Mrs. Cormier."

"Hi Layla. Taylor sweetie, I'm going to go to bed but I'll be up in a few hours."

"Sure Mom, we are just going to hang out around here. I'll see you when you get up."

"Love you," Sarah called out as she turned and headed towards the stairs.

Layla waited for Taylor's mother to be out of earshot. "Can you please get a phone?"

"I don't do phones; not going to start now."

Layla rolled her eyes in annoyance, "And you don't do Facebook or Snapchat or Instagram, I know, but God could you just please get a flip phone like the one my grandmother has? She can at least call 911."

Taylor's mouth turned up slightly and her eyes glanced toward the staircase as Layla's rant continued.

"You have a phone! Seriously? When did this happen? Why didn't you text me?"

"Because I don't text, and nothing about this phone changes that. I have this tool to call the police if I need it."

Taylor walked into the kitchen and poured herself another coffee while filling a new mug for Layla. This argument had gone on for years between the two of them. Neither one having ever admitted defeat.

"You know all those social media sites are just a way for people to see inside your world. You might as well put a sign on your front door that says 'Gone for the day, come on in.'"

"I know, I know," Layla waved her hand being dismissive of what she felt were her friend's crazy precautions. "I'm so excited, can I see it?"

"See what?"

"The phone!"

Taylor couldn't help but smile, Layla could make a rainy day seem like an adventure. "It's upstairs, come on."

The two spent the rest of the morning in Taylor's room talking quietly about the trip and what Layla had been doing with herself. She filled Taylor in on all the latest gossip and the latest rounds of breakups.

It was after lunch when Sarah emerged from her bedroom, her eyes red and hair disheveled. Bed head would have been a kind description. Sarah had heard of people who woke up pretty, she wasn't one of them.

"Oh, good you're up," Taylor said opening her bedroom door. "Can Layla and I go get ice cream at The Barn? I want to check my schedule for next week anyway."

"I don't see why not, just be careful."

Taylor and Layla were halfway down the stairs when Sarah called out, "Who's driving?"

"I am, Mrs. Cormier," Layla answered. "No one wants to get in that death trap Taylor calls a car." The familiar reference to Taylor's car had no sooner exited Layla's mouth than she realized what she had said, and to whom.

"Oh my god, Mrs. Cormier, I'm so sorry, I just meant . . ." Layla's eyes widened, her neck turned crimson, embarrassment creeping to her cheeks. Taylor kept a close eye on her mother's reaction which was, for the most part, even keeled, but sleep deprivation could make her less than understanding.

Mrs. Cormier stood for a few heartbeats, letting Layla stumble over herself before she turned her head and winked at Taylor. Taylor immediately started laughing as did Sarah.

"Oh ha-ha, very funny you two," Layla said, not enjoying being the butt of the joke.

"It's OK," Sarah assured her still smiling. "That car is in rough shape; so is mine for that matter."

"Don't hate on the Stratus," Taylor said coming to her car's defense. "It may look like it hit a few too many branches on the ugly tree but she starts up every morning."

Sarah smiled, "I know darling. Go have fun. When will you be home?"

"Before the sun sets. Thanks Mom, love you."

"Love you too," Sarah called out before heading into the bathroom for a shower.

"Want me to drive us up to your house?" Taylor asked as she closed the door behind Layla.

"Ha – ha, no."

Taylor stayed at the door for just a second longer, waiting to hear the beeping noise the alarm made when it had re-armed itself.

Layla had only known Taylor for two years, but had witnessed first-hand what happened when Taylor didn't feel safe. The last time had been when they'd been doing homework last spring in Taylors' room. They came downstairs to have a snack and the front door was ajar, the alarm not set. Taylor launched into a complete panic, screaming for her mother. She had already started dialing 911 when Mrs. Cormier ran into the house through the front door, her face pale. Her mother had uncharacteristically disarmed the alarm and left the door open while she went to the bottom of the driveway to get the mail.

Taylor sobbed hysterically for hours following.

Layla had been told of Taylor's abduction and knew she was cautious and hyperaware of things like locked doors and alarms. But it wasn't until witnessing her intense panic that she began to appreciate the type of fear she lived with every day of her life.

"Why didn't I drive? It's so hot," Layla complained. The humidity had reached an uncomfortable level, even for Taylor who loved the heat of the summer and was sad that it was coming to an end.

"Want to race up to your house?"

"No I don't want to race. What are we, twelve? Do you see these shoes? I got them at Bloomingdale's in New York City. I barely like to walk in these things much less run."

"Why would you buy a pair of shoes you don't want to walk in?"

"Because they're adorable, and they go amazingly with this outfit."

Layla looked disapprovingly at Taylor's footwear. "Something besides sneakers wouldn't kill you."

The girls would regularly bicker about clothes and shoes, Taylor for the most part thinking they were pointless and Layla constantly trying to convert her friend to things slightly more in style than leggings and tank tops.

"Yeah, yeah," Taylor said with an exaggerated eye roll.

Chapter 3

The center of Templeton looked like the backdrop for prom photographs: a grassy center with a few park benches and a gazebo. Churches dotted the outskirts along with a small smattering of shops and one restaurant. The Barn was a restaurant and ice cream shop, it did the majority of its business from May through September. Taylor was one of the few employees who worked for the owner, Jan, all year long.

It wasn't air-conditioned, but it did have huge ceiling fans which at least pushed the oppressive August air around. In the three weeks since she'd been gone nothing had changed. Mr. Moriarty was still sitting in the corner booth having his tea and reading the paper. There was a manageable line at the ice cream counter and Mario could be seen in the kitchen cooking away.

"Get in line, won't you?" Taylor asked Layla. "I'm going to go in the back and take a look at my schedule."

"Sure."

The back room smelled like fried onion rings, a familiar, comforting scent. Taylor glanced at the notice board which didn't have anything new on it except the schedule.

"Taylor?" A short, heavy-set woman stood in the door. "I didn't expect to see you until sometime next week."

"Hi Jan. I got home late but figured I'd come in for some ice cream with Layla."

Jan's hair was a light brown and gray color. It looked like the perm she got in 1980 never grew out but instead morphed into a permanent poof on top of her head.

"Looking for your schedule? I've got it right here." Jan held out a plain envelope, letting Taylor reach forward to retrieve it.

Taylor opened it, scanning it quickly, always appreciative of Jan's considerateness. "Do you think there is any way I could get next Wednesday off? I thought I had asked for it but maybe I didn't."

Jan's version of paperwork was usually a post it on the wall or a note written on her hand. "Did you? I'll check my desk but try to switch with one of the veterans if you could. It's the first day back to school so I think it will be busy. Need my best team together."

"Yeah, sure," Taylor said disappointed.

"See ya," Jan said absentmindedly as she trudged back into the kitchen to check on an order.

"What's up?" Layla asked as soon as Taylor got back in line, which hadn't looked like it moved at all.

"I've got to work next Wednesday."

"On your birthday? That's ridiculous. Call out."

"I can't."

"Did you tell her it's your birthday?"

"No. I asked for the day off, but she must have lost her note. I should have called her from the camp last week to remind her. It's my fault."

"That sucks though; maybe you can find someone to work for you."

"Maybe," Taylor let the subject drop for now.

Layla in her typical I'm bored with this topic what else is going on started looking around as the line slowly crept forward.

Taylor saw her friend surveying who else was in the restaurant.

"Hmmm," Layla said.

"What?"

"There's a boy in the corner, opposite of that old guy you always wait on."

"Mr. Moriarty," Taylor began to turn her head.

"Don't look," Layla hissed. "I think he's looking at you."

Taylor's anxiety kicked in. "Is he a boy or a man?"

"He's a boy; he could be our age."

Taylor stepped forward in line and waved her hand, dismissing Layla, "Then he's not looking at me."

"He's cute, whoever he is." Layla commented, turning her attention, finally, to what ice cream she was going to get.

Taylor did manage to turn her head as nonchalantly as one can do that type of thing.

The boy smiled at her just before he got up and walked out into the sunlight.

A few minutes later whatever concerns there were of next week and the mysterious boy were being drowned in double chocolate peanut butter ice cream with whipped cream and sprinkles.

* * *

Days later Taylor still hadn't found anyone to cover her shift for her birthday. That wasn't the only thing tormenting her sleep though. The squealing transmission of the Cherokee broke the silence of the morning, promptly at 7 a.m. as Sarah returned from work.

"Why are you up?" Sarah asked, surprised to see Taylor folding the laundry she'd left on the couch the night before.

15

"Couldn't sleep."

"Couldn't sleep since when?" Sarah probed for more detail.

"4 a.m.," Taylor admitted.

"Oh baby, we go through this every year. It's going to be fine. Have you set up an appointment with Dr. Perna yet since you've been back?"

"No," she knew that he wasn't going to be able to help her sleep.

"I thought maybe this year you wouldn't go through this but obviously that's not the case. You shouldn't start your senior year like a zombie. It's not healthy."

"It's not exactly a choice!" Taylor shot back. "I'm sorry," she said instantly regretful. "You know I don't mind going to see him; I was just hoping to get through this on my own."

Taylor's kidnapper wasn't her only concern. Various online conspiracies existed surrounding the abduction, and how she escaped. Some people just gossiped. Others took advantage of the anonymity of the internet and did more than sit behind a keyboard. One year after her escape the police discovered that someone was taking pictures of Taylor and trading them like baseball cards online in various chat rooms. He lived in Maine, just a few hours north of her house. Police found hundreds of pictures, spanning months.

When she was about to turn sixteen the message boards put up a countdown to her birthday, they called it 'Deathteen'. She spent her sweet sixteen barricaded in her house afraid to go outside.

"I know going back to school makes you anxious. I understand that having to be at the same place at the same time is difficult for you, but it's one more year of this and then you will be off to college. New place; new people. This won't always be a part of your life. I promise."

Taylor paced the living room like a caged animal. Her muscles bunched as her fists clenched and unclenched, rhythmically, methodically, compulsively.

Sarah took inventory of her daughter's reaction.

"Why don't I call Dr. Perna's office and set-up something for you, I'm sure he'll be able to make some time for you today."

Taylors stomach tightened into a familiar knot making it hard to breathe.

Sarah smiled as she picked up the phone. "Go and take a nap, you look horrible."

"Ha-ha," Taylor said slowly but was grateful for the dismissal and headed right for the stairs knowing a nap would solve at least one of her problems today. The rest, though, she would need to figure out and soon.

Despite her racing mind, once snuggled into her bed she dropped off to sleep with relative ease.

"Taylor," a soft voice and a gentle touch pulled on the fabric of Taylor's dreams.

Always the same dream. She's sitting on a basement floor as the door opens, light hurts her eyes and she hears boots coming down the stairs. She looks up and something darts past the door. His boots stop in front of her, she wants to look up and see his face but she can't, she can't move. Adrenaline floods her system, she tries to scream, but the sound won't come out. He pushes her down onto the cold dirt floor. Together they chant, *"I love you, Daddy."*

Sarah's voice pulled at Taylor's consciousness again. "Sweetie."

Taylor's eyes flew open, panicked.

"You're fine," her mother assured her.

Taylor's eyes darted around the room for a moment more, verifying her mother's words that she was, in fact, fine.

Taylor clenched her eyes closed, tighter and tighter willing away the images. Blinking a few times, her eyes adjusted to the light.

"Dr. Perna had an appointment this afternoon at four. I figured you would want to go."

"Yeah," Taylor said, shoving her face back into her pillow. "I'm up, I'm up."

"You slept for a long time are you sure you aren't coming down with something?"

Sarah's hand instinctively reached out to Taylor's forehead. Taylor indulged her mother, allowing her cool hand to conduct the quick mother fever test.

"Nah, I'm fine just didn't sleep a lot last night before I decided to get up."

"Let's not make a habit of sleeping all day OK? You'll be staying up all night with me pretty soon."

"I'm going to hop in the shower before I head downtown." Taylor stood and headed to the Jack and Jill bathroom that attached her room to the guest room.

Taylor's parents had always meant for there to be a Jack to their Jill, but a series of miscarriages followed Taylor's birth and after that they never got pregnant again.

Sarah pushed away the errant thought and watched her daughter close the bathroom door behind her.

Chapter 4

D r. Perna's office was modest in all aspects of the word. He had a woman that answered the phones in the mornings, but after lunch he took care of them himself. Wood paneling lined the walls throughout the waiting area and inside his office. The rug was old and worn, but clean. His walls were bare except for his diplomas and one motivational poster with a ballerina on it.

"Heya Taylor. I was beginning to think you didn't want to hang out with me anymore. How was your trip?"

"Hey Dr. Perna," Taylor shuffled into his office and took up a position on the chair opposite his couch.

Dr. Perna's hair was scruffy and always uncombed and unkempt. He was attractive with olive skin, dark hair and blue eyes. Taylor figured he was in his early forties.

"It was good," she said happily. "It's so amazing there. I really love California and it was great to spend some time with Kristen."

"I know I've said this before, but I am really glad that you and Kristen have become friends. It really is so important for people who have been through trauma to have others to talk about it with. In some ways those relationships are more important than any others."

"More important than our relationship?" Taylor said pretending to be shocked.

Dr. Perna smiled, indulging her. "So, what's going on?"

Taylor looked back at him, her face blank. "Can't sleep."

Counseling Taylor had always been a chess match. When she was shuttled in by her father four years ago she had refused to even put her pieces on the board. Instead she spent two whole sessions staring at the poster he had in his office. Saying nothing but taking everything in. Since then she had on occasion opened up, but mostly he felt used by her. He taught her breathing techniques to control her anxiety when it became overwhelming. He talked about her routine, ways that she could go about a normal life without becoming predictable. It was his idea that when she did get a job her schedule should only be given out to her.

Generally, though, he never felt like she was really working on recovering from her trauma. She pushed it away which only exacerbated her severe PTSD; it also didn't allow her to heal her mind. Taylor suffered from dissociative amnesia. There were sections of her abduction that she had blocked out and couldn't remember. From Dr. Perna's understanding these sections were important to the investigation and without this information the case had gone cold. Her guilt in a lot of ways had become psychological bear trap. The pain it inflicted, kept her trapped to her abduction, regardless of her belief that she was free.

"How are the dreams?"

"The same, there's never anything new."

"Let's talk about some memory therapies to help you resolve the dream."

"No."

"Taylor, do you know how telling it is that the only dream

you can remember for the past five years is that single frag-mented memory? If we can unpack that you could regain those memories that are handicapping you. You could truly begin your journey forward."

"NO! How many times do we have to have this conversation? The things I do remember are enough for me to know I don't want to remember anymore. It's been five years! I'm fine, it's a bad dream! Who cares?!"

Dr. Perna retained his composure, despite Taylor's outburst.

"Do you think it's the dream that is keeping you from sleeping or is it the stress of the school year starting again?"

Taylor sighed. She wasn't trying to be antagonistic and she knew that Dr. Perna was trying to help.

"Both. I'm worried about going back so I stay awake thinking about that. And then when I do finally fall asleep he's there and he's coming down the stairs all over again. I don't feel safe when I wake up; it's like I'll never be safe."

"Why do you say that?"

"Because it's true," she said clearly before her voice dropped to a whisper. "It's always been true."

"You know that pedophiles who act on their perversions do not typically maintain that attraction once the child has grown up."

"He isn't just a pedophile," Taylor said whispered. "He's different, I don't remember why but he's different."

And they are never going to catch him, she thought to herself.

"Tell me about the day he took you."

Taylor's eyes lingered on the floor. Dr. Perna insisted talking about that day gave her ownership and control over what happened. He also kept notes to see if she ever added more detail signaling that she might be recovering new memories.

21

"Everyone was going to Shauna's house after school, but I told mom that I would go straight home. My friends were disappointed, but I was excited. James had said he would call me that afternoon."

Taylor's voice continued on as if she was there, but in her mind she was 13 again.

She climbed on the bus and sat down next to her sometimes-friend Jessica. They made small talk as Taylor willed the bus to drive faster. Finally, her driveway came into view.

"Bye," Taylor said and hurriedly headed for the door.

"Hey!" Jessica called. "Your backpack."

"Oh," Taylor's eyes rolled, "thanks!"

"No problem," Jessica said smiling, "I'll see you tomorrow."

"See you tomorrow," Taylor called over her shoulder as she took the three steps down onto her driveway. She swung her backpack around to her front and grabbed the key out of the front pocket. When she got to the door though there was a note taped to the outside..

Change of plans come meet me at the park.

- James

Taylor checked her watch. She promised to call her mother when she got home. That was their deal for her being able to be home alone. She looked to the sky, the clouds were ominous, threatening rain. She read the note again. If she ran, she could meet him and tell him to come back to the house so she could call her mother. She'd tell her the bus was late. Taylor dropped her bag on the porch and took off at a sprint. The wind was starting to pick up, thankfully the park was close. She saw him at the edge of the woods not facing her.

"James," she called out to him. He didn't turn around.

As she got closer she realized that the man standing there wasn't James. She looked around but there was no one else at the park. The man turned and smiled at her.

"Taylor, right? Jacob," he said touching his chest. "We met at the park a few weeks ago remember?"

"Hi."

He smiled again. "Were you meeting someone down here? I lost my dog in the woods and a young man offered to go in there and look for me. Bad knees."

Taylor looked into the woods not seeing anything.

Jacob continued to ramble on about his dog and his knee all the while taking a few steps closer to Taylor.

"Rain's coming," he warned. "Would you see if you could help him out?"

Taylor heard a dog bark and boy's voice yell at the dog.

"James?" she called stepping just over the divide between the park and the woods.

Suddenly a body slammed into her pinning her arms to her sides. A cloth went over her face reeking of pine. She struggled, kicking her legs and flailing her head all the while sucking in the sickly smell.

She started to get dizzy and her body felt sluggish. She struggled like it was the last thing she would do on this earth, finally getting one good kick to Jacob's knee.

He yelped, and the hand temporarily moved away from her face letting her suck in a breath of air until he slammed her onto the ground. Jacob used one hand to push on Taylor's back right between her shoulder blades pinning her down onto the earth. The other clamped over her mouth like a vice grip. Taylor was still kicking her legs and trying to push up with her arms but the cloth on her mouth was doing its job.

Her shirt was damp from the earth and a stick jabbed uncomfortably into her stomach. The edges of her vision blurred and grew dark. Despite the panic which registered in her mind, her body would barely respond until finally it gave up entirely and she fell into a shallow and fitful unconsciousness.

Time is a funny thing to an unconscious person, what seems like minutes could be hours or days.

Before she was even awake she knew her head hurt, and her mouth felt like it had cotton stuck in it. She was confused and unclear why she was so uncomfortable. It took a few more seconds for the terror to register in her mind and her eyes snapped open, nostrils flaring like a caged animal. Adrenalin pumped through her system making her heart race and her muscles springy. She was lying on a dirt floor on her side, her hands tied behind her back; her feet were bound too. A quick tug on the ropes told her that her hands and feet were tied together. Like a hog, she thought. The ground smelled damp like earth and rain. There were fieldstone walls and a ceiling—a basement she slowly registered, a very old basement. She surveyed her body and besides the headache she didn't appear to be hurt, so she tried to roll herself over so she could see the other side of the room. She squirmed and turned, and eventually got herself onto her stomach. Turning her head she saw a hose dribbling water into a pool and an apple placed on the ground. The house was silent above her and so she screamed.

"Help! Someone help me!"

She screamed as loud and as long as she could. She screamed and cried and screamed again until, finally, the sobs overtook her body and she had to stop to breathe. The panic had begun to set in the second she realized where she was, but now it threatened to overtake her. It sat with her in the dark, caressing her cheek while she sobbed. It draped her shoulders while she screamed. She could feel it begin to settle in her chest, like a cancer. Hours had passed, yet there had been no noise, no sign of life except the faint trickle of water from the hose. Slowly she wormed her way over to the water.

She lapped at the pool in the dirt like a dog and tried in vain to find a way to eat the apple. Every time she tried to take a bite it rolled away, mocking her. The rain had stopped and the sun had set long ago. She didn't want to sleep but her head still hurt, and her body was exhausted from straining against the ropes. First in a failed attempt to free herself; then to move her body to the water; finally ending with her chase of the apple around the basement floor. Her throat hurt, and her voice was now barely a whisper. Sleep her body begged, yet panic gripped her. Eventually her mind succumbed to exhaustion and she fell into a light sleep, her body twitching like a fish on a line.

She lay there for two days and no one came for her. She woke. She screamed. She drank. Wrestled with the apple. Screamed again. And slept. Over and over and over again. She was able to measure time only by the sole window in the basement. She knew if it was day or night, but that was all. Occasionally she would hear footsteps above her head but there was never any indication that the person even heard her scream.

She had soiled herself repeatedly. Lying in her own excrement she could feel the shreds of her humanity slipping from her mind. The next time she woke she didn't scream, she just wiggled over to the water and drank her fill. The apple had been eaten some time ago, core and all. Twice more she woke, drank and slept. She started to mark a spot on the dirt floor. She didn't want to lose track of how many days she's been there. Five. It had been five days.

Taylor's eyes slid back into focus on the wood paneling in the office for the first time in what felt like hours. The pains of hunger fresh in her mind.

Dr. Perna studied her face as she came back to herself. He let her do so quietly, she rarely allowed her memories to gain the upper hand, they clearly had that afternoon.

"It was that one word you know: 'Hello.' Such a simple word, you say it, what, twenty times a day? I opened that door and he slipped right in. That was where my path changed from a regular kid, to this. 'Hello,' that was all it took."

"Whose fault was it Taylor?" Dr. Perna prodded.

Taylor paused knowing what she felt and knowing what the correct answer was. "It was his fault," she said in a practiced type of way. "I was just a kid saying hi to someone. I should have been able to do that . . . it was his fault."

Taylor sat quietly for a few minutes more, letting the memories dissolve on their own rather than try to push them away.

As she sat, something occurred to her. "I never told James that Jacob used him to get me to meet him. I think when I got home I thought for a while that James was in on it; that he helped Jacob take me."

"Did you ever tell the police that you thought that," Dr. Perna asked, as he made a note.

James new territory

"No," Taylor said staring off into space. "James would never hurt me, I know that. Jacob knew though; he knew that I liked him and he knew that I would come if I thought it was James asking."

"It's likely he had been watching you for weeks."

"I know."

"Maybe you should tell him," Dr. Perna offered. "Maybe that would help."

Taylor didn't discuss many friends with Dr. Perna. He had no first-hand knowledge that Taylor didn't speak to James, but it seemed likely she wasn't particularly close with him anymore.

The two sat in silence for some time after that. Taylor wasn't sure exactly how long.

Dr. Perna cleared his throat forcing Taylor to look at him.

"Is there anything else you want to talk about?"

The scheduled hour of their session had passed an hour ago.

"No," Taylor said somewhat despondently.

Dr. Perna nodded, "I want you to continue your breathing exercises and I want you to come in with your schedule before school starts so we can work through it and see where it can be altered and adjusted to give you as much flexibility as possible. In the meantime I'm going to give you a prescription for a mild sedative."

Taylor immediately looked alarmed.

"We do this every year. You don't have to take them but having some on hand so you can get some sleep may help you with the transition."

Still Taylor looked alarmed and wary.

"Just fill the script and if you don't use them that's fine."

She nodded.

"Keep up with your running, though no strenuous activity at least an hour before bed or it will keep you up. Stay away from the screens and all that type of stuff; try reading a real book," he said with a smile.

"Your hilarious," she chided him, knowing he was making fun of her generation's inability to do anything without a screen of some sort in front of them. "I'll do my best."

He smiled and rose from his seat, "All right, let's see you back here on Friday at two. Pick up your prescription this afternoon so you have it for tonight, sound good?"

"Yeah sounds good. Thanks Dr. P."

"Anytime Taylor."

Dr. Perna sat down behind his desk almost as soon as Taylor

shut the door behind her. His computer sprang to life while he reviewed his notes from their session. He opened her file and began typing.

Patient remains concerned for her safety.

Sleep disturbances continue but are not uncommon at this time of year. Patient continues to refuse therapies aimed at memory recovery.

Recommend twice-weekly sessions and will monitor behavior for future recommendations.

Chapter 5

Taylor breathed deeply as she descended the stairs and stepped out onto the pavement. The sun had disappeared while she was inside. Dark clouds loomed overhead and the wind was whipping. She heard a distant thunder and hurried to her car, eager to get home. The skies opened up a mile from her house and she had to slow down. She didn't like to be in the rain, and it didn't matter that she was in a car. Heavy rain made her re-live the day he took her. It had taken eighteen months before she could even listen to the rain from inside her secure house. Being out in it still made her edgy and uncomfortable. Like at any minute he would smash in her car window and drag her out by her hair. The children's song 'You Are My Sunshine' filled the car, drowning out the sound of the rain. She was singing before she even realized she was doing it. It comforted her, she didn't know why.

Pulling into her driveway she could see all the house lights on and her mother pacing in front of the window.

Her mother opened the door, "Hey, how was Dr. Perna? Some rain, huh? You OK?"

The questions ran into each other manically.

Taylor could see her mothers favorite family photo clutched in her arms. Sarah had her own demons with rain. Like being told that the dogs couldn't pick up the scent because of the downpours. That the teams were going to have to wait until the rain let up to go back out to look for Taylor, they just couldn't see anything.

All those were nothing though compared to what her daughter had gone through and she could see the tension show in Taylor's shoulders as she tried to shrug it off.

"I'm OK . . . really." Taylors eyes rested on the photograph of her father, clutched in her mothers arms.

"I can't believe it's already been three years since Dad died. Sometimes I wonder what he would say if he could see us. If he'd be proud of me."

Sarah put the picture down, her face grimaced, she hated that her daughter had endured so much pain in her short life.

"I feel him whenever I look at you. You have his strength and his perseverance. You make him proud every day, I know that."

Sarah crossed the space between them in three long strides and opened her arms for the type of hug that teenagers rarely give their parents. The two embraced and Sarah could feel Taylor melt into her body like she used to when she was just a child and a mother's hug could cure all that was wrong with the world.

Tears welled in Sarah's eyes and her breath was heavy. "I love you so much," she whispered in her daughter's hair.

The magic broken, Taylor pulled away, "I love you too, Mom. Go make dinner; I am starving."

Chapter 6

S arah gently pushed Taylor's door open, "come on, darling, get up."

Taylor's body was mostly covered by her bedspread, except her finely toned leg which hung off the edge, almost comically.

Sarah's voice took on an edge, "Taylor."

"I'm up," she grumbled, "I am."

"I'll start the shower for you."

Slowly the comforter transformed into a five-foot tall ghost and slipped off as Taylor trudged past Sarah into the bathroom.

"Thanks Mom," she mumbled and shut the door.

"Happy Birthday, sweetheart," Sarah called out to the closed door.

Twenty minutes later Taylor emerged freshly showered and dressed with a light touch of makeup and perfume. On her eighteenth birthday she had grown into a truly beautiful young woman. Sarah was in awe of the transformation from the child she once was to the woman standing in front of her.

"You look great."

"Is there coffee, please?"

"One step ahead of you," Sarah pushed the cup towards Taylor. The two sipped in silence.

"Do you want your present now or after school?"

Taylor's face broke into a smile, "Now."

Sarah reached into one of the drawers in the kitchen island and pulled out two boxes carefully wrapped in a red ribbon.

"This one first," she pushed the smaller of the two boxes toward her.

Taylor easily tugged the ribbon free and opened the box. Inside a small silver globe for her charm bracelet. Turning it she could see the continents outlined in gold.

"Oh Mom, I love it."

She took off the bracelet on her right wrist and started to thread the new charm on it. Dangling at every angle, shape and color, it was their non-conformity that she loved. Each charm was a little piece of a memory from someone. The most important one from her father. He had given her the bracelet and its first charm when she turned eight.

Her mother knew where her daughter's thoughts would stray as her eyes settled on the teddy bear charm that Richard had picked out for her in the jewelry store.

"It'll be her first real piece of jewelry," he had said to Sarah. *"I want it to remind her of her childhood as she grows older."*

"Now this one," she said as she pushed the larger of the two boxes across the counter.

"Can I wait and open this one tonight before you go to work?" Taylor asked.

"Of course."

"I like the anticipation," Taylor said with a smile. "It's nice to know there will be a surprise when I get home."

The closer she got to the high school the worse the traffic became. Templeton's high school was unique in that it was shaped like Mickey Mouse's head. It made parking look like a

32

game of musical chairs but with teenagers in cars.

Taylor finally pulled into a parking spot and began climbing out of the car. She hit the lock button before absentmindedly shutting the door; it was a millisecond before her car door hitched that she realized her keys were still in the ignition.

"Shit!"

"Good morning to you to," Layla came walking around her range rover and over to Taylor's Dodge Stratus.

"I just locked my keys in the car, Dammit!"

"No one cares," she dismissed Taylor's obvious frustration.

"Can I get a little sympathy, please?"

"That sucks," she said apologetically. "Now focus; it is our first day of our senior year!" Layla squealed. "I'm so excited!"

Despite the car situation, Taylor couldn't help but smile back at Layla. Her mood was infectious.

"What the hell am I going to do about my car," she moaned.

"I'd call AAA for you but we are barely going to make it to homeroom if we don't hurry up. We'll hang out after school and wait for them."

"I can't," Taylor groaned, "I've got to work."

"Blow it off, it's your birthday, you aren't supposed to work on your birthday. Speaking of . . . happy birthday," Layla bellowed in the parking lot. "I have a present for you, but you can't have it yet."

Taylor couldn't help but laugh out loud, "Thank you."

"Don't worry about your car. I'll figure something out and have it to you at The Barn before the end of the night, I promise."

Taylor knew her friend would take care of it; Layla had a way, with just about everything.

The two walked arm in arm across the parking lot and into the building. Winding their way through students and over to their lockers, conveniently located right next to one another. That may or may not have had to do with Layla greasing the school's secretary at the beginning their junior year so the two could have lockers right next to one another, even though they were assigned alphabetically by last name. Taylor had heard later that the secretary had claimed a typo when questioned by the principal.

She smiled at the memory.

"What's that?" Layla said peering around Taylor's shoulder.

An envelope was taped to her locker, it was beige and thick, the type made from stock instead of just thin paper. It had a gleam to it that was almost shimmery.

Her name was handwritten in fancy lettering. The ink was a deep rich black. It reminded her of calligraphy.

"I don't know," Taylor said, intrigued but at the same time concerned. Her eyes darted from person to person as she scanned the hallway.

Layla watched her.

"Don't go there," she insisted. "It's a birthday card. Everyone knows it's your birthday, just open it."

Taylor knew Layla was right. She took the envelope from her locker, being careful not to tear it from the tape, and slit it open with her finger.

"Shit!"

"What now?" Layla asked, slightly irritated.

"Paper cut," Taylor answered sucking her pointer finger. The blood welled in her mouth and her finger stung.

She grabbed the card inside which was just a single panel:
Happy Birthday

Tied to the card's corner was a heart for her charm bracelet. Taylor untied the charm, and placed it on the top shelf of her locker along with the card. Part of her wanted to throw them both away immediately, things like this made her incredibly uncomfortable. She didn't want to cause a scene though and so she promised herself they would both go into the trash later that afternoon.

Layla peered over Taylor's shoulder, "So fun!"

"What's so fun?" James Scott came up behind Layla.

Taylor's eyes fell on him just for a moment, James had light hair and dark brown eyes. He was tall, at least six foot and played soccer as well as baseball.

No one knew of their almost romance. After her abduction, it was as if it never was.

James and Layla were very on again, off again. This past summer he had visited family in North Dakota and had been gone since the middle of July. Absence had obviously made the heart grow fonder.

James acknowledged Taylor with a nod as Layla turned to him and pressed her body into his in a way that made anyone near them uncomfortable.

Two years ago when Layla had moved to town, Taylor knew the student body would happily accept her. She was exuberant, excitable, pretty and rich. She had everything that made high school worth attending. The only strike against her was that she had made friends with Taylor over the summer before anyone knew who she was. Taylor had tried to warn her new friend that she shouldn't hang out with her at school, but Layla wouldn't listen. She kept insisting that kids at school just needed to give Taylor another chance.

Before Taylor was taken, she was one of them, part of the group. After was different, she couldn't fit back in, and in a lot of ways, didn't want to.

"So what's fun?" James asked again now that Layla had let him go.

"Taylor has a secret admirer; that's what's fun."

"That's interesting. Who do you think it is?"

"No idea," Taylor said with a shrug, "I don't care either; probably someone just playing a prank."

"Yeah, probably," James said.

Layla hit James on the chest with her palm.

"Don't be an ass and wish the girl a happy birthday."

James glowered, "happy birthday," he mumbled in Taylor's general direction before taking off to a group of guys a few lockers down.

Seconds later the first tone rang signaling the students should head to their first period class. Taylor and Layla finished gathering up their stuff and shut their lockers one behind the other.

"Who do you think it is," Layla asked?

"Honestly, I have no idea. I couldn't even imagine who would want to date me."

"Don't say it like that," Layla admonished. "Any guy would be lucky to go out with you."

"Hmmm," Taylor said lost in her thoughts for a moment.

"This is me. Find me at lunch and we'll figure out what to do with your car."

"Will do," Taylor said over her shoulder as she continued down the hall.

Taylor didn't need to run but she did decide that bigger steps were probably a good idea. The second tone was just beginning to sound when she slipped into her chair.

Chapter 7

At lunch Layla got Jessica to agree to wait with her for
AAA so they could drive Taylor's car to The Barn, and
then Layla would drive Jessica home.

"Hey thanks," Taylor said stopping Jessica at the end of lunch,
"I really appreciate it."

"It's no big deal," she said, awkwardly tucking her hair behind
her ear, glancing around as she spoke.

Taylor and Jessica rarely talked anymore, but there had been
a time when they had been close. Occasionally little bubbles of
that friendship came to the surface, otherwise the two were left
with too many unsaid words and strange silences.

"Well," Taylor said, "thanks, all the same. I have to get to
next period."

With that she left without waiting for Jessica to say anything
else. Taylor's whole life was like this. Friendships that she had
before had all abruptly ended. Some had tried when she first
got home but she couldn't be near them. She would scream if
a man or a boy got too close to her. The girls were worse. They
wanted Taylor to talk about it. She couldn't leave the house for
almost an entire year—she would go to therapy or the police
department but that was it. And after a while her friends stopped
trying. She had done three years of school from home, when her

father died she had to go back. Her mother couldn't afford to stay at home with her anymore.

Taylor was a good student, she had a 4.0 GPA. The time she'd spent homeschooling had set her up very well for her remaining years of high school. She was enrolled in all advanced placement classes all of which would earn her college credit.

As she went through each class she felt they were being given too much homework and reading to even be legal on the first day. There were at least four major papers that were due before Thanksgiving. She had stopped reading the rest of her syllabi because she could feel herself getting overwhelmed with the work load.

By the end of the day her iPad was about to overheat. She switched-out books and supplemental reading between her back pack and locker. Trying to figure out where to start, she had forgotten about her mystery card until it fell out of her locker and flew across the floor.

She turned to retrieve it but a wall of junior football players paraded down the hall forcing Taylor to flatten herself against the lockers to avoid being touched. The card had at least a few shoe prints on it. She looked around, considering just leaving it there.

"Is this yours?"

The boy from the barn stood across the hall with the same smile he had given her just a few days ago.

"Umm, yeah," she responded holding out her hand for the letter, being careful to only grab the edge.

His skin was tanned from the sun, his eyes were a warm shade of brown, his hair hung a bit long but was also dark. He smiled. "I'm Peter, Peter Trellis," he said, his voice rich.

Taylor said nothing.

38

"And you are?" Peter asked.

She shook her head, unaccustomed to people asking her name. Her story and her reputation of being standoffish usually preceded her.

"Taylor," she said, "my name is Taylor."

"It's nice to meet you, Taylor," Peter said. "I moved here over the summer, I don't know a lot of people."

Taylor pursed her lips not knowing what to say to that statement. The silence stretched out, slightly too long.

"I've got to go," Taylor said slamming her locker shut and tucking the card under her arm.

"Yeah sure, maybe I'll see you around sometime. Happy Birthday," he called out to her down the hall.

Taylor ran towards the door her bag bouncing on her back. Coming out into the open air relieved her sense of claustrophobia. Her eyes squinted at the sudden onslaught of sun. She didn't need to see well though for she could hear Layla long before she could see her.

"Oh my god, did you see that paper we have to do for AP English? It's twenty pages! I can't even begin to imagine what Mrs. Leete was thinking." She was complaining loudly perched on top of Taylor's car surrounded by James, Jessica and a few others. Each nodding in agreement, at least the few that were actually in AP English were.

"Taylor there you are," Layla said as she shielded her eyes from the sun.

"Sorry, I got stuck in History. Mr. Dribble would just not stop talking; I'm not even sure he heard the bell ring."

"I had him last year," someone echoed. "The man must be deaf. He. Just. Keeps. Talking."

"Awesome," Taylor said, "something to look forward to."

The group started to break up and Jessica climbed in the back of Layla's range rover.

"All right lady, so we will bring your car to The Barn later as soon as AAA gets the thing unlocked for us. I think a few of us are going to stay and have dinner, too."

"Good deal. Call when you are headed that way and I'll get a table cleared for you."

The three sat in semi-comfortable silence until Layla shattered the peace and almost drove them off the road in the process.

"Hey! I forgot, what about your secret admirer? What's the deal? Do you know who it is?"

"Nope," Taylor said, lips pursed, "no idea."

"What's this?" Jessica asked leaning forward in her chair. No high school student could resist a bit of gossip.

Layla relayed the story for Jessica quickly and the two spent the rest of the ride trying to figure out who it could be.

"Someone creative," Jessica suggested.

"Yes, definitely, and someone shy maybe," Layla offered.

They each tossed out a half dozen names during the car ride and at the end decided that it really could have been any of them. Taylor could see The Barn in the distance and was happy to be exiting a conversation that she wasn't really a part of anyway.

"We will figure out who it is before we get here for dinner," Jessica promised.

"Great, thanks," Taylor said. "I really have to get to work. Thanks again for my car."

Taylor leapt from the car as Layla shifted into park, fishing her apron out of her backpack while giving them both a quick wave.

Chapter 8

The Barn's interior was dark, in contrast to the sun outside. She took practiced steps to the back room and clocked in before wrapping her hair up into a messy bun and tying an apron around her waist.

There were usually only two-three waitresses on at one time along with the kitchen staff and then, of course, Jan. Everyone was happy to see her, they were used to not knowing when she was working. She was always grateful that she worked with such awesome people, even if they were all at least fifteen years older than her.

"Hey Taylor," Kate said giving her a big hug. Her overweight frame nearly swallowed Taylor. Kate was a single mother who had been there for a little over a year. She did a good job even if she often called out of her shifts because she couldn't find people to watch her little boy.

"Was that Trevor in the corner when I walked in? It's so bright out I can still barely see you."

"Yeah," Kate said. "My mother couldn't watch him again and I knew Jan needed a good crew in for tonight. She's so great; she never gives me a hard time about bringing him in with me."

"Well," Taylor said, "he's probably the best kid I've ever seen. He just sits there, does his homework and then reads a book."

"And eats treats that you all bring him," Kate chided.

Taylor laughed, "Yeah that too."

Kate smiled and gave her a wink. "Better get back out there, those tips aren't going to make themselves."

"Oh my, darlin', look at you. I swear you got more beautiful while you were gone. We missed you sugar." Taylor turned toward the sweet southern drawl.

"Hey Deb, I missed you too."

Deb gave her a quick hug and a kiss on the cheek. Deb was about sixty years old and had moved up to Massachusetts to be near her son after her husband had died. She had lived in Troy, Alabama, all her life, and her drawl was as thick as pea soup, which is exactly what she would tell you if you asked her.

"It's always good when you come back at the end of the summer. How was your trip this year, how is your friend?"

"Good, Taylor answered, "really good."

"It's Kristen, right?" Deb asked.

"We had an amazing time; it is always nice to get away from . . ." Taylor paused, "everything."

"I bet," Deb responded knowingly. "You've got a good friend there. It's nice that the two of you have one another. Anyway, I've got an order coming up, or at least it better be coming soon!" she shouted towards the kitchen.

A spoon hit the steel counter in reply.

Mario was the cook for The Barn. He was a genius, a bit temperamental and, well, kind of crazy. But the women loved him, and he loved them. They were a family there and the group that was working tonight was the nucleus.

The afternoon flew by and it wasn't until 6 p.m. that Taylor got a call from Layla saying they were on their way. Five of them ended up coming in: Layla, James, Jessica, Shauna and Mike.

Taylor was out straight all afternoon, so by the time they got there she had easily made $100 and knew if she kept up this pace she could probably get to $200. She quickly took their orders and brought them out a round of drinks. She enjoyed hearing their conversations almost as if she weren't there.

"Sucks you have to work on your birthday," Shauna offered, when Taylor deposited her diet coke in front of her.

"It's OK. Thanks for remembering."

"I've always remembered," she said back seriously.

An hour later Layla was harassing Taylor to sit down.

"Layla, I've got, like, three tables still, I can't come and sit down with you."

"Just for a minute please," she begged.

Taylor hated it when Layla begged and felt her resolve crumble. "Fine, give me ten minutes. I need to get a few things taken care of first."

"You can have five," she shouted towards her back.

Five minutes later Taylor sat down between Shauna and Mike, and for a minute joined in on their jeers and lively conversation.

Out of the corner of her eye she saw a flame. Her heart began to pound hard in her chest, she couldn't breathe. Flashing back she saw the lighter in his hand held next to her cheek. She could smell her hair burning, his icy blue eyes stared back at her through the fire.

"*Happy Birthday to you, happy birthday to you ....*"

Taylor's hands clenched and unclenched as she willed herself to inhale. Closing her eyes she shoved the memory into the recesses of her mind.

"He will not steal another birthday from me," she said to herself.

Gritting her teeth, she smiled, to her friends.

She knew that Layla must have organized the whole thing—her friend was like that. Refusing to believe or accept that Taylor was anything except just like everyone else.

"Thank you," she said wiping her eyes. "I can't believe you did this," she said to everyone.

"It was Layla's idea," Jan said. "Take ten minutes with your friends. I'll cover your tables."

Taylor ate a huge piece of cake with her friends and even laughed when they made fun of her about the panic in her eyes when she saw the candles.

"It was a perfect birthday," she said. "Thank you."

"Anytime," Layla said seriously.

Taylor hugged Layla goodbye a few minutes later and thanked her again for such a special birthday before she started to clean up the tables.

"Happy Birthday," Mr. Moriarty said from the corner. The Barn had died down enough at this point that Taylor could hear his soft-spoken voice.

"Thank you, sir," she said to him.

"Eighteen, is that right?" He asked.

"Yes sir."

"Enjoy it."

"I will, sir, thank you."

Taylor watched as he used the table to push himself into a standing position before gingerly taking steps toward the door on the uneven wooden floor. Generally speaking she didn't like waiting on the old man, he stared at her too much and smelled funny. It was nice that he wished her happy birthday though.

An hour later all the tables were clear, the door was locked, and the salt containers were almost refilled. It was just after 10 p.m.

"Get outta here," Jan said from the doorway, "we can take care of the rest in the morning. Get home before your mother heads off to work."

Taylor was happy for the release. "Thank you," she said.

She punched out quickly and stuffed the stack of bills from her apron into her back pack before grabbing her keys and heading out the side door towards the parking lot where Jessica had left her car.

She got in quickly and began to pull out of the parking lot before she saw the present perched precariously between her windshield and the hood of her car.

Putting the car in park she scanned her mirrors before stepping out and retrieving the small box. Her name was scrawled familiarly on a tag. Andy, she said to herself and smiled.

A necklace with a police shield on it and a small diamond was inside, along with a note.

Happy birthday kid.

How about breakfast this Saturday?

Call me

- Andy

She smiled again, looking forward to the invitation and to seeing him—it had been too long.

Andy Fisher was a state police detective for Worcester County specializing in sexual assault. A million years ago he had been Taylor's father's closest friend. They had both been police officers in Templeton, but after Taylor's abduction he had become a state trooper and then a detective a couple of years after that. He had maintained his friendship with her and her mother after her father's death, but then suddenly, last year, he moved down to Worcester. He had promised Taylor before he left that if she ever needed anything she could call him. She

45

knew that if she ever did he would drop everything and come. She fastened the necklace around her neck and pulled out of The Barn's driveway eager to get home.

Chapter 9

The lights were on in the house, though she knew her
mother needed to leave for work any minute.

Sarah worked the overnight shift in the ICU at
Highfield Memorial Hospital. Her mother loved being a nurse.
After the kidnapping it became clear that both parents couldn't
continue to work. Her mother quit and the family stuck to their
budget. It had worked too, but when Richard died suddenly
in a car accident while on duty, Sarah had to go back to work.
She worked the overnight shift on purpose—there was extra
money in what they called a shift differential. Because less
people wanted to work overnight, she got paid more money
to do it. Her income could pay for their living expenses but they
didn't have a lot of extras. When Taylor had gone back to public
school it took her almost a year to see how tight things were
for her mother. She hated to see her struggle, she got a job at
The Barn so she could take care of some of her own expenses,
like her car and clothes. It wasn't so bad. Sarah worked while
Taylor slept; she was home and awake when Taylor got back
from school, though on the days that Taylor worked they were
like two ships passing in the night.

"Hey Mom," Taylor called out as soon as she opened the door.

"Hey sweetie, I thought I was going to miss you. Late night

tonight, huh?"

"Yeah, it was super busy."

"Come open your other present before I have to leave OK?"

The small box was on the counter. Taylor gingerly untied the ribbon and noticed, for the second time that day, her bracelet, and thought of her father.

He should be here, the errant thought flew through her mind.

Inside the box was a key chain. It was heavy and cold in her hand.

"Thanks . . . Mom," she said, confusion running through her mind.

"Do you like it?" her mom pushed.

"Yeah, it's great . . . thanks," disappointment painted her words.

"Good," Sarah said, "I wanted you to have something to hold these."

Dangling from her fingers was a set of car keys.

Taylor's face broke into a smile.

"What is this?" she asked, excitement resonating throughout her voice.

"Your new car."

"Seriously?" Taylor hugged her mother. "Where is it?"

Her mother broke out into laughter. "It's being dropped off in the morning. I got it from a guy in town—I met him at the hospital. It's a Jeep Compass. It's a good car and it has four-wheel drive."

Taylor was still bouncing around the house threading her new keys onto her key chain.

"Here's the deal," her mother said, "you've got the car this year. Once you go to college, though, I'm going to keep it here. You won't be able to have it on campus anyway and four-wheel drive would be nice in the winter."

"Oh yeah, it will," Taylor exclaimed, paying little attention to her mother.

Sarah laughed again. "All right, I'll talk to you about the details later. Try and get some sleep OK?"

Taylor, despite her excitement yawned, "I will." Between school and work she felt more tired than she had in a week and was looking forward to her bed.

"I've gotta run, I love you," Sarah called out, grabbing her keys from the bowl next to the garage door and blowing her daughter a kiss.

"Love you too, Mom."

Sarah headed out and, as always, Taylor listened for the alarm to beep indicating that it had re-armed itself.

Looking around the kitchen she decided to clean the remaining dishes in the sink and cleared off the countertops before she saw the empty laundry basket by the basement stairs. She knew she had laundry in the dryer. There was a pair of yellow capris that she wanted to wear to school tomorrow. The basket taunted her sitting in front of the stairs. All she had to do was go into the basement and get the laundry. She took a deep breath.

"You can do this, just pick up the basket."

Basket on her hip, she laid her hand on the basement doorknob. She hadn't even touched the door to the basement in a year. It was progress from when she required a deadbolt be on the top and bottom of the door so that it couldn't be opened by accident.

She twisted the knob and pulled, hard. A wall of air slammed into her face. The smell of fieldstone foundation and dampness mixed with the scent of dirt flooded her nose and mouth. She couldn't breathe. The basket fell from her hip, she stumbled, grasping for the edge of the door. Every second that ticked by felt like an eternity, her fingers connected with the edge of the door and she shoved it closed.

Her breath came hard now, and the room swung in front of her. She tried to get a grip on her breathing. Don't pass out, don't pass out, she thought.

Eventually her pulse slowed. It was still beating wildly, but not as fast as before. The room stopped spinning, she straightened her back and took a deep breath.

"Next year," she said into the ether.

She checked the alarm one more time, re-checked the locks on the doors and windows eventually heading upstairs to find something else to wear for the morning.

Taylor woke to a pile of laundry being dumped on her legs, her yellow capris on the top of the pile.

"You're the best, Mom. Thanks."

"No problem, now get a move on; you've got like ten minutes to get out of here."

Taylor dressed quickly and headed downstairs.

"That's pretty, is it new?" Sarah asked admiring the necklace Andy had gotten Taylor for her birthday.

"Andy got it for me."

Sarah stepped toward Taylor, fingering the necklace. It wasn't overly expensive but it was more than she was comfortable with him spending.

"Can I go get breakfast with Andy this Saturday?"

Taylor could see her mother's face tighten. Sarah didn't like it when Taylor brought Andy up in any context, but less so when she wanted to see him.

"Sure," she said dropping the necklace and changing the subject. "The car should be here when you get home OK, and then we need to get your car up on Craigslist and try to sell it.

We should be able to pay for your insurance with what we get for the car."

"I'll do it today. I think I can come home before I have to work. I have last block free. Will the car be here by then?"

"Yes, and I will be up when you get here."

Taylor downed the last of her coffee and filled a to-go mug before slipping her backpack over her shoulder and heading out to the garage.

Sarah grabbed a glass of water, turned off the coffee pot and made sure the doors were locked before she headed up to bed. It was coming up on 7:30 a.m. when she finally collapsed into her own comforter which swallowed her thin frame. She snuggled deep into it. Relishing the room-darkening shades and blackout curtains that made her bedroom seem like it was night time instead of the beginning of most people's day.

She was too preoccupied to notice the top of the head that ducked under the window sill as she went upstairs.

Chapter 10

As per her agreement with her guidance counselor, Taylor had stopped into the cafeteria and let the teacher who was monitoring the free block know that she was leaving campus.

Thinking about her car she walked up to her locker and saw a white rose wedged into the grate on the front. She smiled despite herself, roses were her favorite. Glancing in both directions there wasn't anyone in the hallway. "Not that it would take long to put a flower in a locker," she thought to herself. Fingering the rose gently being cautious of the thorns she tugged, freeing it from her locker. It's fragrance was wonderful it clung to her fingers and made her smile again.

"You ditching?" a voice from down the hallway said to her.

Her hug swung around, vaguely aware of who the voice belonged to.

"I get to leave during free blocks, so I'm headed out for the day."

"How did you manage that?" Peter asked, genuinely interested.

He had continued walking and now stood a comfortable distance between the two of them.

"I've got a good shrink," Taylor joked. Hoping he didn't

realize the truth within her words.

Peter laughed, "Yeah, me too, but I didn't get that good a deal."

His warm brown eyes lingered on hers. She had been privy to the leering glances, the hungry stares. In some ways she was more comfortable with what she knew. She wanted to say something quick and witty, some teasing flirty chit chat that would have come easily to Layla. Her mind was a blank so instead she just stared back at him.

Peter walked past but turned as he was about to open the door to a nearby classroom. "Do you need help carrying your bag out to your car?"

Taylor was thrown off. No one had ever asked if they could carry her books for her. It was sweet.

"No, really there aren't that many, and I don't want you to get into trouble."

"OK," Peter said with a shrug of his shoulders as he opened the door. "See you around."

"See you."

Taylor swung her bag on to her shoulder and smiled as she walked out to her car replaying the scene in her mind. She was painfully awkward around boys and she knew it.

Although he did offer to carry your bag, she thought to herself. So maybe not so awkward after all.

As she drove home, she could see a red Jeep Compass in the driveway. It was gorgeous. She hopped out of her now almost-sold car thanks to Craigslist, and ran over to the Compass. The doors were unlocked and she eagerly pulled the drivers' side door open. The interior was cloth and, while it wasn't brand new, it still had that new-car smell. It was so clean inside she almost didn't want to get in it . . . almost.

"Do you like it?" Sarah asked standing on the porch.

"Oh my God, I love it!" Taylor squealed. "Thank you, thank you, thank you."

Sarah tossed her the keys from the porch. "You deserve it."

Taylor had trouble graciously accepting compliments, and yet her mother continued on.

"You have done great in school, you help around the house. I know money has been tight these last few years and you don't have all the newest things that your friends do."

"Mom stop, it's not a big deal."

"No, listen to me," Sarah said as she walked down the steps and into the driveway. "You never complain. You don't ask me for things you know we can't afford, you pull your weight and work so you can afford some of your own stuff. You do deserve this." Sarah's hands reached out and squeezed Taylors shoulders. "Now," she smiled, "try not to destroy this thing so I can enjoy it next year."

Seconds later Layla pulled over in front of the house. "Nice wheels," she yelled out the window.

"Thanks!" Taylor yelled back.

"Now maybe you can drive somewhere for once," Layla yelled before pulling back out onto the road and heading up to her own house.

Sarah worked a rotating schedule meaning that sometimes she worked all weekend, sometimes just one of the weekend days and sometimes not at all. This weekend she was working on Friday night but that was it until Monday.

"We'll do something fun this weekend, if you want to?" Sarah asked.

"Sure," Taylor said, distracted by the shininess of her new car.

"Why don't we drive into Boston and go look at the university," again Sarah offered. BU was her alma mater and she had been pushing it a bit hard.

"That doesn't really sound like that much fun. I really want to go to either Stanford or Colorado State—you know that."

"I know, sweetie. It just scares me you being that far away."

"I know, but I love California and I'll be closer to Kristen over there and you could come visit me whenever you want, it would be warm, we could go to the beach." Taylor's voice was teasing but playful. "And Colorado is just gorgeous. Do you remember their dorm rooms? They were amazing."

"All right," Sarah said hands in the air. "BU is still a backup though, right?"

"Yes, it's a backup. Can we just go and walk around Boston? We haven't done that in forever."

"Sure sweetie, we can get up first thing in the morning and head out."

"Not first thing, I'm having breakfast with Andy remember?"

"Oh right," Sarah said unenthusiastically. "After lunch then. I'll take a nap while you are gone."

"Perfect!"

Taylor glanced at her watch. "I've got to get going. When do I get to drive this thing anyway?"

Sarah smiled at her daughter, "You can take it to work. I took care of the registration and insurance today while you were at school."

Taylor hugged her mother and started moving things out of her old car and into her new one.

"If you are home after 9:30 I won't be here OK? I'm going to head in a bit early and get my paperwork going so I can get out right at seven."

Taylor was distracted and didn't respond.

"Did you hear me?"

"Yeah, work early, out at seven."

Sarah laughed. "Go to work; enjoy your car. I love you!"

Taylor beamed back at her, "Love you, too!"

Chapter 11

Wanting to get a run in before having breakfast with Andy, Taylor stretched her legs in the living room. She tightened her shoes and grabbed her running stick, as well as the can of mace from the basket on top of the shelf above the coats. The weather had turned cold in the mornings, she contemplated grabbing a long sleeve shirt but ultimately decided against it.

The sun was just starting to rise as she disarmed the alarm system and opened the door, making sure to hear the beeps before she walked down the stairs. She didn't like to go out of the house through the garage. A couple of years ago she watched an episode of 60 Minutes where it showed people robbing houses by waiting for people to pull out of their garages, then they would sneak in while the door was closing.

Most of the houses were dark. She turned her head towards the development and but at the last minute changed her mind and headed down the street away from town. Being the weekend she wasn't surprised the roads were quiet. She allowed her mind to wander, looking forward to the day she had planned. Her thoughts also drifted towards Peter. She liked his smile, the way he spoke to her. She also liked that he didn't know anything about her. It had been a long time since she thought of any boy as anything other than a threat. She knew she wouldn't allow anything to happen with Peter, but here by herself, she imagined, for just a moment what it would be like if she did.

After two and a half miles or so Taylor stopped running to check her watch and, noting the time, decided to head back. The sun shone through the woods across the street, and out of the corner of her eye she thought she saw something move.

Her head on a swivel she turned immediately, her hand poised to grab her mace.

The woods, though, revealed nothing out of place.

She stayed motionless for a minute, the only movement coming from her chest. Breaths puffing into the air.

She turned and headed home, her pace faster than normal.

* * *

Bagels and Friends had been around since Taylor was a kid. Tucked into a small plaza near downtown, it always smelled like bacon. They actually made their bagels from scratch, which was why most people said it was so successful. The artwork on the windows was from a local artist and the booths were old but still in good condition. Taylor scanned the restaurant searching for Andy. His head bobbed to the song that was playing in the background while he sat up at the coffee bar. He must have heard the door close because he turned around not long after and, on seeing Taylor, swung his frame off the stool and crossed the room in three huge strides. He wrapped her in a bear hug that was fatherly. He was the only man other than her father that she could stand to touch her. She hugged him back warmly.

"I've missed you, kid," he said, his voice soft-spoken.

"I missed you too, Andy."

"Let's eat," he suggested, motioning to the stool next to him. "How was your birthday? I see you got a new ride."

Andy was freakishly observant, it could be unnerving if you weren't used to it.

"Yeah, Mom got it for me," Taylor grabbed a menu and started to figure out what she wanted.

"What else is going on?"

"Not much," Taylor offered, ordering a coffee for herself as the waitress generously refilled Andy's mug. "Been working a decent amount, school just started and I'm going to start my early admittance application for college."

"Nice! Where are we going?"

"Stanford or Colorado University."

Andy whistled. "Wow, are you smart or something?"

Taylor smiled at him, "Turns out, I kind of am."

The two sat in companionable silence for a few minutes.

"Any guys I need to run background checks on?"

Taylor could feel the heat rise on her neck, "Umm, no."

"Who is he?"

"No one!"

Andy raised his eye brows at her.

"Really!" she insisted.

Andy wasn't buying it.

"There is this one boy who seems nice and is always asking me about my day—he even offered to carry my books out to my car."

"What's his name?"

Taylor took a sip of coffee and opened the menu again. "Peter"

"Does Peter have a last name?"

"You are not actually going to run a background check on him."

Andy looked at her quizzically, "Of course I am."

Taylor's face pouted, "Please don't; I have to stop seeing ghosts everywhere. Not everyone is out to get me."

"You're right," he admitted, "but I'm a cop so I'm going to keep thinking that everyone is out to get everyone, if that's OK with you."

"It is," Taylor assured him. "He's a nice, normal guy."

The bell above the door rang as it opened and in walked Peter Trellis with a handful of wildflowers.

Taylor's face burned with embarrassment as if she had just been caught talking about someone behind their back. She kept her eyes on her menu hoping he wouldn't notice her.

Andy noticed Taylor's reaction immediately and glanced at the boy at the front of the restaurant.

"Is that him?" Andy whispered leaning into Taylor.

She nodded not saying anything.

Andy raised his eyebrows. "Huh," he said, "this should be interesting."

Taylor swatted at his arm. "Shhh!" she whispered.

"Yeah, yeah, yeah," he muttered, turning back towards his coffee. "You teenagers are so dramatic. Just go talk to the kid."

Taylor sat for a minute more trying to decide if she could ignore him. Feeling guilty though she slid off the stool and wound her way through the busy restaurant as only a waitress could.

Peter was tall, he easily dwarfed Taylor's short frame. A T-shirt was all he wore, his arms looked muscular but in a thin kind of way.

"Hello," he said warmly.

"Hi Peter, what are you doing here?"

"I didn't mean to interrupt your breakfast, please go sit back down, your coffee is going to get cold." Peter motioned towards Taylor's chair.

Taylor glanced back over at Andy, he was doing a good job pretending he wasn't paying attention to anything. With somewhat of a sigh, she headed back towards her stool, Peter in tow.

"I love these bagels, and I saw you come in. Here," he said passing the wildflowers to her, "these are for you."

"Thank you," she smiled, enjoying the attention.

"It's nothing," he said sheepishly, "they were on the side of the building."

"Is this your father?"

Andy turned eager to get a look at the boy who had stolen his little Taylor's heart.

"No," Andy said using his most authoritative voice. "I'm more like the uncle who's a detective with the state police."

Andy put his hand on his hip which pushed his coat back revealing his gun.

"Oh," Peter said, not reacting to the tone or the gun. "It's nice to meet you," he offered his hand to shake Andy's.

Peter turned back toward Taylor, "umm, listen I know this is stupid, me showing up like this. It's just, I wanted to ask you out. A few people at school told me you wouldn't want to, that you didn't date because of what happened. I mean I don't really know anything about your past, but I've heard some things and so then it just seemed dumb, but then I was walking by and there you were, so now here I am. "

Taylor stared at him, unsure of what to say in response to his rambling.

"I'm sorry, that was a horrible version of the English language. Let me start again, would you like to go out on a date with me?"

Taylor's anxiety had kicked into high gear as Peter spoke. She wanted to say yes, but she was afraid. Her mind did it's best interpretation of Dr. Perna, "scared of what? Saying yes won't put you in any danger."

"Yes," Taylor blurted out as her answer like the release valve on a pressure cooker. That would be great. Why don't you sit and have a coffee with us?"

"I, uh, can't, my dad needs my help with something—I told him I would just be a few minutes."

"Oh," Taylor said somewhat disappointed.

"Can I call you tomorrow?"

"Call my house," she said turning towards the counter and asking the waitress for a piece of paper and a pen.

"You don't have a cell?" Peter asked.

Taylor laughed. "Nope. Call my house and leave me a message. I don't usually answer numbers I don't know. I'll see you at school."

Peter smiled, a warm inviting smile that drew Taylor's attention towards his lips. "OK, I'll see you at school."

Andy watched this exchange carefully. He was surprised at Taylor. She'd never shown any interest in anyone. Not since, what happened. *It's been 5 years*, that little voice in his head reminded him.

"So," she said as she slumped back on the stool, "what are we eating?"

Taylor got Irish eggs Benedict, her favorite. Andy got a meat lovers omelet.

They chatted while waiting for their food but dug in eagerly when it was finally set down in front of them.

"I think my stomach may explode," Taylor complained upon finishing her meal.

Andy grunted in agreement.

"So, what's up with the kid? Kind of bumbled the date request didn't he?"

"I think it's sweet; so he's a little shy."

Andy faced turned to disbelief. He may have stuck out his tongue as well.

"He still asked, which is something no one else has done, you know, ever."

Taylor had, for the most part, no interest in dating. It had not been lost on her though, that no one had even asked. It wasn't like she was unattractive, but her baggage was large and well known. No one wanted to get anywhere near her. It had begun to bother her over the summer as she realized she would go to college without so much as having been kissed.

"I don't know. I don't love it."

"Would you love anyone?" Taylor quipped back.

"No, probably not. I owe it to your dad to keep an eye on you and I'm always gonna do that, got me?"

"Got you," she replied. "Hey, speaking of Dad, what happened after he died? Between you and Mom, I mean."

Andy inhaled sharply. What Taylor had just done was an interview tactic, lull someone into a false sense of security and then switch the direction of the conversation quickly and abruptly. Even though her father wasn't a detective, he was a damn smart cop—she must have picked it up from him.

"What do you mean?" he said keeping his tone passive.

"I don't know," Taylor replied not really noticing his body language. "It's just after he died you were at the house all the time; you helped out Mom when things broke, you took me to get my learner's permit but then one day you just didn't come around anymore. Now whenever I bring up your name, or that

63

I'm going to see you, Mom acts like I'm talking about her . . ."
Taylor's voice trailed off

"Her what?" Andy prodded.

"She acts like I'm going to see someone she doesn't like."

"You know what darlin', your mom and I were just using each
other too much as a crutch for our grief. We had been close for
so many years and so in a lot of ways when your dad died we
kept that closeness up, the only difference was your dad wasn't
there anymore holding the three of us together."

Andy took a sip of coffee.

"We were pretending in a lot of ways that we could be friends,
but without your dad there it was just different. We needed to
stop pretending that it was the same."

"I don't get it."

"I know, but that's just the way it is right now."

The two gathered their things and paid the bill,Taylor
promised to meet him again in a few weeks. They hadn't
seen each other much over the past 3 months of summer, it was
nice just sitting together.

"Let's get together again in a few weeks ok?" Taylor asked.

"Of course kid, I'll give you a call."

Waving goodbye, Taylor headed home looking forward to the
rest of the day with her mother. Even the foreseeable argument
about the many benefits of Boston University and living close to
home.

Chapter 12

T aylor was quiet when she got into the house, assuming her mother was still sleeping.

"Taylor, is that you?" Sarah called out from the top of the stairs.

"Why aren't you sleeping?"

"Couldn't. Want to get going early?"

"Sure."

"Do you want to drive in or take the T?"

"Let's take the T; it's cheaper."

"Sounds good to me." As Sarah had lived in Massachusetts her whole life and had gone to school in Boston, taking the T was a pretty normal way for her to reference the antiquated version of Bean town's subway and train station. Taylor liked it because it was the oldest subway system in the United States. Sarah hated it because it was the oldest subway system in the United States.

Once, Taylor in passing had made the same reference to Kristen. That kicked off a whole 'Who's on First' conversation that ended in both girls laughing hysterically on the floor. Taylor smiled, she'd have to call Kristen later and remind her about that.

There was a train a few towns away that would take them right into the city. Taylor had only taken it a handful of times, but

Sarah used to do it all the time. Before Taylor's abduction, she had been a part of the Alumni Board at BU.

Sarah often thought of those days and how everything was broken up into before and after. As if their path had been changed so dramatically by the incident. Whatever was destined to happen for them prior, now wouldn't. They were on a new path. They were on the 'after' path.

They made good time and the two decided to hit up Faneuil Hall just before lunch. It had turned out to be a nice day; the sun was warm and there were a fair amount of people just milling about. The cobbled streets always fascinated Taylor. She liked to think of who may have been walking where she stood hundreds of years ago.

They did some window shopping and stopped for sandwiches before Sarah finally convinced Taylor to just take a stroll around BU.

"What's up with the balloons?"

"I don't know," Sarah said, fake innocence dripping from her lips.

Taylor looked at her, her eyes narrowing. "What is this?"

"It's nothing," Sarah said shaking her hands.

"It's nothing with balloons. Balloons always mean something."

"It's a small open house," Sarah grimaced.

"What?" Taylor exclaimed. "Come on, we did this last year." Taylor huffed, and her face pouted.

"I didn't plan it. I just checked their website when we decided we would come into town and they happened to be having an open house. Sometimes things just work that way. Come on, we missed most of the formal programs anyway, let's just walk around and maybe you'll see something that interests you. You

66

never know."

Taylor didn't hide the roll of her eyes as she took her mother's arm.

For the most part her mother was right, the open house was just about over. Parents of what looked like high school juniors were still talking to staff or faculty members. There were a couple of tables with refreshments, and a small activities fair—mostly tables with clubs or other offices but there were a few fun things like a ring toss, an inflatable obstacle course and a psychic fair.

Sarah lost at ring toss three times before giving in. "I think my eyes are getting bad," she commented.

"Oh yeah?" Taylor said. "I beat you and now your eyes are bad, huh? You put needles in people's veins with those eyes, don't you?"

Sarah laughed, "OK, so maybe you are better than me at a few things. Don't get used to it, I made you, remember?"

"Yeah," Taylor said, "made me better than you at ring toss."

"Do you want to do the psychic fair?" Sarah asked. "They used to do these when I was in college and I loved them."

Taylor's first reaction was to say no—it was always her first reaction. But she saw her mother and how happy she seemed, and she didn't want to rain on that parade.

"Sure."

Sarah smiled happily at her daughter. She had asked before she even thought about the question and was surprised that Taylor said yes.

"Let's go then; we'll do it together."

There were four different types of psychics sitting in a small circle, each behind their own table. Sarah and Taylor were the last two people, so each got to pick who they'd go see. Sarah chose a tarot card reader and Taylor chose a palm and tarot reader.

Taylor smiled as she approached the woman and sat down. The woman was older, probably mid-fifties, and had a black cloth on the table that had all sorts of glitter all over it. As soon as Taylor sat down the glitter covered her knees.

"So," the woman said without introducing herself, "do you have a question for me?"

Taylor hadn't been prepared to ask a question. "Uhh, no," she stammered, "not really."

The woman smiled. "Let me see your palms."

Taylor held out her hands, her palms facing the sky. The woman took Taylor's fingers, opening them and moving her palms back and forth in the light. The woman's hands were strong and cool—they felt good on Taylor's skin.

"Your path is broken," the woman said simply. "You were supposed to be going in one direction and then something changed it, and now you're going in a new direction."

Taylor looked in this woman eyes and she continued.

"This new direction is harder than your life would have been but better, richer. Everything that is harder is worth more in the end."

Taylor was shocked, looking at her palms wondering how someone could have gleaned all that from her hands.

"Is this new life shorter?" Taylor asked quietly, careful to make sure her mother couldn't hear her.

The woman's milky eyes fixed onto Taylors. "Your life line is strong but broken. It starts and stops. I think your life will be short, but will then start again. A rebirth of sorts, or a death depending on how you look at it."

"Pick three cards," the woman said, unceremoniously dropping Taylor's hands.

She skillfully spread out a stack of cards in front of Taylor. Taylor took three and turned them over.

"Ahh," the woman purred. "The Chariot, Death and the Tower. These are all very serious cards."

Taylor sucked her breath in when she saw the death card.

"No child, Death does not mean what you think it means. Death in Tarot is the ending of a cycle, the conclusion of a journey, something is about to end in your world. The Tower tells me that there will be chaos and confusion; there will be unexpected action that will have widespread repercussions. The Chariot indicates that you will show creativity in the midst of this chaos, and that you will gain determination and control, that you will find value in positive aggression. Something in your world is about to get very messy but you are going to find a way to fix it."

With that the woman stood and directed for Taylor to get up and rejoin her mother. Taylor did, but as if in a haze, still confused from all the things the old woman said.

"What did yours tell you?" Sarah asked excited as the pair left the fair.

"That something was about to change."

"Mine too," Sarah exclaimed. "She said that there would be big changes in the year ahead and that I should open my heart to new possibilities."

"That's cool," Taylor said.

She shook her head pushing the women's words from her mind. That stuff wasn't real anyway.

Chapter 13

The first few weeks of school went by without incident. Taylor settled into her non-routine, routine. She even managed to get one of her four major papers that were due before the holidays pretty much done, which made her feel better. For senior year, they really were piling on the homework.

Taylor sat in AP English, Mrs. Leete's class, discussing Theroux when the door opened bringing with it the smell of cologne. In the doorway stood Peter, looking slightly confused.

"What is it, Mr. Trellis?" Mrs. Leete stood at the smart board looking annoyed. "I'm in the middle of a lesson."

"Sorry, Mrs. Leete, I'm transferring into this class. My placement tests finally came in with my records from my other school."

"Do you have something from the office?" Mrs. Leete said, now abandoning her position at the head of the class and walking over to Peter.

Peter's eyes scanned the room, resting on Taylor.

She smiled and could feel the color rise on her neck. If he was in this class with her, maybe he would be transferring into AP History or Advanced Calculus with her as well.

Peter handed Mrs. Leete the paper from the office.

"Take a seat next to Taylor, please,"

Peter did as he was told, tucking his backpack behind his new chair. He leaned over to Taylor, "Will you help me find these other classes, too? I don't want to be late to everything all day."

"Sure" Taylor said taking his schedule out of his hand. She looked it over quickly and realized that it was the exact copy of her schedule.

"You're doing all AP classes?"

"Yeah, looks like it. That was what I did in my other school too, but this place seems harder. I didn't think I would test into them, but I guess I did."

Mrs. Leete, who had returned to the front of the classroom, cleared her throat and gave Taylor the cut-the-shit look. Taylor leaned away from Peter and he took his cue from her, focusing his attention on the remainder of the lecture.

Taylor spent the morning bringing Peter up to speed on the teachers and what homework he had missed so far. She also dropped the bombshell about all the papers that were due.

"Seriously! Four papers before Thanksgiving? That's insane."

"Yeah, it's rough but if you get started you'll be able to get them done, just don't wait. It's always worse if you wait."

They walked over to Taylor's locker.

As Taylor spoke she could tell Peter wanted to say something. Rather than continue on, she paused and waited patiently.

"I have a confession to make, but I don't want it to freak you out."

Taylor couldn't help but be a bit on guard. "Okay."

"I saw you a few times before school started, I saw you running and then I saw you at that restaurant in town."

"The Barn"

"Yeah, there. I just, I thought you were pretty and I asked some people about you. They said your birthday was coming up

71

and so I may have left the note on your locker w/ the charm."

Taylor was taken aback. "I'm not really sure what to say."

"Don't say anything please, I thought at the time that it would be cute, that you would like it. I didn't realize ... "

"You didn't know who I was."

Peter's eyes were downcast.

"Did I screw this up?"

Taylor expertly spun the combination on her locker and reached up to the top, her fingers finding the heart shape charm that had settled there just a few weeks ago.

"No, you didn't screw it up, hold this."

She handed the charm to Peter and took off her bracelet. He handed it back to her and she wound it on with the other charm.

"Word of advice though, I'm probably not the best person to try and surprise."

"Words of a wise person," he joked.

"Who's wise?" Layla interjected.

Taylor hadn't even seen her approach as the two had stopped at Taylor's locker.

"I am apparently." Taylor said smiling at Peter.

"I'm gonna go drop off all these books before lunch. I'll see you later?"

"Yep, I'll see you after lunch."

"You two seem cute," Layla said watching Peter walk away. "Anything I should know?"

Taylor had until that moment kept Peter somewhat of a secret. He had been playing into it here and there, leaving notes on her locker or a flower occasionally. It had been nice, having this piece of information that no one knew. Though enjoying the anonymity, she had begun to feel a little guilty.

"It's him, it's Peter, the notes, the flowers."

"Yeah, no kidding I've just been waiting for you to tell me. Why didn't you? You seem happy. Do you like him?"

Taylor grimaced, she felt stupid whenever she asked herself that question. Even if she did like him it didn't matter, he had no idea what he was getting himself into. Pretending to be normal was something that she was used to. Actually being normal though, that was something else entirely.

"I don't know," Taylor said. "What's going to happen when he tries to hold my hand and I scream, or if he kisses me and I vomit all over him."

"Wow! You are just full of sunshine today, aren't you?"

"Sorry," Taylor said glumly. "I'm just nervous; I feel like I'm leading him on."

"What if it's fine, what if you just hold his hand and what if when he kisses you you're ready for it and you like it."

Taylor shrugged for the moment choosing to not believe her friend's words.

"Fine," Layla said, "don't listen to me but I'm telling you one day something will happen and it will be OK. How else are we going to have kids together, huh?"

Taylor smiled. Layla's life was just so, she stopped, thinking, trying to find the right word . . . normal.

Chapter 14

The door to the office was slightly ajar, Taylor knocked gently before pushing the door open, Dr. Perna?"

Dr. Perna didn't look up from his desk.

She tried again, "Dr. Perna?" She said louder.

He glanced up and seemed surprised to see her.

"Hey, Taylor, is it three already? Sorry, our schedule changes so much I forgot you were coming in today."

"That's OK," she offered, "I can go if you have something you need to do."

"No, no, no, that's not, no, come in please," Dr. Perna stumbled over his words. "Come in, sit down is what I meant. I'm sorry, I was just working on a speech I'm giving in a month."

"That's cool, what's it about?"

Dr. Perna hesitated before answering, "Post-Traumatic Stress Disorder in teenagers."

Taylor didn't say anything at first. "It's about me," she said matter of factly, feeling slightly betrayed.

Dr. Perna shook his head emphatically, his hands raised, "Taylor, it's not really. Yes, you were the one that gave me the idea when they asked me to speak on PTSD, but that was my specialty before you. I have treated countless people with this disorder, yet there is a whole other subset to treating teenagers and there are a lot of good clinicians out there that don't know what to do with your age group. This is about telling other people what methods I have used and letting them jump into the conversation, so we can all learn from one another."

"Will they know it's me?"

"No. I have changed your name to Belle from *Beauty and the Beast*. They won't know specifically what your trauma was; just that 'Belle' was assaulted and separated from her family for a significant period of time. I would never put you at risk or betray your trust."

Taylor nodded, feeling better.

"Now, what's going on in the world of Taylor?"

"I think a boy likes me."

Dr. Perna's eye brows raised. Victims of sexual assault typically struggled with developing relationships, especially as those relationships became physical in nature.

"How do you feel about him?" he asked, keeping his tone neutral.

"He's nice, he's smart, he's in all AP classes just like me—he's cute, too."

Dr. Perna smiled, classic Taylor sidestepping the question.

"That's nice, how do you feel about the fact that you think he likes you?"

"Scared," she admitted. "Excited too. Does that make me weird?"

"That makes you normal."

"Well that's something you don't call me every day."

Dr. Perna laughed out loud. "I guess it isn't. Has he asked you out?"

Taylor smiled, "Not yet, he asked if he could ask me, but we haven't gone anywhere yet. He always seems to find me

75

at school, walks me to my locker, that sort of thing. "

"When you get to the date point, be honest with him regarding your expectations, he'll understand. How's the sleeping going?" he asked changing subject.

"Decent," Taylor answered. "I have some off nights, but I get six–seven hours usually, which isn't too bad. As a general rule I'm feeling less anxious about everything."

"Do you want to talk about your dad?"

Dr. Perna had been waiting to bring up Taylor's father. Before she left for California over the summer she'd mentioned the fact that before her father had died her parents had been fighting a lot. She normally spoke of her father with reverence but Dr. Perna sensed that something else had been going on toward the end.

"Did I ever tell you that he came and found me, basically insisted that I take you on as a patient?"

Taylor's head picked up. "No," she said, suddenly more interested in the conversation.

The only people who told stories about her dad were cops and she didn't see them much anymore. Her mom didn't like to talk about him. She did right after his death, she talked about him all the time, but then one day she just stopped.

"It was about a year after you came home, and I think he was desperate as far as counselors."

"I didn't talk to any of the first ones; no one until you."

"You didn't talk to me for a while either."

"But you hung in there," she smiled.

"Yes, I did," he smiled back.

"Your father showed up in this office. I had only been here for maybe two months and I had barely any patients. He said, 'You have to see my daughter!'"

76

"I just stood behind my desk staring at this man who I had seen on TV. He hadn't introduced himself, but it was like he assumed that I knew who he was and if I didn't, it didn't matter to him. He had a daughter and I was going to see her. That was it."

Dr. Perna paused, lost in his thoughts. "He really did take up the room, didn't he?"

"Yeah, he really did. When he told me he had found me a new therapist I told him I wasn't going to talk to you anyway, and he was just wasting his money. I was pretty mean that year." Regret painted her face.

"He understood," Dr. Perna offered. "He knew you were in pain. If memory serves, you were doing pretty well when his accident happened. I think he was very proud of you. You overcame a lot."

Dr. Perna adjusted his seat, studying Taylor carefully.

Taylor stared out the window wistfully, "I just wish he could see this. This year is going so well, I'm going to graduate high school and go to college. He's missing it; he'll miss all of it."

Dr. Perna glanced at the clock behind Taylor noting that they were over their slot by five minutes. He cleared his throat. "It's normal to feel regret as you come up on big milestones in your life and your father can't be a part of them. As long as those feelings don't lean into depression and you can't find the joy in your milestones. Allow yourself to be sad, no one expects you to forget that your father isn't there for any of them.

Dr. Perna paused, letting his words hang in the air as Taylor continued to stare out the window. "Let's be done for the afternoon. I want to see you next week though."

"OK," she said gathering her book bag and heading toward the door.

"I'll see you next week."

Dr. Perna circled his desk once Taylor shut the door to the outer office and made some notes in her file.

Patient is exhibiting a positive attitude and seems hopeful about the future. She mourns for her father but in a healthy way, anniversary of her abduction is coming up in a month. The fall is a difficult time she tends to waver from hopeful to hopeless easily. Will continue to see her once weekly and monitor progress. Sleep is acceptable.

Finishing out her file he returned to his notes for his speech.

Chapter 15

Saturday Morning

Taylor loved weekends. It was finally time for her to just relax. She still had a mountain of homework that she needed to take care of but having breakfast again with Andy was going to be the high point.

She was walking up to him when she heard his phone ring.

"Hello," Andy motioned for Taylor to wait for him. "Speaking," he said. "Hello sir, yes of course . . . No, I wasn't aware."

Andy turned away from Taylor.

"Yes, sir . . . I'm actually already here, sir. I was meeting a friend for breakfast . . . Yes sir, I'll call the local chief . . . Yes, sir, I'll keep you updated."

He turned back toward Taylor who was staring across the street, watching an older couple walk together.

"Hey kid, I gotta go, something has come up."

Taylor's face immediately turned into a pout. "You suck, I was starving."

"Don't say 'suck,'" he chastised her. "I'm starving too; let's get something to go, quick though."

Taylor and Andy ordered at the counter and had a cup of coffee while they waited for their breakfasts.

"What's going on?"

"Not sure yet, I've got to make some phone calls when we get outta here. We'll meet though again in a couple weeks OK?"

"Yeah, no big deal."

The waitress handed them each a bag of hot food over the counter. Andy paid, and they grabbed covers for their coffees.

"You headed home?"

"Well, I was going to have breakfast with a friend since I've got a ridiculous amount of homework to do. Breakfast was going to be my only break all day so, yeah, I'm going to go home and work on that."

"You know, no one likes a smart-ass, right?"

Taylor smiled in his direction. "You know I have heard that before."

"All right kid, get home, I'll talk to you soon."

Andy gave Taylor a quick hug and watched her get into her car. His eyes kept watch on the street, making note that nothing seemed out of the ordinary. He felt bad not telling her what the phone call was about considering it was all about her. He had also seen the stress that it caused a victim when they thought that there was some kind of break in a case that ended up being another dead end. It didn't seem worth it to put her through that until he knew more.

As he walked to his car he dialed the local chief's number.

Chief Naughton was the kind of man who wanted you to think he was a gruff and grumpy curmudgeonly type. In reality though he truly cared about his town and the people in it.

The chief picked up on the second ring.

"Chief, it's Detective Fisher."

"Fisher, well this is a surprise. How are you?"

"Hello sir . . . I'm well, thank you. Something has come up I need to discuss with you, it's concerning the Cormier abduction."

The Chief paused for a moment, "how long will it take you to get here?"

"I'm in town, I can meet you at the station in ten minutes."

"I'll be there in 5."

"Yes sir, see you there."

Andy's specialty as a detective was sexual assault cases. Taylor's abduction had changed all their lives in many different ways. He had read once about the ripple effect and he could see it everywhere in the small town. People didn't let their kids play in the front yard anymore, the local parks were more closely monitored and random people just sitting around on park benches near children were almost always met with a police presence. The parents of the community took what happened very seriously. Taylor's tale was a cautionary one and without an arrest, fear settled in to the town and never really left.

The station looked exactly as it had years ago, maybe just a bit more disheveled if that was even possible.

Walking through the door brought back so many memories.

Richard had liked the street. He loved being a cop and it was all he ever wanted to be. Andy loved it too, but he saw decisions being made and he wanted to be a part of that. Following Taylor's return home after the abduction, he decided to apply for the state police, intent on becoming a detective. He'd made detective six months after Taylor's father had died in the car accident. Richard had been upset when Andy applied for the state police job. Andy hadn't gotten around to telling him his plans to go for detective when he died.

"Fisher," a voice called out across the precinct. The chief was standing in his office behind his desk.

"Good to see you, sir."

Andy extended his hand and the chief grasped it warmly. "Good to see you too, Fisher. You look well. Being a suit suits you."

Andy smiled, the chief loved a good pun. "Thanks sir."

"So, what's going on?" the chief asked moving on from the pleasantries.

"You saw that a 10 year old girl was abducted in Virginia?"

"I did," the chief responded. "Horrible."

"The detectives in Virginia believe that this abduction may be *our* Jacob again."

The chief sucked in his breath. "What do they have?"

"Juliana Seville reportedly told her babysitter that she had made a new friend at the park. That his name was Jacob. The sitter didn't think anything of it until a couple days later when the little girl disappeared from her back yard and police started questioning her."

The chief sat silent for a minute.

"Have you seen her picture?" Andy asked.

The chief looked confused. "No, why?"

Andy grabbed his phone, pulled up the photo and turned it around.

The chief let out a whistle, "this girl looks just like Taylor did, it's uncanny."

The girl had a faint smattering of freckles, long blond hair, fair skin, and an innocent smile.

"This is the other reason they think it's Jacob. They think he's recreating the abduction so he can finish whatever he started."

"Do they have any leads?" the chief asked, still staring at the picture of the little girl.

"Possibly, you remember the FBI's CARD team?"

The chief nodded."They got a hit on a message board, someone posted that there was a girl, J.S., who looked just like T.C.".'"

"He used their initials instead of their names?"

"Looks like it, the interesting part is that it was posted a couple hours before she was reported missing. They tracked the IP address down to a house in Newport News, Virginia. The guy's name is Samuel Bishop. They're waiting for him to come home and are going to bring him in for questioning."

"OK," the chief said, encouraged, "so what's the next step?"

"You remember that the FBI had believed that Taylor's case was connected to three other abductions? In each one the children mentioned that they had made a friend—Jacob. Two girls, one in Utah and one in Colorado, and a boy out of New York. The children all ranged in age from eight to ten, with the exception of Taylor who was thirteen when she met Jacob."

The chief nodded having suspected something along these lines. During the hunt for Taylor the FBI had swooped in on the scene pretty quickly. They had resources the chief only dreamed of, but there were also chain of command issues and jurisdiction problems. It made things more difficult and he wasn't looking forward to having to get back into bed with them.

Andy sensed what the chief was thinking. "Listen, I remember what a pain in the ass they were to work with and I was just a cop back then. I've worked with these guys though, they are good people doing the best they can with the hand they're dealt. I don't know if they are going to be sent here or not, a lot of it will have to do with what they find at Bishop's house. Either way, my boss wants me to get started and make sure I'm up to speed on everything just in case this guy turns into something more."

"All right," the chief said, "what do you need from me right now?"

"It would help if I could go back through the old case files. I'd like to review everything."

"OK." The chief was a man of action; he preferred a task than to sit and wait for the FBI to fill him in on whatever they were working on. "Morse!" he shouted from inside his office. Andy sat in awkward silence waiting along with the chief for Dan Morse.

"MORSE!" The chief bellowed again.

The one patrol officer who happened to be in the office rose from his chair and darted out to the parking lot.

Minutes later, Dan appeared, somewhat out of breath, wiping his filthy hands with an equally dirty rag.

"Sorry Chief, one of the patrol cars broke down, again." Dan's face registered shock as he realized who else was in the room, "Andy?"

It had been a few years since Dan had seen the man he had once considered a mentor. Dan was a large man, not overweight but bordering on it. His eyes were kind and his mouth almost always looked like it was smiling. He was one of those people for whom the trials of life seemed not to touch.

"Hey, Morse," Andy said affectionately, "it's good to see you."

"Good to see you too, buddy. Look at you, all fancy now."

Morse jabbed at him, but Andy didn't mind. Morse had the type of personality that eased the tension in a room. Andy had missed that about him.

"Morse," the chief interrupted, "I need all the case files from the Cormier abduction. Everything you've got down in the basement, go get it. Set it up in the empty office so Fisher can get to work."

Andy turned. "Why do you have an empty office?"

"Budget cuts, we used to have a deputy chief and the captain position but a couple of years ago the city council—in their

84

enduring wisdom—decided that those roles could be done by the same person." The chief's voice dripped with sarcasm.

"It's why I need a raise," Morse joked.

Andy turned back toward him. "Oh yeah? I didn't realize you had made your way up in the world."

"That's what happens when you leave us for the big city."

"Yeah, yeah."

Morse motioned for Andy to follow him and led him to the empty office a couple of doors down from the chief's room.

"I'll go get the files for you."

"Thanks."

Andy looked around and considered for a moment turning on the computer that sat on the desk, but he remembered how slow they were a few years ago and decided to stick with his laptop instead.

He was still full from the breakfast sandwich he had eaten in the car. Coffee though, would be good. He hunted down the last cup at the bottom of the pot. The cup was warm in his hand. He drank his coffee black. Something he had picked up from Richard years ago. Richard used to make fun of the guys that drank cream and sugar with a little bit of coffee in it. Andy had learned that good black coffee could dance on your tongue like chocolate. Since Richard's death he had become a bit of a coffee snob. The smell coming from the cup in his hand warned him that this would not taste like chocolate. Although nothing had prepared him for the bitter, burnt, horrifying taste that assaulted his entire mouth.

Morse chuckled walking past him with two boxes stacked on top of one another. "Careful. That shit could peel paint off the walls. The chief started making it when you left as he said none of us did it right. Now we all have to go out and buy coffee because he refuses to admit that he's probably going to kill us with that."

"I'm going to start making the coffee again."

"You going to be here that long?"

"Not sure yet . . . maybe."

Morse dropped the boxes on Andy's new desk. Dust covered the tops of them and they smelled like the basement.

"Thanks."

"No problem. Let me know if you need anything else."

The boxes covered the entire desk and stood as tall as Andy. It had not been a small caseload.

Almost hesitantly he grabbed box number one and mumbled under his breath, "let's get this over with."

Andy spent the next three hours going back over his notes from interviews with Taylor following the abduction. Almost everything he remembered with glaring detail.

The files were archived in the computer system, but they were also on a thumb drive Andy had left in the bottom of the box. The red USB stick was small and clicked into his computer, automatically opening the files.

Audio interviews 1–4 stared back at him. Although he knew he should listen to them in the interest of being thorough, he didn't want to.

He needed a break, pushing back his chair he stood up and paced in front of his desk. "There's nothing there," he said to himself, "you know there's nothing there."

The tapes had been a point of much contention within the department. Typically, under more normal circumstances Andy's relationship with the Cormier family would have made his involvement ill-advised. The CARD Team at the time had refused to have someone of Andy's rank interview Taylor. The problem was whenever one of them went into the room she screamed like she was going to be killed. With Andy or her father, she just stared blankly at a wall. Eventually it was determined that this was the best option given the circumstances. The District Attorney had warned that any defense attorney would rip the interview to shreds. So, when the interviews ended up to be a waste of time on everyone's part, it was almost a relief.

He stared at the back of the laptop.

"Fuck it."

With purposeful steps he came around the desk and sat down. Reaching down he grabbed his ear buds and pulled his chair in.

Seconds later he heard his voice as clear as day, like it just happened.

Interview 1, 8 a.m., November 1, Heywood Hospital Andy Fisher performing the interview.

Victim has been examined by Doctors. She is malnourished, not dehydrated. She has been bound by both the ankles and the wrists. Doctor did a rape kit: they say multiple sexual assaults, one assailant. They note victim has not spoken. Only female Doctors have attended victim as she becomes extremely agitated if a male comes too close to her. She has been moderately sedated for the purpose of this interview. Doctors highly recommend more sedation. Toxicity screen came back negative. Victim is otherwise in acceptable medical condition.

For as long as Andy had been in police work he used recorders. It was why he was better at his job than most people. It wasn't just about the report someone writes or noting certain phrases a victim said. The truth could be heard in the cadence of speech, the inflections, the pauses. The details that would lead a good detective to the next question. Andy could hear the stress in his voice as he had tried to not say Taylor's name and not appear

87

as close to the situation as he was. For all the interviews he had done with her, he'd recorded them with his phone—he remembered leaving it on the hospital table in front of her. For a long time he had kept them on his phone, afraid that someone would lose the thumb drive.

"*Taylor*," he heard his voice say.

She hadn't spoken to him during this interview or the three after that. The police had lost valuable time because of this. She couldn't have run that far so wherever she had been held was close to where she was found. If she had just given them something maybe they could have gotten this guy, but she didn't; she just hummed through the entire interview staring through Andy like he wasn't even there.

He could hear her now, the popular children's nursing rhyme haunted his memories. Why parents would sing "You Are My Sunshine' to their children in an effort to comfort them astounded him.

The song was now the creepiest thing he could think of, especially when put in the context of a child abduction case.

"*Taylor, it's Andy,*" he had smiled and leaned in at this point, he remembered, hoping to connect with her on some level. "*Hunny, you've got to help me so we can find who did this to you.*"

Taylor stopped humming at the end of that statement. Andy could see her in his mind's eye. She almost focused on him for one minute but then phased out again and continued humming,

"*Taylor*," Andy said more sternly hoping to snap her out of it, she stopped humming.

"*You are safe.*"

Taylor had laughed at this, just once, loudly. The type of laugh that made Andy think she had lost her mind. He had begun to question over the next three interviews whether or not Taylor would ever really make it back to them.

Andy knew there was no more to the interview even though the timer on the screen said he had left the phone on for another fifteen seconds.

He placed his coffee down on the edge of his keyboard, which turned the volume up on the computer and through to the ear buds he was using. The empty static noise of the too-loud volume hurt his ears as he realized what had happened and moved the cup before trying to turn it down.

As his hand reached across he heard something. It was a voice. Her voice. But he couldn't tell what she said. It was mumbled and so low it's no wonder he hadn't heard it before. She was barely whispering. He pondered whether he'd turned around or something at the end of the interview. He had. He remembered now. Her laugh had scared and frustrated him. He had stood up from the chair and turned around staring at the wall.

His excitement was tangible he pulled the buds from his ears and turned his computer volume up as high as it could go. The seconds ticked by to the whisper. At first the words were indecipherable, but slowly he picked them out, playing it over and over again.

Her voice was a whisper, ghostlike in its transparency.

"*I'll never be safe.*"

He could hear it now he was sure of it.

His heart broke thinking of her sitting in that hospital room. He'd told her she was safe and she laughed, not because she had lost her mind but because she thought what he said was funny.

He wondered then what else was on the tapes. There were three other interviews when she had said nothing the entire time . . . or, at least, that had been what he thought originally.

He opened the advance audio setting and pulled the base and

high-end tones down as low as they would go knowing that human speech used the center audibles. He hoped by turning down the other two he could clean it up a little bit and maybe make it easier to hear anything that she said.

The state had a lab that he could send the audio to but it would be weeks until he got it back, he wasn't about to wait that long.

On the second and fourth tapes he couldn't hear anything, but the third one he remembered at one point Richard had come into the interview insisting that Andy stop and give Taylor a break.

Andy had taken him into the hall and talked him down. It had been three days and Taylor still hadn't spoken to anyone. She couldn't stand to have any men near her and the doctors were talking about admitting her to the psych ward, afraid that if left unsupervised she would try to harm herself.

Richard's voice came through loud and clear as it always did. *"Andy. You are done; she has been through enough, you've been in here for twenty minutes. Give it a rest."*

"Rich, I need to ask her these questions. We are losing valuable time."

"You think I don't know that?"

Richard's voice strained in an attempt to whisper what he clearly wanted to scream.

"She won't speak! I've asked her every different way to say something so that we can find this guy. I've even offered to kill him myself. She reacts to nothing! It's like she isn't even there!"

The voices were moving away from the phone and Andy could hear the door open and close, the muffled sounds coming from the other side of it. He turned the volume all the way up.

Taylor's voice barely a whisper came through the speakers. *"So many faces. He has so many faces. He could be you."*

This was huge. Andy couldn't believe he had missed this. He

was excited and needed to talk to Taylor. He was about to call the house when he noticed a shadow in his doorway. Agent Michael Knight stood there not moving or speaking.

"Fisher," he said slowly, "good to see you again."

"Agent Knight," Andy said back to him, secretly pissed that out of all the guys they could have sent, this was the one that he got. He was also surprised the FBI had sent someone out so soon . . . unless they had their own suspicions that there was more to Samuel Bishop than any of them knew.

The FBI had a special group called the Child Abduction Rapid Deployment Team. They were called CARD for short. Andy had worked with a number of them throughout the years—all seemed to be good guys with decent heads on their shoulders. All except for Michael Knight; he was an arrogant asshole.

"Something interesting?" Knight asked, pointing at Andy's computer.

"Maybe," Andy said elusively. "I'd like to look into it a bit more before I bring it up though. It could be something, but it could also be nothing."

Knight cocked his head to the side. "Let's start off on the right foot shall we? I know you aren't my biggest fan but I am here to do one job. This guy is my guy. I've been hunting him for the better part of five years and if you have anything that can help me I want to know what it is. You and I can either work together or I'll have you re-assigned so fast it'll make your head spin."

Andy took a deep breath, it didn't look like Knight had gotten any nicer since he'd seen him last. Andy pulled out the head-phones from his laptop and hit play. Knight was going to make this difficult, he knew it, but he also knew that Knight had the highest case-solving stats on the team. So while Andy didn't particularly like the guy he wouldn't argue with his results.

Andy had to spell out for Knight the last bit that Taylor said. Even with the adjustments he had made to his computer the audio was difficult to understand at best. He'd listened to it so many times he could hear it more clearly.

Knight's eyebrows raised. "Do you think our guy is a cop?"

The thought chilled Andy to his core but he had read once how cops and psychopaths had eerily similar psychological profiles. No one knew what the deal with this guy was. He could be just a pedophile, which the idea of him being 'just' anything upset Andy more than anyone could know. The point was, while Andy believed there was a more serious title attached to this person, like psychopath, he couldn't prove it.

"I don't know," Andy said, "I need to talk to Taylor. I don't even know if she remembers this—I doubt she does. Really these could be just hopeless ramblings of a deeply traumatized child. But there was something in her voice . . . something, something real I can't describe it but my gut tells me that there was something to her statement."

"How bad is her memory, no bullshit,"he said seriously.

Andy shrugged his shoulders. "The things she remembers she remembers with clarity and has stuck to the same story this entire time. The stuff she doesn't remember sometimes catches her by surprise and she gets a fragment of it but she can't piece them all together."

"How much does she remember if you had to put a percentage on it?" Knight inquired.

"Twenty-five percent," Andy responded. "Probably another fifteen or twenty-five she has in bits and pieces, and she could probably recover those memories if she tried."

"The rest?"

"I don't know. She may never get the rest back."

Knight nodded. "I came to tell you that Bishop came home; they brought him down to the station in Newport News."

"Does your team have someone there already?" Andy asked, referencing the CARD team.

"Yeah," Knight said, "Agent Gonzalez should have gotten there by now. We are all working on this; thankfully it's been a slow abduction month for us."

Andy left Knight's joke on the table, refusing to start joking about the children who hadn't been taken.

"I like Gonzalez," Andy noted. Andy had never met him directly but a few times they'd gone back and forth via email on different things. He seemed sharp and quick witted.

"They are going to start questioning and hopefully we will get something from his statements to allow a judge to give us a warrant for his home and his DNA. With any luck we'll find the girl and if he's a match to the Cormier rape then we've got ourselves a ball game."

"One step at a time. Who's doing the questioning?"

"One of the locals," Knight answered back. "We are trying to not completely take over until they prove that they're incompetent."

There was his arrogance again, although Andy didn't love the idea that they were leaving the questioning of this guy to some local cop with who knows what kind of experience.

"I've arranged for the interview to be streamed over a secure server so we can weigh in if we need to."

Andy nodded, impressed for a moment with Knight's foresight. "The conference room is across the precinct and I can log on with my laptop."

The two left Andy's office walking across the bullpen area to the conference room. The chief joined them.

"Chief, have you met Agent Michael Knight?" Andy asked.

"I haven't," the chief said, stretching out his hand to shake Knight's. "It's a pleasure to meet you, we are happy to have your help with this. Hopefully something pans out here."

Knight didn't respond but did force a half smile in the chief's direction before turning his attention to the computer screen.

Chapter 16

Saturday Afternoon

Samuel Bishop was in a small room, seated in a small chair in front of a small table. He didn't move or look around, he simply stared at the table until the detective came in. Only then did he pick his head up.

"Hi Samuel," the detective said to him.

"Call me Sam," he said warily.

The detective and Sam exchanged pleasantries for at least an hour. At no point did Sam ask why he was there or do anything to further the conversation. Andy and Agent Knight watched from a laptop in the conference room at the Templeton police station.

Samuel Bishop was slightly overweight, balding and wore glasses. He looked like the type of guy that would fold once the smallest bit of pressure was put on him. But his actions belied his appearance. Instead of cowering he seemed to be enjoying the attention, like he was happy to just sit and talk with someone.

The Detective flipped a picture of Juliana in front of Samuel. "Do you know this girl?"

Bishop's lip turned up crudely. "She's the one that's missing, right? She's pretty."

"She's ten years old," the detective said, a warning in his voice. "Do you know where she is?"

"You know I heard that she liked to play hide and seek, so I would check places where she could hide."

"Are you admitting to something?"

"Nope," Sam answered slowly, "just trying to be helpful."

Somewhere in the second hour, just when Andy was about to reach through the screen and kill someone, the detective asked, "Have you ever been to Templeton, Massachusetts?"

Sam smiled, "No, I can't say that I have."

"Are you sure?" the detective prodded again.

"I think I would remember a trip that far north, don't you? Did something happen up there?"

Sam was toying with them, Andy could feel it. His impatience rose. Knight seemed unperturbed, he just stared at the screen taking in all of Bishop's movements—his facial expressions, everything.

"You took a vacation five years ago, in the fall. Where did you go?"

"Did I? Huh, I took a hunting trip I think, but who can remember?"

"Hunting?" the detective said, not believing a word of what he was being fed. "You don't really look like the hunting type."

"What does the hunting type look like . . . you? Give anyone a gun and they can kill something, doesn't really require a type."

The detective was frustrated and he showed it in his tone, his body language, he was an open book. "What were you hunting?"

"Does," Sam said simply.

This went on for another hour. The detective would lead Sam to an answer and he'd counter it with a question or with an answer that let you know he wasn't going to give you anything to work with. Finally, the detective took a break leaving Sam in the room alone. Andy was about to look away when Sam looked right at the camera and smiled.

"It was the apples, wasn't it? Does she not like them anymore?"

The room erupted into chaos as two officers rushed in chasing the detective who was advancing toward Samuel with murderous intentions.

They managed to pull him back just in time slamming the door as they dragged the detective out. Samuel started laughing, at first a chuckle but then it grew to hysterics.

Andy turned to Knight, "Your guys had better get a judge to give you those warrants."

Knight nodded, the two united in that moment.

"Chief," Andy said as he strode to the door, feeling tired and slightly disheveled. "Two things: I think you should consider sending an officer down to the Cormier's. This is going to get out. When the judge grants those warrants the media will pick it up and they will be all over them. The five year anniversary is coming too—"

Andy tried to continue but the chief held up his hand. "I agree, no need to convince me. We should call Sarah though and warn her."

Andy nodded.

"What's the other thing?" the chief asked.

"Huh?" Andy said, momentarily distracted by the thought of Sarah. "Oh, no more making the coffee. If I'm going to be stuck here for the foreseeable future I'll make it myself."

The chief furrowed his brows. "My coffee—"

"Is horrible," Andy finished for him. "Please don't make me drink it."

"Fine," the chief acquiesced, "have it your way."

Andy smiled at the old grizzled man as he turned back towards his office. It was nice to be home in some ways.

"Somebody go tell dispatch I want to talk to Sarah Cormier in the chief's office," Andy called out to no one in particular.

Moments later Line 1 was blinking as Andy, Knight, Morse and the chief huddled around the phone. Knight pressed the button despite the fact that it was the chief's phone.

"Sarah, this is FBI Agent Michael Knight. I'm with the FBI CARD team. I have some news regarding the case involving your daughter."

Andy smiled inwardly imagining Sarah rolling her eyes at Knight's awkward phrasing.

"Where are you calling from?" Sarah asked carefully not giving away anything.

"I'm at the Police station in Templeton."

"Who's with you?"

"Hi Sarah," the chief said. "How have you been? How's Taylor?"

"Hi Chief, we're good."

"Hi Sarah, it's Dan Morse."

"Oh, hi Dan," her voice warm, "I haven't heard from you in quite a while."

Dan Morse was a rookie before Taylor's abduction. A few times Andy and Rich had taken him out drinking or some other form of mild debauchery. Sarah had always liked him. She paused on the line

"Hi Sarah," Andy said.

"Hi," Sarah responded shortly, the chief shot him a quizzical look which Andy ignored.

"Mrs. Cormier, another girl has gone missing in Virginia; we believe this is related to what happened to Taylor. A car has been sent to your house and will remain there for the time being."

Knight laid out the situation with Samuel Bishop and why they believed that he was Jacob. He did this without taking a breath and without giving her a chance to respond. Sarah was quiet. Andy knew she was taking stock of her reaction and being careful to keep it together.

"When will it go public?"

"We don't know, Sarah," Andy said. "It's very possible that the news outlets will pick it up when the papers are filed for the warrant. We'd like to have someone at the house with you just in case."

"OK."

"Did Taylor get home OK?" Andy asked, the conversation felt like it was just between the two of them

"Yeah, she's upstairs," Sarah said.

The room could feel the relief in that statement.

When Taylor ran screaming into a quiet residential neigh-borhood at 6 a.m. forty days after she had been taken, it was a national sensation. The world watched the small New England town where a 13-year-old girl just vanished with very few leads and then one day she was running through the streets screaming at the top of her lungs and banging on doors in a frenzied panic. She was only one mile from her house.

It was a miracle, the media reported. Everyone wanted an interview with Taylor, her nurse mom and her cop dad. Taylor, however, was deeply traumatized and was in no position to talk to anyone. Richard dealt mostly with the requests. Sarah hated the press; hated seeing their names out there. The media was a circus and they were relentless in their pursuit of the family. Richard, though, wouldn't listen. He wanted the attention for the case, so he said. With Taylor refusing to speak the only chance they had was that someone had—or would—see something, and he wanted to make sure that the world was watching. Sarah and Taylor though, were reclusive. Whenever something broke in the case or there was a flimsy connection, the rabid dogs would jump all over it. Since Richard's death there hadn't been any major breaks, but Sarah feared what would happen without him there to serve as the buffer between them and the world.

"Is it him?" Sarah asked.

"We think it is, Mrs. Cormier," Knight answered.

"Andy?" Her voice was raw.

"There are some encouraging ties from him to this location and his general profile fits what we are looking for."

"Andy?" Her voice more serious now.

Andy paused and looked around the room. "Sarah, I don't want to get your hopes up if it isn't the guy."

"Andy!"

He sighed. "Yeah, I think it could be him."

"I need to talk to Taylor and let her know what is happening, I'm turning our phones off so if you want to talk to us send your officer to the door. And Chief . . ."

"Yeah?"

"Keep them off my lawn," Sarah said and then promptly hung up.

Andy stood up and paced around the office. "Do we know if they have actually gone for the warrant yet?"

Knight was staring at his phone. "Gonzalez says the lawyers are working on it. Looks like the judge is a real ball buster."

"Awesome," Andy said, "that's fucking awesome."

"Fisher," the chief said sternly, "go get some air."

The chief was fine with outbursts of cursing as long as he was the one doing it. If one of his officers started, he sent them for a walk.

Andy left the precinct and went through the neighborhood. It was cold, somewhere in the forties, and the sun was lost behind the clouds making it feel colder than it was.

He had made the loop around the neighborhood twice, it was probably time to go in. That and Morse was standing outside looking for him.

"You've gotten angry in your old age, Detective."

"Yeah, yeah."

"I like it," Morse smiled with his hands up. "It's about time you stopped being so blasé about things."

"Is there a reason you're out here?"

"The judge issued the warrant."

Five seconds later the familiar tones from *Law and Order* rang in his pocket. Long ago Andy had set up Google Alerts for any kind of reference to Taylor or Jacob, which made it easier for him to keep track of things that were going on.

A reporter in Newport News down in Virginia had just tweeted: *Local Police are questioning a man related to the abduction of Juliana Seville. This abduction may be connected to the infamous Cormier abduction in Templeton, Massachusetts, 5 years ago.*

"Shit!"

The tweet had already been shared a hundred times.

Morse shifted his eyes, looking at Andy's phone. "Is it me or does it seem like social media is making this job harder."

Andy's mouth formed a hard line. "Harder, definitely harder."

Morse turned toward the precinct, Andy followed, an uneasy feeling filling the pit of his stomach.

Knight stood in the corner of the room, focused entirely on

his phone.

"We got the warrant," he said without looking up. "We only got it for the house; the judge wouldn't give us one for his DNA, said we didn't have enough evidence."

"If this is our guy, he has not evaded capture for so many years by leaving evidence lying around his house. We are going to need more."

Andy was irritated, and it showed. "Morse!"

Morse, who hadn't left Andy's side, stepped into his line of sight.

Andy lowered his volume. "I need you to get some background on this guy. What other properties does he own? What does he do for work? I want to know everything about him."

Knight, still glued to his phone, bristled, "We are already doing that. This isn't our first rodeo."

Andy ignored him. "I want it all in an hour, so call in whoever you need but make this happen. If this is our guy we need to know and, if it isn't, we need to know. Got me?"

"Yes, sir."

Seconds later Morse had a handful of people around him and he was laying out instructions. "I want you to get into this guy's life, I wanna know what his mother ate for breakfast this morning." Morse scanned the group, letting the seriousness of his tone and demeanor sink into them. "Do you understand me?"

He got a series of nods and dismissed them before turning to Andy. "These are good people and they'll get you what you need."

"Thanks, Dan."

"Of course, sir."

"Fisher," the chief called from his office. Andy turned,

followed closely by Knight.

"You need to see if Taylor can ID him."

The chief pushed a picture of Samuel Bishop over to him.

Andy hesitated, "I may not be the best person to do that."

Knight's head popped up from his phone and he stepped in front of Andy, blocking him from the chief's sight.

"I can take it to her. Would be good to be introduced—it looks like I may be here a while."

"No." Andy wasn't about to let Knight within a foot of Taylor, at least not until he had to. "I've got it."

On Andy's way out, he asked dispatch to inform the officer stationed at their house that he was on his way over. Coming out of the precinct he saw clouds gathering. A storm was coming.

Chapter 17

Saturday Evening

Saturday Evening
Pulling up to Richard's old house was like was walking into his childhood home. The ghosts of the past pulled at Andy and begged to be remembered.

He could see him and Richard playing polish horseshoes on the side yard next to the house while Sarah busied herself in the kitchen and a toddler version of Taylor played on the porch. He could remember barbecues in the yard, Taylor riding a bike for the first time, and a thousand other moments that had all been inconspicuous. He even remembered the night he showed Richard the 'Be On The Lookout' from New York.

Some memories weren't so nice.

Richard, Sarah and Andy sat at the far end of the patio, a small fire going. Having grown up in small towns all three of them had a special affinity for having a fire on a summer night. Richard kept a small cooler always stocked with beer on the patio. He stood and grabbed both him and Andy another drink before returning to his seat.

Sarah had just finished ushering Taylor upstairs before she joined them outside. "So, what's going on down at the station?"

They always waited until Taylor had gone to bed to talk about

Richard's job. Sarah didn't feel that a 12-year-old should be subjected to the topics that inevitably came up when your husband and his best friend were cops.

Richard took a sip of his beer. "Not a ton really—the regular stuff. Couple parties got out of hand over the weekend down at the sand pit. They emptied one out and like two hours later another party with a whole other set of kids had started down there."

"The owner really needs to figure out a way to keep people out of that area if he doesn't want them trespassing. Those sand pits just beg for teenagers to trash them and there were a few on ATV's that we weren't going to get a hold of no matter what we did, so we just let them go into the woods. We're lucky that none of them crashed into a tree in the dark."

"Did you see the BOL out for that guy?" Andy shifted in his chair, unsure if he should have brought it up.

"No," Richard leaned forward interested.

"What's a BOL again?" Sarah asked. "You know I hate it when you two talk in code."

"'Be on the Lookout.' It'll be from out of state."

"It was sent out by the Corning police in upstate New York," Andy said, confirming Richard's previous statement. "Looks like they had a boy go missing a couple years ago and it looks like they finally have a person of interest. They sent along a sketch; his name is William Lange."

As Andy was talking he had grabbed his phone and pulled up the notice before turning the phone to face Richard and Sarah who were seated next to one another on the love seat.

Sarah got up to pour herself another glass of wine from the cooler, disturbed by the thought of a person like that being anywhere near her home.

Richard grabbed the phone and scrolled down to see the picture.

"I'm going to print this, OK?"

"Yeah, man, go ahead."

What made Richard such a good cop was that he was always a cop. At no point did he turn off. Sarah watched his wheels start turning and she knew that he was already thinking about who he had seen that day and the day prior. He had a memory that was incredible, and Taylor had inherited the same trait. She could just recall things in incredible detail. The two of them would play a game sometimes where they would be in a store and one would yell out close your eyes. The person with their eyes closed would have to recall everything they had seen in front of them and on their sides and anything they thought seemed out of place.

It annoyed Sarah to no end as it made it incredibly difficult to actually get any shopping done, but at the same time she truly admired how good Taylor had gotten at it. She could at any point tell you exactly who was around her and what seemed out of place. It was a genius game for a kid . . . especially if you were grooming her to be in the FBI, Sarah always thought.

"Richard, give Andy his phone back," Sarah said as she walked back toward him and sat down curling her feet up under her body and tucking her toes under his leg.

"Huh? Oh, sorry buddy, here you go."

Andy smiled at him. "I'm sure he's not here. Besides, they sent it out because they only recently decided he's a person of interest and apparently he moved away over a year ago. I assume they have a reason for thinking he headed this direction. I wouldn't worry about it, Sarah, really."

She smiled, comforted by his words. "Thanks, Andy."

"I'm going to bed," Richard said suddenly standing up. "What are you two doing? Getting drunk by yourselves again?"

Sarah smiled, "Probably, I don't have to work tomorrow."

"I do, but I bet my buddy will cover for me."

Richard snorted, "Andy, you're in charge of the fire. I'll see you in the morning."

Richard leaned in toward Sarah, his mouth and breath caressing her ear, "And I'll see you in bed."

Andy watched Sarah smile, her face tilted up ever so slightly towards Richard's as she leaned in for a kiss. Andy looked away as their lips met.

Without Richard to keep her warm, Sarah crossed the patio to the outside storage bin retrieving her favorite blanket. It smelled like fire and leaves and she loved to curl up under it at the end of most evenings. The fire sparked and crackled, dancing in its own hypnotic way that made conversation unnecessary . . . except.

"Why did you break up with Jennifer?"

The magic broken by Sarah's abrupt question.

"Who says I broke up with her? She called it quits, not me."

"That's not what happened, and you know it. You two dated for as long as you could reasonably expect her to wait. What did you think: that you could just date forever and she would never want to get married and have children?"

"It wasn't that long," Andy said, disbelief in his voice.

"It was three years!"

"That's not that long."

"Andy, we're not that young anymore. What were you waiting for?"

"I don't know . . . it just never really felt like the time to get married. Still doesn't."

Sarah shook her head and smiled, letting the subject drop for the moment. She watched him through the flames as he tried to pretend their conversation hadn't upset him. He was lonely, Sarah could tell. She could feel his eyes on her sometimes and it never made her uncomfortable. She knew it was loneliness that drew his gaze.

Her glass was empty and it was getting colder. "I'm going inside; can you make sure the fire is out, OK?"

"No problem," Andy said, standing up as she stood for a quick embrace and a kiss on the cheek. Andy sat back down and watched as Sarah climbed the stairs into the kitchen.

The rain continued to fall, harder now than when he arrived. In some ways he couldn't wait to get out of the car. Yet he sat for one more moment letting the scent of the fire and the image of Sarah drift softly from his mind. Gathering his resolve, he pulled up his collar, opened the door and walked into the rain. Bypassing the front door, he ran toward the back and stared at the now abandoned fire pit before he tentatively knocked on the door.

Sarah's anxious face lightened, just barely, at the sight of Andy on her porch and not a reporter. That relief was temporary as her eyes then registered the pain of seeing him. She paused as her hand reached the door knob, for a heartbeat, before she yanked it open.

"Why are you here?"

Andy didn't move and hardly dared to breath. "Sarah . . . I did what you asked, I stayed away. I didn't come back for Richard's remembrance mass and I've kept my distance from Taylor even though she doesn't understand why. Please . . ."

He was going to continue but Sarah held up her hand and her face softened just a bit. "Just tell me why you are here."

Her voice echoed exhaustion and stress, and while he desperately wanted to shut out what was happening around them and have the conversation that absolutely needed to happen, he couldn't.

"I need to talk to Taylor."

Her eyes narrowed, sensing a threat. "Why?"

"I need her to look at a few mug shots and tell me if any of them look familiar."

Sarah's eyes grew dark, her lips pressing into a straight line. In the first year following Taylor's abduction it would happen monthly, the police would ask her to visit the station to look at a series of photographs. Taylor would always say that none of them looked like Jacob. She claimed she remembered what he looked like but her description of his face would change. The sketch artists didn't know what to do with her. Sometimes he was thin, others he was heavier. She would waver on the size of his nose or his cheekbones. Inevitably she would become agitated and retreat into herself humming that damn song. As the years went on the requests of Taylor grew more sparse. In part due to her unreliability, in part due to the fact that there was no one new to look at.

Sarah stepped into the doorway, blocking Andy from entering.

"I don't think so. I assume you need her corroboration for something, otherwise you wouldn't be here." Sarah's eyes searched Andy's for information. "What is it? The babysitter didn't recognize him? He has an amazing alibi? The judge won't give you the warrant you need?"

Andy's eyes wavered, just for a second. Sarah saw it and attacked like a shark that smelled blood in the water.

"Get off my porch, I'm not putting her through this again, if you think that you can just show up here and –"

"Sarah!" Andy had stepped forward rather than retreat, "I have something else. I heard something on my interview tapes from the hospital after her abduction. She said something and I need to know what she meant."

"Which interview?"

Andy stepped towards the ledge of the doorway. "The third one."

Sarah repositioned her body, forcing Andy to step back into the rain. She knew he wouldn't touch her and she was using it to her advantage.

"She didn't speak in that interview. She didn't speak for two more days after that interview."

"She did. I have it . . . it was just a whisper, but she spoke."

Sensing her daughter, Sarah turned and saw Taylor standing in the kitchen watching them.

"Hey, kid," Andy tried to act nonchalantly, not knowing if she had heard him or not.

"I didn't say anything," Taylor said defiantly.

"Sarah," Andy said with a fair amount of force. "It's fucking pouring can I come in?"

He could see the faint smile on the corners of her mouth as she turned to the side, forcing him to squeeze past her body.

Andy stood in the kitchen for a moment before he took off his wet coat and brushed the rain off his backpack. Taylor handed him a towel from the downstairs bathroom which he took happily. Everything was wet and the cold added a chill to his bones that would be difficult to get rid of. It was warm in the house at least and the towel helped dry his hair if not his shirt.

"So what's up with this guy?" Taylor asked sitting down at the island in the kitchen.

"Samuel Bishop," Andy said.

"Right," she responded with a cookie in her hand, "Samuel Bishop. Is it him?"

"I don't know, I was hoping you could look at a few pictures and let me know what you think."

110

"What happens when I tell you that none of them are Jacob?"

"Not much. You know the drill, we'll keep working on it. And the lawyers will note if it goes to trial that you couldn't identify him from mug shots."

"You are going to need much more than me to make a case stick in court." She may only be eighteen, but she had done her homework when it came to what a lawyer would need to get a conviction. The DNA they pulled from Taylor's rape kit was good and her physical injuries told them things. But any lawyer worth their salt would rip Taylor's recollection of the events to shreds. Her memory of what she remembered was almost infallible. Her story never changed, she never added or removed detail. The problem was once she got past her solid memories the rest didn't make sense. Jacob's facial features were inconsistent, she had no idea how she had escaped, she was obsessed with that nursery song. The only thing they could hope for at this point was that any memories Taylor got back would lead them to real physical evidence. Going on her word alone had potential to damage any case against Jacob.

"Can we skip the mug shots for now?"

Andy was disappointed but tried not to show it. "Yeah, of course." He pulled out his laptop and opened the audio file. "I need you to listen to this though."

He played it for Sarah and Taylor three times before either one said anything.

"What did you mean?" Sarah asked Taylor.

Taylor looked white as a ghost. Andy thought she might pass out.

"I don't know, I don't remember."

"Are you sure? Listen to it again."

Andy hit play again. Taylor's voice came through the computer speakers. *"So many faces. He has so many faces. He could be you."*

She said it in a sing-song way. She sounded crazy. It sent chills up Andy's arms and he could see the goosebumps on Taylor's as well.

Taylor sat in the chair as still as a statue with a chill in her heart. There was something to that phrase, something that sat on the edge of her memory threatening to return. She saw faces flash before her eyes but there were so many and too fast to really see them. The only similarity was the cold blue eyes, always the same eyes. It was like a flash of lighting, and as quick as it came it went. She blinked trying to get the memory back, but it was already gone.

Andy could tell when a person was remembering something, though it certainly wasn't hard to spot. The eyes went unfocused and stared through you instead of at you. With Taylor, because so many of her memories were unrecovered, when she did have any kind of flash there was no mistaking it.

"I think you sometimes remember more than you realize. I think it's hard to think about it and I think maybe you don't want to think about it. If you tried though, really tried, I bet you could tell me what all those faces mean to you. Are they different people? Is it the same person do you think? Talk to me, Taylor, please, I need your help. Juliana needs your help!"

Taylor's eyes filled with tears spilling over onto her face and shirt. "I can't!"

These tears were hopeless and her sobs echoed their despair. Sarah wrapped her in a hug and moved her from the kitchen to the couch in the living room. Andy looked out the window and saw the news crews starting to arrive. The cop outside appeared to have a handle on it and at the moment it was just two vans, both of them small local news stations. It was dark in the house,

Andy turned on the lights.

"Don't," Sarah said sitting Taylor down next to her on the couch. "It makes it easier for them to see inside with the cameras." Andy pulled the shades on each of the windows protecting them from the glare of the lights as much as he could.

Taylor sat so close to her mother it was hard to tell where she ended and Sarah began. Andy took up a position opposite on one of the chairs, perching himself on the arm.

Taylor's sobs had settled down to hiccups as she attempted to clean her face. Sarah extended her hand towards a box of tissues on the other side of the room. Andy moved quickly to hand her the box.

Her face now dry with the help of a small handful of tissues, Taylor spoke. "I don't remember. I want to help you, I really do, and this thing with the missing girl, I wish I could help you. Do you have any idea what it's like to have these fragmented memories of the most horrible experience of your life? It's actually worse than knowing exactly what happened and in what order because I don't know if he raped me first and then starved me or starved me before raping me.

"I don't know anything: if I fought, if I gave up, if I escaped, or if he just let me go. I don't *know*! It's all a jumbled mess in my head and it flies in front of my eyes without warning when I'm not ready."

Taylor was on a roll and Sarah and Andy just sat there knowing she needed to just get it out.

"If I smell something familiar I flash back to the basement, but just a few seconds and then it's gone. And I don't know in what order anything is supposed to go. It's like I've been betrayed by my own brain." Her anger had been building but now it was in full fury and it was directed at Andy.

"Don't you think I wanted to tell you who did this to me?" Taylor shouted. "It's my fault he hasn't been found. It's my fault Juliana is missing. It's my fault ..."

She succumbed to her sobs, letting them roll over her like waves. Each one pulling her deeper and deeper into the ocean. She went into the darkness willingly, knowing it was wrong but she didn't care. The painful memories enveloped her soul and instead of pushing them away she reveled in them. Sobbing harder and harder until she couldn't breathe . . . she couldn't breathe. Her stomach emptied itself on to the carpet.

Sarah had watched her daughter with increasing concern and, in spite of herself, glanced to Andy for reassurance. She was just about to tell Andy to get a bowl when Taylor vomited all over their shoes and immediately, Sarah was on the floor with her, holding her hair up and rubbing her back like she would have for a much younger child. Andy went to the kitchen and got some towels, a glass of water and a large bowl.

Sarah had coaxed Taylor back up to the couch and Andy knelt to clean up the mess.

"Andy," Taylor hiccuped between syllables. "I'm s-or-ry." Hiccup.

Sarah handed her another tissue.

Andy was still kneeling on the floor and looked over at her.

"Sweetheart, you have nothing to be sorry for. I'm sorry, I pushed. I hoped that if you heard what you said that maybe you could tell me what you meant or that maybe you had remembered some things that you didn't understand and that this would help. I love you; I never want you to feel this way."

Taylor lunged at him and hugged him, hard. He knew when she was upset like this it was harder for her to touch anyone but her mother. He hugged her back, being careful to pay attention

114

to her cues when she needed to pull away.

"I'm going to go upstairs, take a shower and go to bed," Taylor said, pulling back from Andy. "I love you, Mom."

Sarah kissed Taylor on the forehead, pausing for just a moment to feel the warmth of her daughter's head.

"I love you, too."

As Taylor headed upstairs Andy finished cleaning up, hoping to delay the wrath he felt certain Sarah was about to unleash on him. Instead she said nothing and walked into the kitchen.

He followed her, deposited the bowl in the sink and started washing it. Andy didn't have any siblings, so Taylor was like the niece he would never have. Cleaning up after her didn't make him squeamish at all. It made him feel closer to her as even at her worst moments he was still there. That was how he wanted both of them to feel, somehow, he hadn't communicated that to Sarah, at least, not well.

Sarah reached up above the sink and grabbed a bottle of Jameson. Putting it down on the counter she grabbed two glasses and filled each one with ice.

"Come on, you're starting the fire."

The rain had just ended, and the smell of water still hung in the air.

Tucked behind the house, in the corner, the fire pit couldn't be seen from the street, which was all Sarah cared about. She opened the news report on her iPad while Andy cleared out the pit and gathered kindling and logs they kept under a crudely made shelter. Thirty minutes later the fire burned at a steady rate.

The two had nursed their drinks but they hadn't spoken. Now the fire was really going, and Sarah was tucked under her blanket on a chair.

"Can I watch it with you?" Andy asked tentatively.

"Yeah," she said, positioning the iPad so he could see it from his chair, he leaned forward so he could hear.

NBC's familiar local news anchors mobilized on the screen.

"*Our News Right Now is that there is a person of interest being questioned in Virginia connected with the abduction of a 10-year-old girl, Juliana Seville, she has been missing since Wednesday. We have also recently learned it is believed this abduction may be related to the Cormier abduction from five years ago.*"

Taylor's face flashed across the screen. Some horrible picture of her when she was being released from the hospital.

"*The Cormier abduction touched the nation as a then 13-year-old Taylor Cormier was taken after she got off the school bus. Forty days later she returned having escaped from her captor, whom she called Jacob. Since her return there have been relatively few leads.*"

The screen switched to video from a local news station in Virginia showing Samuel Bishop being brought into the station. The second anchor continued with live video of Sarah's house playing in the background. Andy could see the lights in the living room and his car parked in the driveway.

"*We are learning that Samuel Bishop has made multiple appearances on message boards that exist on the internet praising Jacob, as well as suggesting child pornography be made legal. He is also believed to have been in the area during the time Taylor Cormier was abducted. This abduction struck the heart of the small Templeton town; its community mobilized in an unprecedented way, garnering national attention. Since Taylor's abduction the community's response has been used by countless other towns as an example when preparing for natural disasters or large scale acts of violence.*"

"How the hell did they get that?" Andy swore.

"Which part?"

"The part about the message boards. We haven't even gotten a chance to review all the transcripts yet."

Four months after Taylor had gotten home, Sarah had gone on one of the message boards. She wanted to see what these people were saying about her daughter. It was a mistake. One she regretted to this day. The things that people wrote she knew would never leave her brain. She was furious. She unplugged the computer and put it in the recycling bin. When Richard got home that night they got into a huge fight—Sarah wanted him to find these people and arrest them. They had to have committed some type of heinous crime to even say these things.

Richard hadn't had a good day and instead of holding his wife and letting her cry as she tried to purge those memories from her mind, he yelled at her. Told her she was an idiot thinking he could just walk into someone's home and arrest them for writing some vile thing online.

To this day his words that night echoed in her mind: "Don't you know that I've read these already? Did you just show up to this party? What do you think these people are doing, holding bake sales? I don't need this, at work all day and then to come home to this?"

Sarah hadn't realized it at the time but that was the beginning of the end for them. They never really recovered from that fight. They just moved on from it.

The News Right Now moved on to another story as Sarah hit the button on the bottom of the iPad and it went black. Andy leaned back, admiring the mostly melted ice in his drink. He hadn't expected this time with her and he didn't want to pry into why he was allowed it. Instead he got the impression he was there to make the silence feel less lonely. So he sat contently and waited for her to make the next move.

They finished their drinks at the same time and for the first time that night she looked at him.

The words turned over in his mind, long before his lips moved. "I miss you."

Sarah said nothing for a full minute, just looked back at him before a heavy sigh escaped her lips and her shoulders sagged. "I miss you too," she said, sadness in her voice.

The fire crackled and Andy reached over to add another log. The movement was familiar and strange at the same time. Sarah had tucked herself back on to the chair and sat with her left hand covering the bottom half of her face.

"All this," her hand waved towards the front of the house, "all this going on right now, it's just insane. It's fucking insane. Did you know for the three years after Taylor's abduction, Richard was barely here?"

Andy had in fact known that, or at least had strongly suspected it.

"He was always working and if he wasn't working at the station he was trying to find Jacob. He was obsessed, and I encouraged it. I let him drink himself into oblivion. I let him ignore his daughter. I let him abandon our marriage. I wanted him to find that bastard so much . . . and I thought he would. I thought he would find him, he'd go to jail and then we would be able to go back to the way things were. But I was wrong . . . Richard was lost to me long before he died."

Sarah paused and took a deep ragged breath. "And then there's you. You were his best friend and I feel so connected to you that even when I refused to speak to you for a year I still wanted to call you almost every day." Sarah's voice was now thick with emotion and tears had started to fall from her eyes.

Andy's voice was soft and gentle, "I never wanted to hurt you."

The air was cold, and the fire did little to warm their faces.

"I know," she said wiping her nose on her sleeve. "I just wish it wasn't such a mess."

Andy knew she was still keeping him at arm's length. She hadn't opened the door, but he could see the light coming from the key hole and knew he had a chance. That was all he needed; for tonight it was enough.

He stood up and put his glass on the table between them. He put his hand on her shoulder and gave it a squeeze.

"Get inside and lock the door, I don't want you out here by yourself."

Her fingers came up and touched his hand, just for a second, before she gathered their glasses and started up the porch steps.

He headed down the driveway towards his car.

The news crews had multiplied. He counted three major stations, all with anchors on the lawn recording clips for the eleven o'clock news. The officer was doing his best to keep them under control, but it wasn't good enough. As soon as they saw Andy they abandoned their clips and swarmed him.

"Detective! Detective!" they shouted. "Is this man, Samuel Bishop, actually Jacob? Were you inside with Taylor and Sarah Cormier? How are they holding up? Do you have any new information to share with us?"

Their questions were relentless, Andy could barely see between the flashes and the lights on the cameras.

"Ladies and Gentleman," he boomed, stopping their questions mid-stream. "We have no comment at this time."

The reporters gaffed and began to pepper him again with questions. He didn't speak but instead held up his hand.

"Please respect the Cormier's privacy and their property."

The reporters didn't move.

Andy suppressed the rage that threatened to engulf him. Instead he took in a huge breath and yelled, "Get off their lawn!"

The reporters grumbled not enjoying being yelled at.

As they sauntered away, Andy stormed over to the officer on duty, "What's your name?"

"Marrier, sir."

"You need to hold the line. I don't want to see the yard littered with reporters again. They will do it if they think they can. But only, if they think they can, be the reason they know they can't. Got me?"

"Yes, sir." The cop nodded, clearly knowing who was in charge.

"Radio it in to dispatch," he said, "I want to make sure whoever comes on after you is clear on that subject."

Andy opened his car door and got in. Somehow his hand held the warmth of Sarah's shoulder, he smiled as he drove away.

Andy could already feel the toll of a very active investigation. It wasn't as easy as it had been when he was younger. The fatigue settled on his shoulders weighing him down.

Andy lived in a small one bedroom apartment just outside of Boston. The price of his rent would make a normal persons skin crawl but his pay as detective was decent. He didn't prefer the city, wishing sometimes he still lived in the more rural areas he was used to. For as long as this case took, Motel 6 would be home. Situated next to the town's only gas station the motel was exactly what you would expect. He had already spoken to the manager about a monthly rental situation. There were a couple of units with kitchens and the manager had agreed to let him move over into one of those by the end of the week.

Knight had texted him while he was with Sarah but he had ignored it. Wanting to be alone with her for a few moments. The phone though dinged every few minutes reminding him he had missed messages. Pulling into the parking lot he fished his key out of the center console before checking his phone.

Call me, we've got some issues.

Andy inwardly groaned, "Of course there's an issue," he thought to himself.

The rain which had stopped began again with vengeance on his drive home, he ducked his head and ran to his door, fumbling for a moment to get it opened. His car left unlocked, he didn't bother to go back. Anyone willing to steal something in this rain deserved to get whatever was in that car anyway. The nice thing about staying in a motel was that you weren't paying for the heat. Cold and wet, Andy turned the thermostat all the way up. He laid out his coat to dry over the desk chair and grabbed a beer out of the refrigerator before calling Knight back.

"Took you long enough," Knight disregarded the pleasantries of conversation.

"I was busy, what's the problem?"

"No smoking gun inside Bishop's house. We found child pornography on his computer, that alone gave them enough to arrest him. So far nothing has been found connecting him to the Seville girl."

Andy was confused, "That's a start, what did you expect to find, a signed confession sitting on his kitchen counter?"

Knight ignored Andy's sarcasm, "We sent another agent to talk to the babysitter again, she admitted that she looked around for about two hours trying to find the girl herself before calling police. I think the timeline could match up, but we need more."

Andy's hand raked through his hair, "Ok, I've gotta sleep for a few hours, let's start up again in the morning."

Knight with all his interpersonal skills promptly hung up, no goodbye of acknowledgement.

"God, I hate that guy," Andy said to no one.

Andy's room and all its furniture smelled like smoke and piss. It would have bothered him more if he wasn't so tired. Instead he leaned back in his chair, and fell asleep.

Chapter 18

unday
Taylor slept for fifteen hours, waking up just before 10 a.m. After she'd left her mother and Andy downstairs she did something uncharacteristic. She took the sedatives Dr. Perna had prescribed, and was thankful for the dreamless sleep she had fallen into. She was, however, starving and felt just the slightest bit fuzzy. She stretched her limbs, languishing in bed just a bit longer while she replayed the night's events in her mind.

Images jumped in front of her eyes: throwing up, screaming at Andy, her mother looking desperately at each of them. She couldn't shake the eeriness of hearing her voice on that tape. She ran through the words over and over in her mind, trying to remember anything at all, but it was useless.

The first thing she could remember after her abduction, was seeing her mother sitting on her hospital bed, crying.

Confused, she had asked her mom what was wrong, and then she began to feel it, the soreness, the fatigue, the violation. Besides knowing that Jacob had taken her, she barely remembered a thing.

At the time doctors had warned Taylor that her memories could return at any point. It could be all at once, small pieces here or there, but that they should be prepared for it. They said it would likely be very difficult when they did come back. Her situational amnesia was described as a way for Taylor's mind to protect itself by blocking out the trauma, when it felt it was safe, it would unlock it.

Over the years, some things had floated back: her actual abduction and the first few days in the basement. Recovering those memories hadn't been as traumatic as she originally feared. One day she was staring out at the rain and it just floated back, like remembering a dream.

Five years later and Taylor still only had snippets. Of the forty days, she remembered next to nothing. What she did have were the leftovers, the post-traumatic stress of the events even though she couldn't remember the events themselves.

She hated the sound of running water; it sent chills up her spine like nails on a chalkboard.

She hated apple anything: apple pie, apple cider, apple scented candles in the fall.

She despised the smell of basements and was left wondering if she would ever do her own laundry again.

Those things though were manageable. And since those first few memories had come back, she now understood them which made her feel less crazy.

There were things though that she didn't understand at all, and they would send her into a complete panic attack. Masks in particular, or anything that covered or changed a person's face. The smell of latex was particularly hard for her as well.

The first Halloween after her abduction a group of kids showed up at the house for trick or treating. Taylor screamed when she saw the group of 7-year-old's at the doorway with all manner of masks on, threw the bowl of candy at them, slammed the door and ran upstairs. She had to listen to her father apologize to their parents for five minutes. No one came to trick or treat at their house anymore.

The worst one though was the song she sang. It was a learned behavior the doctors had told her, but imagine learning something that made you feel better but you have no idea how you learned it. In a lot of ways it was like her body and her mind had been hijacked.

The scent of coffee was wafting up the steps and she heard her mother taking mugs out of the cabinet. Taylor didn't think her mother had last night off work, she probably had called in sick.

Thankfully the hospital had been more than reasonable with her mother when things like this happened. If her mother lost her job they would certainly have to move, the next closest hospital was hours away.

She got up and steadied herself before trudging downstairs.

"Hey baby," Sarah said when she saw her. Sarah struggled to sleep at night, a product of working the night shift. She knew she would need a nap at some point that day.

The news was on in the living room providing background noise. Taylor wasn't paying attention to it until she heard Juliana Seville's name. She circled into the living room, her mother following her and standing by her side arms crossed like she was holding her insides together.

"We bring you down to our sister station in Richmond, Virginia as local officials are holding a press conference."

The parents stood behind the Chief of Police. Microphones covered most of their faces.

He held his hands up signaling for silence. "Mr. and Mrs. Seville will give a brief statement. Please refrain from asking questions. I will address your concerns following their statement."

The mother and father stood together, both looking like they hadn't slept or eaten in the last week. The father read from a piece of paper which shook either from his hand or the wind, Taylor couldn't tell.

"We would like anyone, who knows anything, about where Juliana is to come forward. We don't care how you have come across this information, we just want her to come home. She is a good girl, she doesn't deserve this, please help us, please." The father's voice, which had started strong, had begun to break down, overcome with emotion and exhaustion.

Taylor glanced at her mother and saw tears fall down her cheeks as she relived her own experience. "They wanted me to do that too, beg for help from the public, hoping someone knew something. They would see me up there, feel bad, and call the tip line. I couldn't do it, your dad had to."

The chief took over the press conference answering a few questions, directing all questions regarding Samuel Bishop over to the district attorney's office.

Taylor felt her mother take a deep breath next to her steadying herself.

"Kristen called; she wants you to call her back."

"I will, just wanted to get some coffee."

Sarah got her a mug out of the cabinet while Taylor poured herself a bowl of cereal and grabbed the cream out of the fridge.

"Were there a lot of messages on the phones?" Taylor asked, somewhat afraid to know the answer.

"Not too many," Sarah lied.

"Are they still outside?" Taylor asked as she pulled the curtains back just an inch.

The swarm of reporters acted like a beehive, as one spotted

something they all turned and came together with interest. Huge trucks with satellite dishes were outside pointing their disks into space.

Taylor pulled the curtains closed, shielding the room from any natural daylight.

"So how many messages?"

"Only like fifty," her mother said forcing a smile.

"That's better than the last time."

While Andy was still a state cop, they thought that they had caught Jacob. Freddy D'Agostino, a white male in his fifties who was a registered sex offender, was found sitting in a park during April vacation a few towns over from Templeton. He'd made the parents nervous and so they'd called the local police. They picked the guy up thinking he was just a pervert. When they walked him to his car though, the backseat had duct tape, a hand saw, rope and lollipops. They identified that he was a Level 1 sex offender and got a warrant to go through his house. Inside he had newspaper clippings on his walls about Taylor. He also had pictures of girls from the park that he was found in, and on the pictures he'd written how closely they resembled Taylor herself. On a few he noted that their hair was too short, Taylor's hair was long when she was taken. Others he wrote, weren't as pretty as Taylor.

All this led the police chief to make an arrest. The media caught wind of it and blew it up. Before they knew it Taylor and Sarah couldn't leave the house. Again, Richard handled the media, praising the police department's work and his hope that this man would be brought to justice.

At the end of it though, his DNA didn't match with the rape kit. Later they found out he was actually on Cape Cod when Taylor was abducted. Video surveillance at a McDonald's showed him buying a coffee and a sandwich and then sitting there for three hours reading a newspaper. There was no way he could have kidnapped Taylor.

At the time Andy had pointed out to his superiors that he was at a McDonald's that had an indoor play area.

"Do they still think it was Bishop?"

"I don't know, hunny. I haven't heard anything from Andy since last night. I'm going to make some cookies for the neighbors—I don't want them to hate us."

"Here's hoping. I'm going to call Kristen back."

In the safety of her room Taylor sat crossed legged on her bed with her bowl of cereal in her lap and her coffee on the nightstand. She grabbed the phone from her table and dialed Kristen's number by heart.

She picked up in half a ring. "Taylor?"

"Hey,"

"You OK?"

"Yeah."

"Is it him?"

Taylor knew she was referencing Samuel Bishop. "I don't know, but who really knows anything?"

"Can you believe this thing with Juliana Seville? My parents already reached out to hers, just through email. It's only been a few days."

"My mother didn't say anything but I'm sure she'll try and get in touch with them, too. She doesn't like to talk to me about stuff like that. It's like she thinks it's going to make me go catatonic again. I feel stupid saying this because I'm here and no one knows where she is but I feel like this is my fault. If I could remember what he looks like or something useful maybe she'd be home right now."

The words, 'instead of dead' hung in the air between them.

"You know this is not your fault, it's his fault, whoever he is, they will catch him, one day."

Taylor paused a moment, "I yelled at Andy last night. He found something in one of the interview tapes from when I was in the hospital, turns out I spoke *before* I started speaking."

"What do you mean? What did you say?"

Taylor could almost see Kristen perched on the edge of her chair. "I said, 'So many faces. He has so many faces. He could be you.'"

The words were etched in her brain and she had goosebumps just saying them out loud.

"Wow."

"Yeah," Taylor affirmed.

"What do you think it means?"

"I honestly don't know. I just wish I could remember. I'm so frustrated and mad at myself. I wish that I could do more. For years I was so happy that I didn't know. I mean, I knew what he did to me physically—the doctors told me those details, which was hard. But I didn't know how he did it and I was happy about that."

"So what's changed?"

"Juliana for one, if she's still alive and I've got the answer to finding her somewhere locked in my head don't I have an obligation to try? Selfishly though, I'm tired of being afraid of things and not knowing why."

Kristen could identify with Taylor in a way that no one else could. She understood being irrationally afraid of things, the only difference was that she remembered her abduction. Anyone who met her now met a junior at Stanford University in California. But when she was eight years old she was kidnapped and held for ransom. Her kidnappers drove up in front of her school and pulled her into a van while she was waiting for her nanny to finish speaking with another mother about a play date. Her nanny turned around as it was happening, but Kristen was already in the van and she was gone before they even had a chance to look at the license plate. They held her for two weeks. Originally they treated her well, thinking they were going to get their money, but the kidnappers figured out that the FBI was watching them when they went to the drop spot. In retaliation, they sold Kristen to a sex trafficker who was bringing girls across the border into Mexico. It was bad for Kristen and she remembered all of it. She escaped by playing dead after a particularly horrific beating and they left her in the dessert. She was found on a street by some kids that had ditched school to go for a road trip. She had been gone for six months.

When Kristen's parents saw the news of Taylor's abduction, they called Richard and Sarah to offer their support. They even donated significant money to help find her. When Taylor came home they flew from California to Massachusetts to help in any way that they could and so that Kristen could meet Taylor. Kristen had been a light in those very dark days. The two had been best friends ever since.

"What does Dr. Perna say?"

"He says memory therapy, I don't love the idea of someone picking around in my brain."

"I think it would be good for you. Take a bit of ownership and you never know maybe you do know something that could be really helpful."

Kristen paused, always wary of pushing Taylor too far.

"No more death and dismemberment talk, what else is going on?"

The two chatted for hours, Taylor told Kristen about Peter and Kristen told Taylor about a sorority she was thinking about joining.

"Are you still running?"

"Yeah, not that I'll be doing any of that for the next few days. I've got to get a treadmill."

"Have you considered one of those self-defense classes at the Y?"

Taylor loved her friend dearly and she wanted to be prepared—it's why she ran with mace—but she also didn't want to live her life like she was under attack all the time. She yearned to be normal, like most kids yearned to be something more than they were.

"You should consider it, even if this is the guy, there are enough psychos out there for all of us. It wouldn't kill you to be able to knock a few of them on their ass."

"I will look into it."

"Promise?"

"I will," Taylor assured her. "I'm going to make some lunch as I'm starving."

"I'll call you tomorrow."

The two hung up and Taylor did feel better. Conversations with Kristen almost always had that effect on her. She grabbed her iPad and sent Dr. Perna a quick email to see if they could talk about memory recovery at their next session.

Her afternoon was mostly quiet, which was a nice change from the past couple days. There were still one or two trucks on the lawn, but most had gotten bored at this point. There had been no newsworthy information from the police, just that they had removed a dozen garbage bags from Samuel's home as well as his laptop. For now, at least, Taylor's news cycle was at a standstill. Taylor watched as the last two trucks drove away just as Layla pulled up.

"Thank God they are gone," Layla called up to the door of the house where Taylor stood.

Layla walked up to the house. "Did you see all the homework you have?"

"No, I haven't checked yet. How do you know how much homework I have?"

A mischievous smile spread across Layla's face. "Peter told me. He asked me to give you something."

"Oh, yeah? What it is?"

Layla held out a neatly folded note.

"It's so adorable that you two are passing notes. So very 1999."

Taylor rolled her eyes but smiled back at Layla. Taylor unfolded it, eager to read it.

"So, what does it say?"

Hey Taylor,

I called your house a few times, but no one answered, your voicemail is full too. I can imagine it's been a crazy few days but if you're up for it I thought we could go to a movie and grab some ice cream after.

Anyway, let me know, here's my cell. 774-632-2486

Layla peered over Taylor's shoulder as she read the note.

"Let's call him," she said, her eyes wide with excitement.

Taylor hesitated, "I don't know, it's been a little insane around here. I'll call him tomorrow."

"Are you coming to school tomorrow?" Layla asked a bit disappointed.

"I don't think so, I don't want to turn the school into a media circus. The next day hopefully," Taylor said.

Layla was disappointed, Taylor could tell. But these situations took a toll on her, both physically and emotionally. It was like her ability to cope with life was a bucket of water and when these types of things happened all the water spilled out and she needed a few days to fill her bucket back up so she could cope with her life.

"I've got a session with Dr. Perna tomorrow at noon. We are going to talk about trying to help me remember some stuff that happened when I was abducted."

"Oh, yeah?" Layla asked sitting back down. "Are you sure you want to do that?"

"Nope, I feel like I have to try and remember, for Juliana at least. I want to know what happened, you know? All of it . . . even if it's bad."

"Call me tomorrow; let me know how it goes."

"I will," Taylor promised.

Andy called later in the day to give them both an update. Bishop had been arrested on child pornography charges. They were still looking into him as a person of interest in the Seville case but it was unlikely that any charges would be filed unless they found additional evidence from what had been taken from his house. Police in Virginia were still confident that the timeline could match up.

Andy was less confident, but he chose to keep that information to himself.

Chapter 19

Monday

It was mid-day when Taylor left for her appointment. Thankfully, the trucks had all cleared out after the last news cycle the night prior. The media is like a child with ADHD who has been given far to much sugar and put in a room full of toys. If there is no new information in 12 hours they move one. Despite relief that she could leave her house without being tailed, she hadn't slept well. Dr. Perna's email back to her had been cordial and encouraging. Reading it, however, had done nothing to allay her fears. The question—what had possessed her to make her suggest memory recovery in the first place?—kept whizzing through her brain. She hadn't told her mother. She didn't plan to either, not until she had something to tell her anyway.

She had purposely arrived early, wanting to walk off some of her nervous energy.

Downtown Gardner smelled like one huge pizza place. It didn't have many highlights, with a bank and a pool hall being the two biggest. She was contemplating getting a soda when the doors to the pool hall opened. Two men emerged, cigarettes already in their mouths.

Taylor instinctively took a few steps away, getting ready to cross the street.

"Hey," one of them said, obviously intoxicated, "wanna smoke?"

"No, thank you," Taylor said keeping her eyes straight ahead. She waited for one last car to go by before stepping off the curb.

"I know her," one of them said pointing at Taylor. "I know her."

Taylor's breath came quickly, the last car passed, and she ran across the street. She was too busy looking back to pay attention and she ran right into the chest of another man and screamed.

"Taylor, Taylor, it's me, it's Peter, are you OK?"

She backed right off and took a few panting breaths before she could see Peter clearly. She could hear the guys laughing across the street before tossing their cigarette butts in her direction and heading back into the pool hall. Adrenaline coursed through her veins and all she wanted to do was run.

"Peter," she said, "umm, yeah, yeah, I'm OK. There were these guys they . . . uh . . . ." Her thoughts were disjointed and she felt jittery. Adrenaline overload. "I need to sit down."

"Over here," Peter motioned.

The two sat down and Peter offered her a bottle of water from his backpack.

"Shouldn't you be in school?" she asked.

"I had an appointment with a doctor down here."

"You OK?"

Peter's face twisted just a bit, amused or insulted, Taylor couldn't tell.

"I don't mean to pry," she said quickly.

"It's OK, I'm fine. I see a psychologist and normally I go after school but it's a tough month for me so I took a half day."

Taylor couldn't believe it. "You see Dr. Perna?

"Yeah," he said, surprised.

"Me too."

"Oh yeah? What are the odds?"

Taylor laughed nervously, "Probably pretty good, how many psychologists do you think work around here?"

Peter laughed, "Yeah good point. What about you? You OK?"

"It's a tough month for me, too."

Peter didn't say anything else for a moment. "Why don't I walk you over there."

"OK."

Peter deposited her safely at the door.

"I'd really like to go out with you on Friday," Taylor blurted out. As soon as she said the words she wanted to take them back, it was so impulsive of her.

Peter smiled but for a second looked the slightest bit sad. Taylor caught a glimpse of it and then it was gone, replaced by his regular smile.

"Good, I'd like to go out with you too. I'll pick you up at seven."

Taylor waved goodbye still puzzled by his face and headed inside.

"Hey Dr. P."

"Hey Taylor," Dr. Perna said walking out to the waiting room to meet her. "Come on in. How are you doing?" he asked as he strode back behind his desk.

"Eh," she said.

"Do you still want to talk about some memory therapy or do you want to save it for another day?"

She took a deep breath and Dr. Perna could feel a decision made somewhere in the exhale.

"I want to try."

Dr. Perna smiled, "All right."

When he had received her email the night prior he had been encouraged, but not entirely surprised. While Taylor was a deeply troubled young woman, she was also a reservoir of strength. He had felt confident that she would feel the need to remember things at some point. He had even spent the last hours of the evening determining the best approach to take when he spoke to her the following day. Deciding in the end that a simple list and brief explanation of each method would probably be the easiest for her to digest.

Taylor sat quietly as Dr. Perna started by explaining the different types of memory therapy. Each sounding as dreadful as the next.

"The last one we have to talk about is hypnosis."

He gave her a quick assuring smile but pressed on.

"Hypnosis is the best type of therapy for your type of amnesia. It isn't mind control or anything like that. It's putting you in a deep state of relaxation and allowing your mind to wander through its memories without fear. Think of it like guided meditation." Dr. Perna could still sense Taylor's uneasiness. "What do you think?"

She took a deep breath, "How do I stop it?"

"You will be aware the entire time, so at any point you just say stop and you listen to my voice and you slowly come back to yourself. You will be safe here with me."

While Taylor did trust Dr. Perna, she knew she would never feel safe. Taking a tour through the most horrific version of memory lane wasn't incredibly appealing, but she had come to try and make some progress.

"OK, let's do that."

"Let's talk about what else has been going on first. How do you feel about Juliana Seville going missing."

"Guilty."

"Is that what prompted the sudden interest in recovering memories?"

"What if she's alive, what if she's in a basement somewhere and I could help her. It's never mattered before, I mean it mattered when they didn't find him and I always felt bad about that. It wasn't affecting anyone else though."

"You know what is happening with Juliana regardless of whether or not Samuel Bishop is Jacob is not your fault."

"I know, but I still feel like it is."

"Have you talked to Kristen?"

"Last night, she wants me to take a self-defense class."

"You don't want to?"

"I don't want to feel like I have to. Like the world is more dangerous for me because I'm me. I want to feel like the girl whose biggest problem is her boyfriend won't call her back." Taylor looked down at her feet. "Why couldn't I have been that girl?"

Dr. Perna had anticipated this would be a long session and blocked the afternoon off. The two talked about Juliana Seville, Samuel Bishop, Detective Fisher, all of it. Taylor, in rare form, unloaded it all. While she didn't delve too deeply into her feelings, she was processing an incredibly large amount of information. More specifically, she was able to process it without shutting down and that was a huge accomplishment for her. It had been just over two hours when Dr. Perna shifted in his chair, his usual signal that the session was ending.

"What about the memory stuff?" Taylor asked.

"What about it?"

"I want to do it."

"I think you've got a lot going on right now, we'll start in a few weeks when things have quieted down."

Taylor stood suddenly. "No! I don't have a few weeks. Look, Samuel Bishop could be the guy and if he is they need real evidence. Something that might be locked away in my head. It's time. I need to do this now."

Dr. Perna sighed. "Taylor, it would be irresponsible of me to do this with you right now."

Taylor's eyes darkened and fixated on his. "If you don't do this with me, you know I could call any psychologist in the country and they would be at my house tomorrow. They'll publish their papers and be on the Today show by next month. I don't want to do that but I'm doing this, with or without you."

Dr. Perna wanted to throw her out of his office and tell her to go do just that. He knew though that she would and he knew that whoever she found willing to do this with her now wouldn't care about her at all. He just hoped she knew what she was getting herself into.

He reached into his desk and pulled out a metronome. He then went to the three large windows in the office and pulled the shades down about halfway.

"Taylor, turn your chair so that your back is to the windows and sit comfortably for me OK?"

"What's that?"

"It's a metronome; it helps musicians keep time." He started it and let it fall into its methodic tick, tick, tick, tick. "Its purpose is to give you something to focus on. When it stops ticking it's time to come back out from your memories. Also, I'm going to record these sessions. It will help with the validity of your testimony if it ever came to that. Sound good?"

"Sounds something," Taylor quipped.

Dr. Perna ignored her. He walked around to the couch in

front of her and sat down. "We will start with the last complete memory you have of when you were in the basement and build from there. Close your eyes."

He could see the struggle going on in her brain. The part of her that never fully trusted anyone, that didn't like the idea of closing her eyes with him in the room.

"Now, listen to the metronome. Just focus on that noise. When your mind begins to wander bring it back to the metronome and my voice. Breathe in and out, in and out, in and out. Slowly."

It took Taylor about fifteen minutes to get to a relaxed enough state that Dr. Perna could start to work with her.

"Remember that you are with me in the office, that you are eighteen years old and that you are safe. Take a deep breath . . . can you smell the basement?"

Taylor nodded

"Good, tell me what it smells like."

Taylor thought back and for the first time, she embraced the basement, "It smells like damp earth and mold. It's cold," She heard herself say.

"I wanted to scream, I had been screaming for days though and that hadn't seemed to matter."

Taylor could see the marks on the dirt floor, six marks, six days.

"When the door opened, it was bright, I couldn't stand it. His boots were so loud coming down the stairs. My eyes watered, his face was dark, all I could see was the light around his head, like a halo. He sat down at the bottom stair and just stared at me, it seemed like a long time."

"'I'm glad you stopped screaming,' he said. His voice had changed. It was huskier, deeper, more menacing than in the park. 'You will find that if you are a good girl, you will be rewarded. If you are a

bad girl, you will be punished.'"

Dr. Perna watched Taylor as she relayed Jacob's words to her. Her hands fidgeted, something about her inflection of the words suggested Jacob would be happy to punish her.

"He knelt down next to me, I could smell his body, his breath. It was like the gloves at the doctor's office mixed with rotting meat and smoke. Like fire, smoke, not cigarettes. I almost threw up. He touched my cheek, his fingers were rough, scabby? Like sores or something, I'm not sure. I tried to pull away and he grabbed me and flipped me onto my back, my fingers were crushed underneath myself. He dragged me to my feet but I couldn't stand, it was like my legs wouldn't work. I could feel him, through his pants, he had an erection."

Taylor paused, the memories were so vivid, so much more clear than they had been. In the hospital they had told her two of her fingers had been broken, it must have been when he flipped her onto her back. She could hear herself talking but it wasn't her voice, it was his.

"I'm going to untie you. There's a box in the corner. There are fresh clothes that you can wear and there is food in there. There's also a shovel. When you have to go to the bathroom dig a hole and then cover it up.

"OK."

"Don't move," he warned as he took a knife out of his pocket and flipped it open to expose a clean sharp edge. With practiced strokes he cut her hands and feet loose.

For a split second she thought to run.

"Don't," he warned. "I know everything inside of you wants to run." He leaned into her and kissed her cheek. She trembled uncontrollably. "You won't make it."

The sentiment that he would make her regret it hung in the air unsaid.

Her shoulders sagged. "That's my girl," he said sensing her despondency. "Get yourself cleaned up; if you are a good girl I'll come see you in a couple of days."

Jacob was halfway up the stairs when he turned.

Taylor lifted her head to him.

"You will call me Daddy when I see you next and you will tell me that you love me."

Taylor could hear the metronome in the background. This was all she remembered in any kind of cohesiveness. The rest of her memories hung in the air around her like bubbles about to pop.

"Taylor," Dr. Perna said, "stay in the basement, don't leave the memory. How did you feel?"

"Mad."

"Mad at Jacob?" Dr. Perna asked.

"I didn't want to call him Daddy."

"What did you do?"

Taylor searched through the fragmented memories in her head looking from bubble to bubble to find one that seemed to fit.

Dr. Perna watched her eyes dart around the room as she attempted to see this unseen thing. Her eyes suddenly fixated and slowly came back into focus and she smiled. A knowing, achievement, proud smile.

"I screamed, I screamed at the top of my lungs."

"What did you scream Taylor?"

"I screamed 'you are not my father.' Over and over again."

"Good," Dr. Perna said, "Keep going."

Taylor thought back, embracing the basement once more.

It took a second but he was on her in a flash. He threw her to the ground and she saw stars. Her cheek and the side of her face stung with the crushing blow of her head slamming into the dirt. Using her hair he threw her to the other side of the basement.

Taylor struggled on the floor of the basement to catch her breath.

Jacob stalked toward her, his hands clenched in rage as he towered over her, shaking his head. "You will say it," he said, his tone solemn. "It would go more easily for you if you would just accept that now." He walked quickly up the stairs and shut the door behind him.

Taylor listened to the locks click into place. Her face and head hurt. She thought she was probably bleeding but she didn't want to touch the area if she was. The bottom of the box had two apples, a handful of beef jerky and one bottle of water. Hungrily she tore into the apples and the meat, gulping down the water in between bites. Her stomach groaned in protest at first but she was so hungry she couldn't stop.

Moments later she was back on the floor throwing everything up. She sobbed as her stomach emptied itself on to the dirt. She was so hungry, and so much food was now wasted. She tried so hard to stop vomiting, she even held her hands over her mouth and forced herself to swallow the last of the vomit instead of spitting it out. Her throat burned but she did it, and after a few breaths she knew she could keep that little bit down. One apple and one piece of jerky were left along with a third of the bottle of water. But at least the hose was still dripping in the opposite corner.

With her new found freedom she slowly explored her cage. The space was small but seemed even smaller now that she was standing. The only structure was the set of stairs that lead to a door at the top.

She didn't scream anymore. She knew that she would end up tied up on the floor again if she did and she didn't want that. For the next two days she didn't say anything. She ate the food in small bits. Drank water from the hose. Dug a hole when she had to go to the bathroom. The ground itself smelled every time she dug into it, which made her wonder if another girl had gone through this before. Twice she dared to walk up three of the steps, but her heart was pounding so hard in her chest she was sure that he could hear it. And she was sure he'd be standing on the other side of the door waiting for her to test the knob.

"I don't know how long he kept me down there. I remember being so hungry. I would have killed for something to eat."

There was a bubble—something about food—Taylor could feel it right there on the edge of her consciousness.

"What is it, Taylor?"

"Food," Taylor said, "someone gave me food."

"Jacob?"

"No," Taylor said, her eyes still closed. She struggled to see through the hazy memory. "My stomach hurt, I had started sitting at the top of the stairs because there was some fresh air up there where the door was. There was a shadow, at first I thought it was Jacob but it wasn't. He walked with a thud, this was just a scamper like an animal."

"Crackers," Taylor said astonished, as if it was all coming together. "A boy, he gave me crackers through the bottom of the door. He wouldn't talk to me, but he sang. Oh my god!" Goosebumps erupted all over her body.

Her eyes opened and she stared at Dr. Perna's face.

"He sang my song, he sang 'You Are My Sunshine', I wasn't alone."

Dr. Perna stopped the recording of the session.

Taylor sat in the chair for some time, too astonished to speak. She couldn't believe that there had been someone else there

144

with her and she forgot all about him.

"Do you remember his name?" Dr. Perna asked. He was familiar with the theory that Jacob had abducted other children before Taylor and he knew that one of them was supposedly a boy.

"No," Taylor said shaking her head. "He never spoke directly to me. I don't think I actually ever saw him. He would just push a couple crackers through the door every couple of days and sometimes he would sing to me."

Dr. Perna stood and Taylor followed suit, he motioned her to sit back down.

"You should sit, here have some water." He reached into a mini fridge under one of the side tables.

Taylor drank half the bottle in one sitting.

"Your mind hasn't had the time to dull the memories like it would have if you had remembered it five years ago. It will feel very real and very intense until you have a chance to process it more. This isn't something that we can do every session. You need time to adjust and to decompress in between therapies where you actually gain back a new memory. This could take a while," he warned.

"It's OK," she said, "I still want to do this and now I have something that I can tell Andy. Something real."

While Taylor didn't outwardly smile Dr. Perna could sense her satisfaction.

"We should talk about James," Dr. Perna said switching gears.

"James? Why?"

"You told me that he has been part of the group that has been more friendly to you this year. It might be time to tell him the role he had in your abduction."

Taylor stared at him.

145

Dr. Perna continued on slowly.

"You blamed him when you came home—even if you didn't realize it at the time. I actually don't think it was him as much as the crush you had on him. That being the reason that you left your house in the first place to go down to the park. Now that you are working on recovering more memories, I think it would be good for you to let him know what happened that day. Maybe it would explain some things on his end as well."

Taylor considered Dr. Perna's comments. Although she initially wanted to reject his thoughts on James. It was possible that he was right.

"One last thing." he said. "It would be completely normal for you to want to get home and go through your routines of locking the doors and checking the windows. I want you to try and channel that energy into something else. Make cookies, clean the bathroom, whatever you think you can do, but I don't want you to slide backwards into the obsessive compulsive behavior that we worked so hard to get you out of."

Taylor nodded. For the first eighteen months after her abduction she had begun a routine of checking the locks and the alarm, as well as checking the windows. She would go through every lock and window in the house and, if for some reason something interrupted her, she would do it again. It got so bad at one point she was doing it four or five times a day.

That was one of the first things that Dr. Perna worked with her on. She remembered the first day she didn't check the locks or the alarm. She felt really good about herself. He was right though, she could sense the tension in her body. It would be a struggle to not check the locks tonight.

"I'll do my best," she assured him.

That's all you can do," he said noting the time. "That's it for today; let's do another session next week. But in all seriousness, if you need me before then you call me, OK?"

"OK."

Walking out of his office she instinctively looked for Peter. It was late though. She'd been there for much longer than she thought she would. She wasn't ready to tell him what had happened but it was nice in some respects that he had his own baggage. She hopped in her car and decided to take a detour to the police station to see Andy.

Chapter 20

Walking into the station was always nice. Everyone knew who she was; most had seen her grow up playing under her father's desk. She said hello to everyone and headed over to Andy's temporary office.

Andy was studying something on his laptop intently. He didn't even notice Taylor standing in the doorway. She cleared her throat.

His head came up slowly. "Hey Taylor, what are you doing here? Everything OK?"

"Yeah, everything is fine. I had a session with Dr. Perna today and I have something for you."

"Oh yeah?" Andy wondered what she could have gotten for him from a therapy session.

"I remembered something. With Juliana still missing, I just started to feel like it was time to try and remember some things on my own, you know? Maybe I'd come across something that could help."

Andy leaned forward in his chair. "That's great, so what did you remember?"

Taylor told him about the basement and about Jacob but she held the best part for last.

"I wasn't alone."

Andy's eyes widened. "Who else was with you?"

"A boy. He was younger than me, I think—he seemed little, his fingers were really skinny."

Andy made a confused face.

"I never saw him," Taylor admitted. "He was in the main house, but he would slip me crackers sometimes. He would sing to me, especially if I was crying."

"Did he speak to you? Did he tell you his name?"

"No, he only sang to me. I don't think he was supposed to help me."

Andy was a little disappointed, but it was a start and he didn't want Taylor to see it, so he smiled at her and gave her a high five.

"That's really great. We thought that Jacob might have had something to do with that abduction in upstate New York. This could be that boy. Maybe the other two girls are alive too. You didn't see them did you, or hear them?"

She shook her head, "Just the boy."

"You keep working at it. Whatever you can give us is a possible lead. You got me?"

Taylor smiled, happy that Andy was happy. "Yes, I got you. What else is going on? Is there any more news about Juliana or Samuel?" It was weird to Taylor to say his name. She'd been purposely not thinking about it too much or getting her hopes up.

Andy shrugged his shoulders, "We are working on a few angles but there isn't much I can tell you. He's still a person of interest in the Seville case, but we haven't been able to charge him with anything yet. We haven't been able to find Juliana or any physical evidence of her. We aren't going to give up though, I can promise you that. Any chance you want to take a look at those photos since you are here?"

Taylor hesitated. It had been a tough day but thanks to her little drive down memory lane she could see his face clearly. There was something though, something that bothered her about what he looked like. She couldn't put her finger on it but something told her not to trust the face she remembered.

"I'll give it a go."

"Let me go get the file."

He left the office and Taylor watched the familiar hustle and bustle of the station. She missed being a part of this family. Once a cop, always a cop was the motto. She and her mother were still part of the family, technically, but it wasn't the same. There were guys on the force now that she didn't know, and they didn't know her, at least not as anything except the town's biggest unsolved case.

Seconds later Andy returned with a manila envelope. "All right, I'm going to lay out about a dozen pictures and I want you to look at them. Any of them that isn't our guy just flip it over.

Taylor turned around keeping the image of Jacob's face fresh in her mind. She heard the turning of pictures on to the desk with that familiar flip, flip flip sound.

"OK, take a look."

Taylor turned, looking up at Andy first and then looking down at the desk.

She scanned the photographs quickly. Slowly she flipped over the ones she was sure wasn't him, until it came down to four pictures. Each face was similar: white man, mid- to late forties, not skinny but not fat either. She wanted one of them to be Jacob so badly, just so this could be over.

She also wanted to be right. Even if these guys were sick fucks, she didn't want to send one to jail for something they didn't do.

The struggle was real inside of her, Andy didn't move but she could feel the tension emanating from his body. She turned all four pictures over and looked at Andy.

"None?"

"No, none of them."

"That's OK."

Taylor picked up on his tone and he quickly said it again. "Really, sweetheart, it is OK. We knew that you would struggle to identify him, it's OK."

Taylor nodded, only half believing Andy.

"I was going to go to your dad's grave this afternoon. I haven't been in too long. Do you want to go with me?"

"Yeah, I'll go, I've got to call my Mom though. I thought I would be home right after Dr. P's—she'll be worried."

Taylor's conversation with her mother was brief, but her mother didn't balk as much as she had in the past when Taylor said she was with Andy. Andy even got on the phone for a second and asked Sarah if she'd like to come to the grave with them.

"I don't think so. I did want to ask you though, you've got someone keeping an eye on the message boards, right?"

"Of course."

"No one is posting things about getting back at Taylor; no one has posted any pictures?"

Andy dropped his voice to a whisper so Taylor, who was standing in the hallway, couldn't hear him. "No," he assured her. "They are up in arms a bit about Samuel. They view him as one of their own. Half of them say it couldn't possibly be him, the other half is convinced he's connected to another half dozen crimes."

Taylor eavesdropped on half of the conversation she could

hear and knew they were talking about the message boards from Jacob's followers. Somehow, even though pedophiles were the most vile creatures in prisons, online they had their own cult following. There were at least three message boards that she knew about. She had even visited them a couple of years ago. The things they had posted about her were the vilest, most scary, insane things she had ever read. She hadn't slept for almost a week after reading them and never looked again.

"Let's get going kid, some of us work you know."

Richard's grave was in the back corner of the only cemetery in Templeton. A backhoe was positioned about twenty feet away and a hole about three feet deep had already been started. The employees, though, were nowhere to be seen. Taylor's heart ached for the family of whoever would soon call that hole home.

She came to her father's grave a few times a year. At first, she couldn't stand the sadness that engulfed her whenever she even drove by it. Now though she felt like she remembered him in her every-day life. She didn't need to stand where his body was to know that he was with her.

"Well Rich, your daughter is doing some pretty amazing stuff. She is trying to remember what happened so we can finally catch this bastard." Andy's voice was gruff. "I miss you buddy. I can't believe it has already been three years."

Andy rambled on about some other stuff going on at the station.

Taylor didn't really listen. She watched the birds in the trees getting ready for winter. She saw a man standing about fifty feet away from them. He was standing in front of a grave, but something was off. He kept looking in their direction. She nudged Andy and turned toward her father's grave.

"See that guy behind us?" she whispered.

Andy tensed and she could feel it through his jacket.

"He's looking at us."

"How long?"

"Not too long, but he's looked a few times."

"Let's go, we'll walk that way. Let's see what he does."

Taylor pivoted and looked towards the grave. The man was gone.

"Huh, that was weird." She looked around—no sign of him.

Andy relaxed immediately and smirked at Taylor. "I'm sure it was nothing. Wound a little tight these days?"

"Yeah," Taylor said distracted, her eyes still scanning the graveyard.

The two headed back to the station exchanging pleasantries. Andy asked about Peter and Taylor let him know she was going to see him that Friday.

"I'm not sure about that kid."

"You met him once," Taylor chided, "I think you may be being a bit ridiculous."

"Just remember that there's a lot of stuff going on, I don't want anything to happen to you, OK?"

"OK," Taylor smiled.

The two pulled up to Taylor's new car.

"I'll see you later."

She was about to get out of the car when she turned back to him. "Hey, what about dinner on Sunday?"

"I don't know, I don't think your mom is going to be up for that."

"Let me deal with Mom; I'll call you on Sunday morning. Make a dessert."

"You mean buy cookies?" Andy laughed.

"Yeah, that's what I meant, chocolate chip," Taylor yelled

out over her shoulder as she sunk down into her car. Taylor felt good about the day but she was also exhausted. The drive home felt long and arduous.

"Mom?" Taylor called out when she walked in the door.

"Hey dear, so what happened?" Her mother rose from the couch.

"What smells so good?" Taylor asked distracted. The entire house smelled like vanilla.

"It's this new tea I found, do you want some?"

"Does it have caffeine?" Taylor asked yawning.

"No. It's 3 p.m., maybe caffeine isn't the greatest idea?"

"I've got to work tonight, so it's the best idea." She walked into the kitchen and filled the coffee pot with water, generously measuring the grounds.

"So what happened?" Sarah asked following her into the kitchen. "You were so nervous last night I was almost afraid to bring it up this morning."

Sarah poured a bit more water into her mug from the kettle on the stove.

"I was nervous," Taylor admitted, "but it worked."

If Sarah was honest with herself, she was more than a little nervous about the road Taylor had begun to go down.

"I understand why you want to do this but I'm scared for you. I'm scared for you to find out what really happened, I'm scared that it will ruin all the progress you made."

"You're afraid that I'll end up sitting on the couch not able to leave the house."

Sarah grimaced, "A little."

"I am too," Taylor whispered. "But you know what? I remembered something today. And it's scary, I can feel his breath on my neck and I am afraid to sleep tonight . . ." she

154

paused and looked at her mother. "But it was five years ago. I owe it to myself and to Juliana to try and remember what happened."

Taylor sat with her mother for another hour and went through every new memory she had recovered. She told her everything and at the end, after saying it again, she felt better about it.

Sarah gave Taylor a hug. "I do love you so much. Are you sure you have to go into work tonight?"

"Yeah," Taylor groaned getting up from the couch and pouring herself another cup of coffee.

"It'll be better than sitting here. I could use the money."

"All right," Sarah relented. "I don't think I'll see you when you get home. I've got a few things I need to take care of before I go to work."

"I'll see you in the morning."

Chapter 21

Taylor's night at work was busy, she made a decent amount in tips, and Jan was glad to have her back at work.

"I was worried about you," Jan said to her at the end of the night.

Taylor still had two tables. Mr. Moriarty sat at the table at the far side of the restaurant. He was the type of man who looked like he had been born old. He didn't speak much and moved slowly. He only ever ordered Lipton's tea and chocolate chip cookie dough ice cream—not exactly a money maker. The other table was a guy on his own Taylor didn't recognize. He at least had ordered a full meal but he kept trying to make small talk with her, which she politely indulged in hope of a decent tip. She had dropped off his check when he stood up very suddenly scaring her. She instinctively backed up, bumping into a chair and knocking it over.

"Taylor," the man said, "I'm Seth Daniels with the Boston Globe. I've got a few questions for you."

"Do you have any insight into where Juliana could be?" he said forcefully. "Do you know any more about the case? Have they started working on the judge for a warrant to get DNA?"

He kept going until suddenly a cane came crashing down on his toe sending him shrieking into a string of expletives and hopping around the restaurant. It all couldn't have taken more than a minute but all of a sudden both Jan and Mario were in the restaurant kicking the man out and telling him he wasn't allowed back in.

Mr. Moriarty had come to her rescue. He had sat back down as soon as he could but his cane sat at his side in case anyone needed it.

"Are you OK?" Jan asked holding Taylor's arm.

"Yeah, I was just caught off guard. He didn't do anything to me."

"Creep," Mario muttered from under his breath as he headed back into the kitchen.

"Mr. Moriarty," Jan started, "thank you."

"Sure," he mumbled. "Got to be heading out—getting late. Need my check, girlie."

Taylor's eyes almost rolled back into her head. She hated it when he called her "girlie."

"It's on us tonight, Mr. Moriarty," Jan called out. "Thank you again."

"All right," he said, and off he went slowly over the uneven floor, cane in hand.

"You know he only comes in on the nights you work, right? I don't know if that's coincidence or just some weird thing but I hardly see him otherwise."

Later the two of them were the only ones left in the restaurant while Mario was still wiping down the kitchen.

"Do they think this is the guy? This Samuel Bishop?" Jan inquired eagerly. She hadn't had a chance to ask Taylor since she came in for her shift.

"I don't know," Taylor said sincerely. "I guess we'll have to see, at least he's locked up for now."

"I'm going to have Mario follow you home for the next week or so, just in case," Jan said. It was a statement not a question, Taylor knew the difference.

"OK." In truth she was OK with Mario following her back to the house. Being brave at 10 a.m. was different than being OK driving home in the dark at 10 p.m., and, she was tired.

They finished the cleaning for the night and Jan handed her the schedule for the rest of the week.

"Thanks again," Taylor said as she took the schedule. Jan grabbed her shoulders and pulled her in for a hug. Taylor always thought of Jan as a crab—not like grumpy, but like the animal. She would be gruff and aloof but then there were moments like this where she would do something so sincere. Jan held her for a few heart beats and then released her.

"Get outta here. Mario! Taylor's on her way out," she called out to the kitchen.

Mario came shuffling out of the kitchen; he'd changed into regular clothes already. His gold chain hung over his shirt, it reflecting the light was the only piece of color against his black clothes and skin.

"You ready?"

"Yeah," she said. She grabbed her purse from the cubby in the back corner of the room and headed for the door.

Mario followed her the whole way home and stayed in the car until she got inside and flipped on the lights. She waved at him from the front windows as he pulled away.

She felt alone now, for the first time that day. Her paranoia started to get the better of her—it was too quiet. Ignoring her promise to Dr. Perna, she went through the house, checking closets and behind doors. She looked out the windows turning on floodlights that light up the entire yard both front and back. Seeing nothing she checked the alarm one more time. She was exhausted. Taking one last look around she went to bed.

Chapter 22

Her sleep was disturbed. Recently recovered memories mixed with the only nightmare she ever had. She woke at 4 a.m. and decided that was enough of that.

She went for a run and did some cleaning around the house before school. She was getting in the car when her mother drove into the driveway.

Sarah rolled down her car window in the driveway. "You look tired. How did you sleep?"

"Not great."

Her mother made a disapproving face. "I'm worried about what you're doing."

"I know," Taylor said, "but I don't know what else to do, and it felt good yesterday—like I got some control back."

"How does it feel today?"

"It feels tiring. I got to go."

"Go," her mother insisted, "I'll see you when you get home."

Taylor was organizing the large amount of mostly overdue homework in her locker, trying to avoid the inquisitive looks she was getting from underclassman, when Layla came bounding up to her.

"Hey bestie," she sang.

"Hey, what's up with you?"

"Nothing," Layla insisted, "just happy to see you. You should have seen the school yesterday. The rumor mill was on fire."

"Ahh."

Taylor loved Layla, and she knew that she was friends with her because she genuinely liked her. But Layla also liked the attention she got from being Taylor's friend when these types of things came up.

"What's up with this Bishop guy?"

Layla served as Taylor's agent when something like this happened. She disseminated information and people felt like they knew what was going on. That way Taylor didn't have to deal with uncomfortable conversations with people who only talked to her in these few circumstances.

"He's still a person of interest in Juliana's case but they haven't found her yet and they can't prove he's the one who took her."

"Anything else?"

"I don't know everything; this is an ongoing investigation so they don't actually include me in their decision making."

"But they tell you whether or not you're safe, right?"

"Yes, they don't think he poses any kind of immediate threat."

"What about his cronies? A bunch of freshman actually didn't come into school yesterday—their mothers were too afraid to send them."

Jacob had followers. They were, for the most part, completely harmless. Behind a computer screen they were scary, terrifying even. In reality they were fat old men in Boise, Idaho with no intention of leaving their basement apartment to travel to New England and do anything. There had been occasions when someone more local would see Taylor and take a picture or stand outside the school across the street, but it had only happened a couple of times in five years. It was scary every single time. Those instances in particular were why Taylor began carrying mace when she ran and why she kept some in her backpack.

"I haven't seen any and Andy has been keeping an eye on the message boards. He said there's been a lot of activity but no one has referenced coming here and there haven't been any recent photos of me posted."

This was Taylor's life. Though there were moments when she said these things out loud and wondered if she was dreaming.

"Hey, listen," Taylor said changing the subject, "I need to talk to James."

"OK, why?"

"I started hypnosis therapy with Dr. Perna this week."

"Oh yeah?" Layla said very interested. "Did you remember something?"

The first bell rang signaling five minutes to get to homeroom. "I'll tell you all about it later, but I really do need to talk to James. Can you ask him to meet me outside during lunch?"

"Sure, I want to know everything later."

Taylor still wasn't sure what she was going to say to James. At first, Dr. Perna's suggestion that she apologize to him seemed ludicrous. James was just like everyone else in that he'd ignored her for years. She couldn't pretend that it didn't feel like a betrayal. But in the last few weeks even Taylor had begun to acknowledge that in her grief she had behaved badly toward James and a few of the others. They were only kids; she couldn't really blame them for cutting her out of their lives and continuing on without her.

Slamming her locker shut, Taylor headed across the hall to first period. She could see Peter in his chair, flipping through pages in a notebook. Almost as though he sensed her, his face turned towards hers and he watched her walk in and sit down. His eyes warmed and his lips turned up into the faintest of smiles.

"I missed you."

Those three words sent heat through her neck and cheeks. Butterflies erupted in her stomach. His attention, at least for the moment, provided a small respite from her jumbled thoughts.

By lunch time, she was a mess of nerves again. She just wanted to apologize to James but she didn't know how he was going to take it. It had only been this year that he had started talking to her more often. She didn't want to ruin their tenuous friendship by bringing up the past.

She waited outside the cafeteria sitting on a picnic table. It was cold. Everyone had given up on outdoor seating and were warm inside. Everyone but her.

The door clicked open and James looked around uncomfortably.

"Hey," Taylor called out.

"Hey, what's up?"

"I need to tell you something."

James just stood there listening.

"Do you remember the day I was taken?"

He nodded, not speaking.

"You had said that you were going to call me."

"Yeah," he said carefully, obviously not enjoying the memory.

"When I got off the bus there was a note on my door from you."

His eyes widened with shock. "But I didn't—" he started.

Taylor held up her hands, "I know, I know that now. But at the time I thought that the note was from you and it said to meet

163

you down at the park."

"So you went?"

"Yeah. Jacob was there, he said that a boy named James had gone into the woods because his dog ran in there. I heard a dog bark and heard a boy's voice, so I assumed it was you. So I went into the woods to help you."

"And that's how he got you?"

"Yeah."

James was silent deciding what to say.

"I'm sorry," Taylor blurted out.

"For what?"

"I was a real bitch to you when I got home. I didn't know why but having you around me just bothered me—it made my skin itch. I wasn't a very nice person to be around anyway but I was mean to you and I'm sorry."

"I would never do anything like that to you," James said earnestly. "I really liked you back then."

"I liked you, too," Taylor said half smiling. "I know you would never hurt me. It took a long time for me though to admit that I had been angry at you, even though it wasn't your fault. I just wanted to tell you why and that I was sorry."

"It's OK, I get that. Do you remember the rest of it? You know what happened after he took you?"

"Not all of it," Taylor said shaking her head. "But I'm working on it."

She shuddered against a cold wind that blew hard against her face. James walked over to her and grabbed her hand. It was warm and covered hers completely. Taylor immediately tried to pull away unused to physical contact.

"I'm not going to hurt you," James said not letting go.

Instead of looking down at her hand, she looked at James, his sincerity shone through and she felt her arm relax in response.

"Come inside, its freaking freezing out here."

"We're OK?"

"We're good, no worries." He led her into the cafeteria and dropped her hand when they got inside.

They walked side by side over to their small group of friends.

"What were you two talking about?" Shauna demurely questioned.

"Nothing, just some stuff that happened a long time ago," James said.

He grabbed a seat next to Layla and wound his hands through her hair, anchoring himself to her.

Taylor sat and watched James and Layla, thankful that she had a chance to talk to him alone. Even though she knew she'd have to tell Layla about it eventually. She absentmindedly picked at her food, letting the trivial conversation of her friends wash over her.

Chapter 23

A ndy was exhausted, unconsciousness pulled at his brain whenever his eyes closed, which was every time he blinked. It was only 9 a.m. A few hours ago he considered making his coffee in the hotel with 5-Hour Energy drinks. He decided against it, not wanting to die of a heart attack in a scummy hotel. Too cliché he told himself. He was slogging through emails when he looked up from his desk to see Knight standing outside his office. He motioned him to come in.

"We need to talk, but not here."

Andy's eyes narrowed he nodded. "This afternoon, 2 p.m., meet me at the restaurant in the center of town. It's called The Barn."

"Of course it is," Knight left without further comment.

Andy turned the papers over. It was the transcript of the interviews done so far with Samuel Bishop. He had been questioned a hand full of times at this point. Normally a person would stop cooperating with police and lawyer up, Bishop hadn't. He also hadn't spoken much during the interviews besides pleasantries and his insane ramblings when he was in the room alone. As soon as an officer or agent would come in he would put his mask back on and have a regular, albeit stunted, conversation like they were waiting for the bus.

It hadn't been without effort either, Andy noted. The detectives had been questioning Bishop pretty aggressively but to no avail. Andy's eyes continued to skim over the paragraphs until he caught something—he re-read it just to make sure.

Agent: So explain to me again the relationship you think you have with Taylor?

Bishop: I told you she saved my life. She belongs to Jacob though. Jacob told us we were his angels. We were there to watch Taylor but not touch her, she belonged to him.

Agent: When did he tell you this?

Bishop: You won't catch him you know. We protect him, all of us.

Agent: Does Jacob know where Juliana is?

Bishop: Juliana was a fail, I failed him.

Agent: Samuel, what does that mean? Where is she?

Bishop: She's missing isn't she? It's really too bad.

Andy couldn't believe it. This was all new. This was different than any information he had gotten from a message board. This was something else.

Why wasn't this pulled out and brought to them directly earlier? Andy fumed, the ineptitude ran rampant. Was it possible that Jacob had formed a network of followers and was actually communicating directly with them?

Andy spent the rest of the morning combing through the transcripts and Bishop's diaries, looking for scraps of information. He also had calls out to the agent who did the interview and the chief in Newport News. No one had returned his calls. The diaries mostly talked about sick stuff he wanted to do to children on a playground or people he worked with. This guy was classic in that nothing was his fault and it made Andy queasy just reading the crap he wrote down. Luckily most of these people would never know what their co-worker thought of them or what he imagined doing to them.

It wasn't long before he found little excerpts that seemed promising. They were only a sentence or two but they all seemed related to Juliana, mentioning her hair or her backpack. He routinely compared her to a younger version of Taylor. Sometimes noting what time she left her house. Other entries just commented on seeing her at the playground.

As far as tying him to Templeton and Taylor's actual abduction, they were still trying to track down where he vacationed five years ago but they hadn't had any success linking his name to any area hotels.

Andy was frustrated, nothing was going the right way.

He was so busy that it was 1:30 p.m. when his stomach started to rumble and he realized the time. His neck and upper back were sore from hunching over all morning. He stood, stretched, and grabbed his car keys, eager for some food, not necessarily the company.

He put on some music and tried to clear the images of Bishop's diaries from his mind. The Barn came into view and he put his blinker on pulling up next to Knight who was still inside the car, staring at his phone, as usual. Andy wondered what on earth he was always looking at. Knight must have sensed he was being watched and picked up his head, nodding at Andy and stepped out of the car.

"Did you read the transcripts?" Knight asked.

"There's some interesting stuff in there. I assume you guys are working to try and figure out how Jacob has been communicating with him."

"The nerd patrol is pulling his computer apart as we speak. They'll call me as soon as they have something."

"I have other concerns though," Knight said leading them

inside The Barn.

"What?"

"If Jacob has been cultivating followers we have no way of knowing what these people are."

Andy raised his eye brows. "What do you mean '*what*' they are?"

"Are they career criminals? Are they pedophiles? Are they hired help? What kind of person is he collecting?"

"Bishop certainly seems like low-hanging fruit. The guy is crazy but he seems crazy in an 'I want to belong' kind of way, not crazy in his own right."

"That's what I was thinking too."

"Why didn't you want to talk in my office?" Andy asked.

"If he has people everywhere, he could have eyes in the precinct."

Andy's mouth hung open in disbelief.

"I only trust one person in this situation."

"You trust *me*?" Andy asked surprised given their interactions to date.

"I think you want to get this guy as much as I do. That's all I need for now."

The two stood in silence for a minute watching high school students get off their big yellow chariot. Silently they watched the clump of students break up into smaller groups of twos and threes all heading in various directions toward home.

Knight turned toward Andy. "I want to flush this guy out; I want to see what happens if we poke the bear."

"This guy isn't hiding in some dark hole, he's not afraid of us."

"That's where you have me wrong. I don't think he is afraid of us, but I think he likes the attention. I think that Jacob's pulling Bishop's strings. He's throwing rocks in the woods and we keep chasing after them. I want to see what happens if we start throwing some rocks back." Knight's phone rang he stepped away to take the call.

Andy had heard this sentiment before. Four years ago Richard had come to him with a similar idea. Richard was tired of chasing ghosts. He thought that they could agitate Jacob into stepping out and taking a risk. Andy had talked him out of it. Maybe it was finally time to see if that theory would work.

"Nerd patrol found something," Knight said, interrupting Andy's thoughts. "Let's go."

Sitting in a room with a bunch of FBI tech geeks was not Andy's idea of a good time. However, they did have some interesting information for him. There were two guys and one girl, each as pale as the next. Andy sat while Knight stood—the three stared at Knight like he was a myth rather than real.

The girl started the conversation with the other two following her lead.

"We've pulled apart everything in the laptop. Besides the typical sick stuff I would actually expect to see—"

"I'm sorry," Andy said, "can I interrupt? What are your names?"

The girl stopped surprised by this question. "I'm Emily, this is Harry and Tom."

"It's nice to meet you," Andy said attempting to fill in the civilities that Knight lacked.

Emily responded with a nod and continued on.

"So . . . most of it looks like normal stuff for this guy. But there was one thing that we saw that's weird. If you notice, a lot of his posts on the message boards are random ramblings. They don't make a ton of sense. Initially we ignored them but then we noticed that there were a handful of profiles that always liked the posts, all of them, without fail. So, we started to look closer.

"If you look at these posts written by Bishop he goes off on a tear about something that isn't even related to the topic the group was discussing."

Andy and Knight nodded.

"If you will notice though, he puts random numbers in the words almost like he's typing fast and it's a mistake. Then he also bolds other words. We ran the numbers through the computer and we think the first number is a time and the second number is a street address. The words in bold while they make sense in his rant are actually all street names within an hour of either Newport or . . ." Emily stopped.

"Or where?" Knight asked.

"Here," Emily said.

The room was silent as Andy digested this information. If what Emily said was right there could be multiple groups not just one.

"Have there been other posts like these from anyone else since Bishop's been locked up?" Andy asked.

"Lots. It's impossible to know which ones are legitimate and which are meant to confuse us. If any *are* meant to confuse us. We have a call into Homeland Security to get permission to use street cameras in and around these areas. Hopefully we'll be able to determine which meeting times are real—"

Knight stopped them with his hand and walked out the door before releasing a stream of curses one right after the other.

Andy followed. "Man, you need to calm down. What are you so upset about? This is good news."

"This guy stalked Juliana, at minimum. Chances are he stalked her, led her into the woods, raped her, then killed her. While that is sad, that's not what I care about, I want to connect him to these other abductions. I want to solve the rest of these fucking cases."

"Listen, with this information, we are going to get him on stalking and child pornography charges. Once he's released into the general prison population, the inmates will rip him to pieces. Pedophiles don't do well in prison, you know that. He will spend years in solitary, 'for his protection' of course. I don't need more than that." He stopped, looking at Knight. "Do you?"

"Yes, I want more than that. I want to put this bastard behind bars for four more abductions and rape," Knight yelled, catching the attention of every cop in the precinct.

Andy grabbed Knight's shoulders and pushed him into his office.

"I want to catch him, too," he hissed, "but I don't want to put this asshole away for crimes he didn't commit. What are you going to tell the Seville's and the three other sets of parents whose children are still missing? Because this isn't about you or putting Bishop away forever. It's about those families who for years now have known that the only possible link we have to their children is Taylor, that she's the only one who came back. Get your shit together and let's stay focused."

Knight pulled away from him and aggressively shrugged his shoulders adjusting his coat before storming out of the precinct.

Andy took a deep breath, calming his nerves.

Gonzalez finally called him back that afternoon. He was quick to inform Andy that Bishop was occasionally giving out small snippets of information and they had found blood droplets in the woods behind Juliana's house. The blood was still at the lab but even Andy knew it would be Juliana's blood, maybe if they were really lucky it would match Bishop too.

Chapter 24

F *riday*

"Are you ready for your date?" Layla asked during lunch.

"Umm, yeah," Taylor said in a hushed tone—she wasn't really interested in sharing this with the group.

"You have a date?" Shauna asked with surprise.

Taylor pursed her lips. "Peter and I are going to go to the movies."

"Peter's the one that never talks to anyone, right?" Shauna asked, obviously trying to be obnoxious.

Taylor may have been accepted back into the group but it wasn't all it was cracked up to be.

"Nah, Peter's a good guy," James chimed in, "he's just quiet."

Taylor gave him a small smile, happy to have him back up her choice.

"Who does he even hang out with?" Shauna asked like a dog with a bone. "I don't think I've ever seen him with any friends."

"I think he does some kind of AP project in the computer lab," Layla offered.

Taylor was surprised. She hadn't paid attention to the fact that as she looked around the cafeteria Peter wasn't there. Normally that type of thing was all over her radar. She had been distracted lately.

"You'll have to tell us all about it on Monday," Shauna remarked.

"You'll be the first one I call," Taylor shot back.

Peter had called Taylor the night before letting her know that he would pick her up around 6:30. It seemed to Taylor, he was making sure their plans were still on.

She was anxious about the date. Peter would have expectations, she was sure of it. The least of which would be holding her hand or putting his arm over her shoulder. In reality, she wished those were the only things he would consider doing. She knew it wasn't though, everyone she knew had been making out with boys for at least a few years. About half had actually had sex already. Taylor couldn't see that as a part of her life, ever.

The bell toned signaling the end of lunch and an end to Taylor's reverie. The group disbursed, and Layla leaned over to her. "You OK?"

Taylor blinked away the thoughts of sex, "Just a little nervous, I guess."

"James and I were supposed to go out tonight—want us to double with you?"

Taylor let out a sigh of relief, "That would be awesome. Let me try to catch Peter before we go into class and just make sure he's OK with it. I'll see you at our lockers before we head home."

Running down the hallway she caught him coming out of the computer lab.

"Hey," Taylor called out.

Peter turned looking disheveled, but he smiled when he saw her.

"Layla and James wanted to know if they could tag along with us tonight."

Peters face tightened. "I guess," he said slowly.

"If it's not cool I guess I can tell her no; I just thought it might be fun with some friends."

His face relaxed but his eyes still held some tension. "It's fine, really. I'll pick you up at 6:30."

"Good," Taylor said, happy that Layla would be there with them . . . and even James for that matter. She felt a little bad that she had rained on his parade, but what did he expect of her anyway?

Taylor relayed the story back to Layla at the end of the day.

"What do you think?" she asked.

"I think you're looking for problems where there aren't any," Layla insisted. "He probably just thought he was spending the entire night alone with you. Now we are coming—it's not like he's friends with all of us. Look, James and I are happy to go and make this an easier experience for you, but you have to acknowledge that it doesn't necessarily make it a better experience for Peter."

Taylor thought about what she said. "You're right."

"We will meet you at the movies at seven. I think the show starts at 7:15."

"Sounds good," Taylor said shutting her locker door.

At home she putted around for a bit straightening the kitchen and sorting through the mail trying to find a way to expend her nervous energy. Her mother was still asleep, which was a bit odd, but Taylor didn't want to wake her.

Her belly was full of butterflies when she went up to take a shower. It was 4:30. Two hours to go. At some point, Taylor ceremoniously threw half her wardrobe on to the bed in frustration, her mother came in and leaned against her doorway.

"How's it going?"

Taylor moaned and threw herself onto the bed. "I don't date."

"Apparently you do, though not very well I'd like to point out. A little nervous?"

"I'm a wreck. I don't even know if I really like him and what if he tries to kiss me. I've been panicking about what to do if he holds my hand. Seriously, what do I do if he tries to kiss me?"

Sarah could see Taylor was circling the drain. She held up her hands, "Whoa, whoa, you need to breathe."

Sarah inhaled, and Taylor copied her; the two slowly breathed out.

"I think you need to have a genuine conversation with him before you go into the theater."

Taylor started to interject, but Sarah stopped her.

"Listen to the words I'm saying before you try to talk. You are always going to have a harder time than most when it comes to dating. You need to tell him what he's getting into. It's the only fair way to do this. You are making a huge personal step here, sweetheart, and I am so proud of you. But most people don't understand what you have been through and they will try to treat you like other girls. You aren't other girls; you have to tell them what you can and cannot deal with.

"If this boy likes you, he will understand. When you are ready, you'll be able to hold his hand or kiss him. But you need to get there on your own timetable."

Her mother was right, she knew. Dr. Perna had said generally the same thing to her before. She just hated pointing out that she was different. It was like having a disability that no one could see.

At 6:30 on the dot Taylor's doorbell rang. Her mother had positioned herself in the kitchen making cookies. Taylor punched in the code to the alarm and opened the door.

Peter stood on the bottom step. He'd changed since school and held a bouquet of flowers. He had a boyish look to him making him appear younger than seventeen.

Peter handed the flowers to Taylor, "These are for your mother."

Taylor smiled, "That was nice. Come on in." She ushered him in and quickly shut the door. "Mom," Taylor said loudly. Sarah came out of the kitchen wiping her hands on a towel.

"Mom, this is Peter."

"Hi, Mrs. Cormier," Peter said formally.

"He brought you some flowers," Taylor said smiling behind Peter's back.

Sarah smiled back to Peter. "Thank you, that was very sweet of you. I can't remember the last time someone brought me flowers."

She took them from him and pulled a vase down out of the top shelf in the kitchen. "What movie are you going to go see?" she asked as she cut the bottoms off the flowers.

"There's a new Bond movie out," Peter said. "I talked to James and he said he'd be cool with seeing that."

Taylor was impressed. "Great, let's get going then." Taylor wanted to have a few minutes with Peter in the car before they started driving.

"Have fun you two, I have the night off, I'll be here when you get home."

"Thanks," Taylor gave her mother a quick hug and a kiss on the cheek before opening the door so Peter could head down the stairs.

Both safely in the car with seat belts on, she could feel her nervousness was creeping up her throat.

He shifted the car into reverse when she blurted out, "Wait!"

He stopped at her abrupt outburst.

"I'm sorry," she said apologetically. "I need to talk to you before we go."

"OK,"

Taylor paused not knowing how to start. "I'm sure you know what they say about me at school. About what happened when I was abducted."

Taylor couldn't bring herself to actually use the word rape with Peter. It made it seem like she was already thinking about sex. Peter nodded that he had heard things similar to that.

"This is a big deal for me, going out with you." Taylor admitted. "I've never been on a date. No one has ever asked, but, to be honest, before this year I don't think I could have gone out with anyone even if they had asked. I need you to know this because I don't want to scare you off but you need to know what you are getting into. I have trouble being touched. I panic if I feel unsafe." Taylor's head hung, "I'm not the girl you make out with at the movies."

Peter was silent for a minute. "I was surprised that you said yes to be honest. I wanted to ask but I wasn't sure you would agree. I've heard the talk and some people have told me a few of your more . . . *interesting* stories."

Taylor's neck burned with embarrassment.

"I don't care about any of that. You aren't damaged to me. I've got my own stories too. I won't do anything you are uncomfortable with. Just tell me what my boundaries are. I will respect them."

Taylor smiled, "OK." That was easier than she thought it would be. "I'd like to just get to know you if that's OK? I know there is a whole physical side to things but I'm just not ready for that quite yet. I would like for us to just be able to talk and work

178

up to," she stopped, embarrassed, "the other stuff."

Peter smiled at her. "I've had my share of rough patches and I understand not trusting people. I think we are going to do fine together and we'll figure out the," he smiled, "other stuff."

For the first time in hours, Taylor felt like she could breathe again. She smiled at him, his face smiling in response.

"OK," she said.

Peter put the car back into reverse, "OK."

With the awkwardness out of the way Taylor tried to enjoy the drive. She noticed the simple cologne Peter wore, not overpowering like most boys their age. His car was spotless, not a trace of trash or dirt. She wondered if he cleaned if for her or if that was just how he was. It was about fifteen minutes to the movie theater in Gardner, they enjoyed comfortable silence. The anxiety that had plagued her the past few hours had settled and there was a warmness in her stomach and limbs.

The two arrived at the movie theater ahead of Layla and James. They picked up their tickets from the kiosk and got in line for some popcorn. Moments later Layla came up behind them.

"Hey love birds," she said.

Taylor grimaced at the reference.

"Hi Peter," Layla said directly. "I'm excited, aren't you?"

Peter smiled at her, "I am actually."

The four of them filed into the movie theater and picked their seats. They munched on popcorn and commented on which previews they wanted to see when the lights dimmed down signaling the start of the movie. Taylor sat between Peter and Layla although Layla was pushed so far over she was practically sitting on James's lap.

Only minutes into the film Taylor heard someone say something in hushed tones. It almost sounded like, "That's her."

179

She stiffened and looked behind her but all she saw were people watching the movie, no one was looking around or at her.

She turned back around.

"You OK?" Peter asked leaning close to her ear, his lips skimming her jawline. His breath on her neck made her quiver. Not from desire. She squashed the impulse to recoil.

"Yeah," she said adjusting in her seat. "Just thought I heard something."

A few minutes later she heard something again. She could have sworn someone said her name. Again, her head whipped around but she saw nothing out of the ordinary. Peter gave her a sideways glance. She tried to smile reassuringly but it was forced. She knew he could tell.

The urge to reach into her purse and grab her can of mace was overwhelming but she tried to fight it.

Layla was busy making out with James. Taylor hit her on the hip.

"Hey," she whispered. Layla untangled herself and James gave her a-what-the-hell look.

"What's up?" Layla said slightly out of breath.

"I heard something," Taylor said.

"Sshhh," someone whispered from behind them.

"It's fine," Layla whispered back, "just watch the movie."

Taylor shifted taking another look around. Everything seemed normal. Peter again leaned over but she shook her hands signaling that she was fine and he turned his head back to the movie.

James Bond was in the middle of chasing down a bad guy along the California coast when Taylor noticed people had gotten up. Instead of going out the main entrance, they walked down to the front of the theater. They were wearing something on their face, all of them.

Others had started to notice them as well. Peter looked at Taylor concerned.

"What are they doing?"

They walked about five rows in front of Taylor and turned. They had masks on. The masks were just faces, not monsters or something you would buy in a Halloween store. They were of people's faces. Taylor's heart leapt into her throat. She couldn't breathe.

They pointed at Taylor and started chanting.

"You killed Juliana Seville, you killed Samuel Bishop. You killed Juliana Seville, you killed Samuel Bishop."

"Oh my god," Taylor flew up in her chair.

Layla grabbed her arm. Taylor could hear James yelling at her to move but it sounded like she was underwater and she couldn't hear him clearly.

It was seconds but it felt like an eternity. James grabbed Taylor by the hand jolting her out of her paralyzing fear. Her hand instinctively grasped his and she finally heard him shouting at all three of them.

"Run!"

As the teenagers got closer to the people in masks, James could clearly see they were all men. They advanced on them now, grabbing at the girls' shirts, their hair. James put his body between them and Taylor, shielding her. He reached around, laced his fingers around Layla's hand and dragged her behind him. Peter ran ahead moving people out of the way like a linebacker. They burst into the lobby of the movie theater James still yelling.

"Get to the door! Get to the door!"

The commotion behind them was escalating as people poured

out of the theater and into the lobby. Not knowing what was going on, people started running for the exits. Peter reached the door first and threw it open. James's arm was now wrapped around Taylor's waist half carrying her to the car. Layla hung onto his other arm, struggling to keep up.

James called out to Peter but either he didn't hear him or didn't want to. Dragging the girls to his Jeep he threw both of them in the back before circling around the car and getting in the driver seat.

Complete chaos was behind them. He could hear sirens in the background and contemplated staying but the sound of Layla crying and Taylor's vacant look convinced him otherwise.

Throwing the car into gear he tore out of the parking lot nearly hitting at least three people. He sped down the highway determined to put miles behind them and the zealots in the movie theater. Layla's phone was ringing but she was still crying hysterically. James tried to quiet her but she couldn't seem to catch her breath.

"Taylor," James said loudly, she didn't respond.

"Taylor!" he shouted at her. Still nothing. He reached behind him grabbing her shoulder and shook her, hard. She finally looked at him, her eyes focusing in on his.

"Get Layla's phone," he instructed pointing at her purse.

"My purse," Taylor said, "I left it."

"It doesn't matter," James said. "Get Layla's phone."

Taylor picked up the purse from the floor Sarah Cormier flashed on the screen.

"Mom?" Taylor said softly.

"Hunny, I need you to come home, now." Her mother's voice was stressed.

Taylor started to cry.

James took it from her fingers which she gave to him willingly.

"Mrs. Cormier, something happened at the theater. She's OK, we're all OK. I don't know where Peter is." James stopped talking as he listened to Sarah on the other end.

"I'll get her home, I promise."

Taylor was crying in the back seat, cradling a sobbing Layla. The girls clung to each other for dear life.

Ten minutes later as James pulled up to Taylor's house. There was already a cop car there, its lights flashing. Another cruiser was flying up the road heading straight for them.

Detective Fisher was at the passenger side door before James had a chance to put the car in park. He saw the girls huddled in the back and a scared pale teenager in the driver's seat. Andy flung open the door and pulled Taylor into his arms, carrying her up the driveway toward the house.

"Get Layla."

James did as he was told and all four of them hurried inside.

Sarah was pale. "What happened?" she demanded as soon as the teenagers got inside.

Andy and James deposited Layla and Taylor on the couch. James paced in the corner like an animal ready to pounce on something. He managed to retell the story of what happened at the theater. Taylor sat motionless listening.

Andy grabbed a radio and spoke to some unknown officer that was already at the movie theater responding to the commotion. Andy told them what to look for even though his hope of finding who did this was already gone. Far too much time had gone by already and it would be easy to pocket masks and run out with the rest of the people.

"Taylor," Andy said.

Her eyes slowly ticked over to him.

183

"Samuel Bishop was charged with the abduction, rape and murder of Juliana Seville late this afternoon. He hung himself a couple of hours ago in his cell."

Sarah stared at Andy waiting for more information.

"At least we'll be able to get a DNA sample now. I assume he didn't confess in a suicide letter," Sarah said callously.

"He left a note, Sarah," Andy paused. "I don't think the kids should hear about this yet—it's been a tough night."

"What did it say?" Taylor asked.

Andy looked imploringly at Sarah begging for back-up.

She sighed. "Tell her. She deserves to know."

Andy saw the scared faces staring back at him. He saw the note in his mind's eye and edited out everything but the simplest facts.

"It said, 'I killed Juliana, Jacob is coming for Taylor,' we are going to run a DNA test as part of the autopsy but we feel pretty certain at this point that Bishop is not Jacob."

Taylor nodded, not saying anything but Andy could tell she was thinking about something.

"How did he write the note?" Taylor looked at Andy, not her mother. "He wouldn't have been given anything to write with, so how did he write the note?"

Taylor's voice was cool, detached, hyper-rational.

"Blood," Andy said, his head tilting as he said it looking for a response from her. "He cut himself with a piece of the toilet he managed to chip off with his foot. He wrote it in blood on the wall."

Taylor's eyes closed and her head hung down as she exhaled loudly.

"You aren't hurt are you?" Andy asked looking over her.

She picked her head up and a version of the real Taylor was

184

suddenly back, her eyes a bit more alive. "I'm OK."

She looked at James, "Thank you. I don't know what I would have done if you weren't there."

Layla had finally quieted down and leaned over to hug her friend.

"Can I stay here, Mrs. Cormier?" Layla asked.

"Of course, call your mother. She's probably heard what happened by now. If she has any concerns I can talk to her."

A few minutes later Sarah was on the phone assuring the girls safety.

Layla's mother was understanding and thanked Sarah for the phone call. Most parents would have wanted their kids to stay away, but Layla's mother seemed happy that her daughter had what she called a "true friend" in Taylor.

James called his parents, letting them know he was OK.

"Can someone text Peter," Taylor asked her two friends. "Just make sure he got home?"

Peter responded instantly, apologizing that he didn't hear James calling out to him and assured them that he got home safely.

"He's really worried about you," James held the phone out to Taylor.

She quickly scanned the texts but made no move to take the phone and text Peter herself. "Can you tell him I'll talk to him later?"

James shrugged his shoulders and began typing.

Andy took official statements from everyone and got Peter's last name so he could get a statement from him as well. It was about an hour later when James finally headed home, giving Layla a kiss and patting Taylor's shoulder before finally heading out the door.

Andy was in the kitchen with Sarah brewing a pot of coffee.

"Girls, why don't you head upstairs. It's been a long night. Try and get some sleep, OK? No TV," she warned.

"Last thing in the world those girls need is to see this playing on television," she whispered to Andy who nodded in agreement.

They waited for the two to get upstairs before they began talking.

"How did he hang himself?" Sarah demanded.

"He used a coat hanger and a shoe lace. I have no idea how he got either of those." Andy said exasperated.

The coffee finished brewing and Sarah grabbed the cream and sugar before reaching into the cabinet above the fridge. Andy saw her struggling to reach what was up there. He stood and approached her, reaching up into the cabinet and brushing his chest up against her shoulder. Her hand came down.

"I was going to get the Bailey's."

Andy's hand came down with the bottle as she was saying the words.

"Great minds," he said. He poured a generous helping into each of their cups and they topped them off with coffee before going over to the couch.

"Who do you have outside?" she asked.

"Marrier again. I'm trying to assign officers' you know, that way there can be no confusion."

His radio crackled to life and he turned it down before answering it.

While processing the scene at the movie theater, they had found a mask. It was on the floor in the screening room. His hip started to vibrate as he ended the radio call to answer the phone. Sarah listened to the first half of the conversation.

"I'm at the Cormier's . . . She's fine . . . That's what I was

186

thinking. How are the masks? . . . Oh yeah? . . . Maybe we can use that . . . let's try and find these guys. Have them finish processing and push everything through, priority. I'll be at the station by six tomorrow morning. Call me before then if you need me."

Sarah stared into her coffee cup.

"It was Knight. The masks were good—well done I mean. Something someone with some skill would have had to make. Narrows things down. They will be processing the scene for a few more hours. Knight is supervising."

What was unsaid hung in the air between them. Andy wasn't expected in the office until 6 a.m.

The phone rang, saving them from more awkward silence.

"Hi Mrs. Cormier, I saw the news out there."

"Hi Kristen, I'm not sure she's still up. She had Layla stay over tonight. Let me check." Sarah's exhaustion seeped through her every word.

"I'll go," Andy whispered.

"Thank you," she whispered back as she sat down.

Andy crept up the stairs being careful to be quiet as possible in case the girls were sleeping. The light was still on but when he poked his head in both girls were curled up together in Taylor's queen bed fast asleep.

He grabbed the phone next to Taylor's bed in case anyone else called and turned off the light. Leaving the door cracked just in case either of them woke up during the night.

He shook his head when he got to the bottom of the stair case.

"She's asleep, Kristen. I'll tell her to call you first thing in the morning."

Sarah hung up the phone and walked over to the couch with her coffee; Andy followed, sitting in the chair adjacent to it. They sipped their drinks in silence. The caffeine attempted to beat the Bailey's but Andy could tell the alcohol was winning.

"Why don't you lay down," Andy suggested. "I'll just hang out in the kitchen, maybe watch some Netflix."

"I don't know."

Andy could see her struggling with something, even though he could tell she wanted him to stay.

"What?"

"Marrier's outside," she said. "I don't want him to think we spent the night together."

Andy flinched, hurt that she was still worried about her reputation with the other cops on the force. It's not like he hadn't considered it but that was last year when he started to realize that they had grown closer than just two friends mourning their loss together. He had made his peace with it, she obviously hadn't.

"Marrier will be fine. I'll be down here the entire time. I'm not leaving you alone right now. Go upstairs and get some rest."

She paused for just a minute but relented, obviously too tired to care.

"No porn," she joked.

"No promises," Andy bantered back.

Andy dozed on the recliner in the living room for a few hours, waking every few minutes. It was 5:45 when he gathered his stuff before making a full pot of coffee for the three ladies of the house, leaving a quick note on the counter.

Went to the station, I'll check back on you this afternoon ~Andy

Chapter 25

Saturday

The station was as busy as Andy had ever seen it. The press had, for the most part, stayed away but Andy knew it was only a matter of time before they came knocking on their door demanding to know whether Bishop was tied into Taylor's abduction.

He had just put his backpack down when Dan Morse poked his head in.

"Hey, you got a second?"

"Yeah, sure."

Dan came in and shut the door behind him and didn't say anything right away.

"Out with it," Andy said.

"I'm worried about Knight. I heard him talking yesterday on the phone. It sounded like he knew something might happen."

Andy leaned forward in his chair. "What did he say, specifically?"

"He said that he'd rather wait and see what came of it than stop it before it happened. He said he hoped Jacob would be there too."

Andy took a deep breath. "OK, let me try and see what I can dig up."

Dan got up to leave.

"Morse," Andy said, "not a word to anyone until I figure out what's going on, understood?"

Andy's first call was to Gonzalez but he was no help. With Bishop's death on his watch he was getting his ass chewed out from every direction.

Andy's next call was to the nerd patrol.

"Emily, this is Detective Fisher. I was wondering if you could tell me what you came up with yesterday afternoon; I haven't been able to check in with Knight yet with all the stuff going on."

Emily paused on the phone. Andy was making a gamble that if she thought he knew, she would tell him.

"Emily … I don't have time for this, what did you tell Knight?"

That did it.

"I let him know about the meeting we thought was going to take place. All we had though was the address of the plaza, a time and some initials. He said he would keep a patrol there and watch it, didn't want to panic people if nothing came of it."

"What were the initials?"

"TIA@JB"

Andy knew that TIA was shorthand for "Thanks in Advance" but that didn't make any sense. He ran through possibilities in his head until he remembered something.

"Emily, hold on, I'm sending a text, I might know what those mean. Did you tell Knight what the initials were?"

Again she hesitated.

"Emily!"

"Yes."

Andy texted Sarah: "What movie did Taylor go to see last night?'

The response was almost instantaneous.

'James Bond'

TIA@JB: Taylor in attendance at James Bond.

Just then Andy saw Knight across the station. He hung up on Emily, not bothering to say goodbye.

"Knight," he shouted from his office door.

Knight looked exhausted and annoyed. Good, Andy thought, I'm in the mood to kill somebody.

Knight lumbered to Andy's door. "What do you want?"

"You knew."

"Knew what?"

"You knew that something might happen at the movie theater and you did nothing."

"I didn't do 'nothing,' I put a patrol on the theater. They were in and out of the lobby and the theaters themselves all night. As soon as there was a sign of trouble they were on the scene. And I didn't *know*, I suspected."

"What about the initials?"

"What about them?"

"Did you know what they meant?"

"No, how would I? Why? Do you?"

This wasn't nearly as satisfying as Andy had hoped it would be.

"TIA@JB, Taylor in attendance at James Bond."

"How would they know that? Did you know what movie she was going to?" Knight tried to turn the tables on Andy.

"You are a real piece of work aren't you. I think you knew TIA was Taylor in attendance and I think if you had put this information out to the rest of us we could have figured it out and stopped her from going. If something like this happens again I expect you to call me. You can't just go off on your own; there are other people involved here."

Knight's eyes narrowed, unaccustomed at being spoken to like that. "I don't appreciate your tone."

"You won't appreciate a phone call to your boss either, which is exactly what's going to happen if you pull this shit again." Andy countered.

"Don't push me," Knight warned.

"Don't push me," Andy shot back.

The two stood toe to toe, neither backing down.

"Fisher, Knight!" the chief bellowed from his office. "Get in here the both of you."

Knight moved first walking next door to the chief's office.

"I've got press on the phone from Virginia to Massachusetts. Fisher, I want a statement from Sarah and Taylor and I want them here when I give it. I'm going to answer these inquiries from the press once and that's it. I'm not letting the town turn into a damn circus again."

"Chief," Andy started, "Sarah—"

"I don't care," the chief yelled interrupting Andy. "Get Sarah to agree and get her here."

That afternoon Sarah released a statement to the press. She had been reluctant to the idea, however the chief convinced her that it would be a quicker way to calm the masses. Especially in light of Bishop's suicide and the discovery of Juliana's body. He read it for her while she and Taylor stood behind him. Every local news station was there rolling unending footage.

"We are saddened by the death of Juliana Seville, our hearts go out to her family and friends. We will continue to put our trust in the investigators and justice system to conduct a thorough investigation. We know they will carry out their very important work quickly and professionally. We truly hope that the other missing children are

found and that their families are able to reunite with them. Thank you for your understanding as we continue to deal with this situation privately as a family."

The crowd, silent while the chief read, erupted in shouts the moment he finished.

Sarah and Taylor stood stoically listening to the questions. Andy stood next to Sarah, their arms touching one another through their coats. Knight stood next to Taylor his eyes scanning the crowd.

Finally, after what seemed an eternity of questions and answers, the chief called an end to it and ushered them all back inside the precinct.

"Let's give them about an hour to disburse a bit and we'll get you home in a squad car. I would expect that they will be around though for at least twenty-four hours," he warned.

Sarah nodded. "Thank you, Chief."

Sarah hadn't been inside the station in quite some time. After Richard's death there just hadn't been any need. The building brought back a mixture of memories. From Taylor's childhood visiting her father, to her abduction and the unraveling of their life leading up to Richard's death. She didn't like being there.

"Do you want a coffee?" The chief's question interrupted Sarah's reverie.

"Yeah, that would be great."

"You OK?" she asked Taylor.

"Yeah, I'm going to go hang out in Andy's office."

Sarah followed the chief down to the break room while Taylor walked two doors down and plopped herself on Andy's couch. Andy was across the squad room talking to Agent Knight.

Knight had introduced himself briefly when she arrived to the precinct that morning. She watched them through the windows. They didn't appear to like each other very much. The conversation ended with Knight storming off and Andy following suit back to his office. He didn't even notice Taylor sitting on the couch until he sat down.

"Jesus," he swore when his eyes found her. "You scared me, kid."

Taylor smiled. "What's up with Agent Knight?"

"Ehh . . . nothin'," Andy brushed off her question. "We just disagree on the way something was handled."

"Something to do with me?" Taylor pressed.

"No, want to get a donut?"

"Sure, so cliché by the way."

He laughed out loud. "Cliché's exist for a reason, kid. Come on."

The two walked down the hall and grabbed a donut. Taylor said hi to some of the cops who knew her. Most had been called in today to deal with the press traffic and just to put everyone's minds at ease. The incident at the cinema had the town on high alert.

Taylor thought about how many times the town had been on alert because of what had happened to her. How many times had there been some kind of concern. She always felt bad like it was her fault that this had happened. It was just one of those things that she carried around with her.

"Did you talk to Peter yet?" Taylor asked forcing her thoughts away from the town.

"Not yet," he said. "The school had an address for him that belonged to an older couple who has never heard of him. I've got to track him down."

"I can call James and have him text him," Taylor offered. "Maybe he just moved."

Turning back toward Andy's office she saw Peter standing outside in the lobby.

"Or, you could go in your lobby and see him."

Andy's gaze followed hers. "That's convenient."

Andy went out and collected Peter and walked him back to his office. Taylor felt exhausted and overwhelmed; Peter in contrast looked strong and confident. She felt better just having him near her. His arm was warm and brushed up against her bare skin, the contact sent shivers down to her fingers.

"How are you?" His voice dripped with concern.

"I am so sorry about last night."

"I'm sorry, too."

"What are you sorry for?" she asked. "You just wanted to take me on a date."

Andy, who had been standing beside the pair, cleared his throat. "Why don't you two talk later? Peter, I need to talk to you about what you saw last night. Can you come this way?"

Andy put his hand on Peter's shoulder to guide him to the left.

Peter practically yelped and pulled away so quickly Taylor wasn't sure what she just saw. Andy's hand immediately retracted.

"Whoa. Are you hurt?" Andy's tone was inquisitive, cop like.

"I got knocked down last night when we were running. I fell on my shoulder. You just caught me off guard."

"Sorry about that, did your father take you to see a doctor?"

"No, it's not bad. I just was surprised that's all."

"All right," Andy said pointing in the direction he wanted Peter to go. "Why don't you head that way."

Peter nodded at Taylor, his air of confidence returned. "See ya. I'll call your house later."

Taylor didn't see Peter finish up with Andy. The chief had sent them home not long after they split up.

"Chief suggested that you just stick to your regular routine for the next week or so. No outings besides school, home and work. He said he would do extra drive-bys of all three just to make sure something like this doesn't happen again," The driver of the squad car said.

"Yeah," Taylor said staring out the window seeing their neighborhood come into focus.

Sarah thanked the officer.

Layla had gone home that morning after breakfast but had said she would call later.

"I've got to call Kristen back," Taylor said as she walked toward the stairs, grabbing the phone from the living room table as she went.

Kristen was astounded when she finally talked to Taylor.

"Wow, just wow. I can't believe this whole theater thing or what happened with Bishop. It's just crazy."

"Yeah, I'm having a hard time believing it too."

"Did you have your mace on you last night?"

"I had it, but I was so freaked out, if they had come at me I wouldn't have gotten it out of my purse in time. I've got to see if Andy can get my purse back; it's still being processed as part of the scene."

"Want me to see if my self-defense teacher knows someone in Massachusetts? I'll pay for them to come out to you. You never signed up for any classes did you?"

"Would self-defense classes have helped me last night?" Taylor said irritated.

"Hey, don't do that I'm just trying to help."

"I know, I'm sorry," Taylor said, embarrassed at her tone. "I'm just tired. I just think in these situations I crumble—I panic.

I couldn't breathe, literally. James was yelling at me to move and I couldn't even understand what he was saying."

"You have to train yourself."

"I looked them up," Kristen said abruptly changing the conversation.

"Looked who up?"

"The other kids that Jacob took. It's so sad. Two of them are girls and have been missing for like fifteen years or so. They were taken in the same state about six months apart. The other one is a boy who actually went missing two years before you did, but he was from upstate NY. I just can't imagine being gone for years . . ."

"I think you are assuming they are still alive."

"I guess I am."

The two didn't speak for a minute, each of their minds going to untold traumas in their lives.

"I remembered a boy," Taylor said quietly. "I did some hypnosis with Dr. Perna and I remembered a boy. He slipped me crackers and he sang to me that song—you know the one I hum when I'm stressed out. It was probably the boy that went missing and Jacob probably killed him already. His poor parents are sitting at home right now hoping that their son will come home, and he won't because he's dead. I left him. I didn't even remember he existed until five years later."

Taylor paused staring off into the distance. "Do you wish that you had died sometimes?"

Kristen was silent on the other end of the phone. "I did when they had me. For a while after I got home I prayed to just not wake up one day. It got better though, I don't feel like that anymore." She paused. "You OK? You're scaring me a little bit."

"Yeah," Taylor said, though she sounded far away. "I just feel really out of control. These things just keep happening to me."

The two finished their conversation quickly after that.

No sooner had Taylor hung up than Layla called. They spoke for a few minutes but Taylor was tired.

"Call me later if you need me."

"Thanks," Taylor was genuinely thankful to be hanging up the phone. When it rang again she didn't even answer it.

"Taylor," Sarah shouted, "it's Peter."

"Can you tell him I'm sleeping?" she shouted back.

She heard her mother make some kind of excuse and hang up. Minutes later she was in Taylor's doorway.

"He sounded disappointed."

"I'm just exhausted and I don't want to be on the phone anymore. I'll see him at school."

Sarah nodded and walked across the room to give Taylor a kiss on the forehead.

"Let's both take a nap, its been a crazy couple of days."

Taylor and her mother spent the rest of Saturday and the entire day on Sunday doing nothing, no cleaning, no meal making, nothing. The shades drawn and the lights off, only the glow from the TV offered a signal to anyone on the street they were home. They watched movies back to back to back, consuming multiple bags of popcorn and at least a dozen sodas. Taylor felt disgusting but suitably satiated. Eventually though, reality came knocking.

"I've got to go to work in a little bit," Sarah said as she got up and attempted to clean up the soda cans and pizza boxes. Then the doorbell rang.

Taylor sat upright. Sarah, seeing her daughter's fear, waved her hand at her.

"At ease, it's just Andy. He's sleeping on the couch the next couple nights while I'm working."

"Jeez, Mom, you nearly gave me a heart attack."

"I forgot. He offered last night and I agreed."

Sarah hit in the alarm code and opened the door. Andy in street clothes looked like normal, every-day Andy. Sarah looked behind him and shut the door.

"I'll be home around seven. Taylor is planning on going to school so I'll probably just be getting here as she leaves. Andy, there's extra linens—"

"In the closet," he finished for her. "I remember."

Andy had spent many nights on this couch when Taylor's dad was still alive. He had been surprised when Sarah agreed the night before to let him come back. He figured with her concerns about what the guys down at the station thought, there was no way she would let him do this for her. Her concern for Taylor though outweighed what she thought the other police officers would say. It probably helped that one of them was no longer stationed outside her house either.

"Little late for you isn't it, kid?" Andy said noting the time.

Taylor yawned. "I'm going to bed. We were just watching some chick flicks."

She gave her mother a kiss and trudged to her bedroom.

"Thanks Andy," Sarah said.

"Anytime, really."

She went through the garage and Andy listened to the alarm system re-arm itself moments after the garage door closed.

He grabbed the linens out of the closet and poured himself a Jameson before putting his gun on the coffee table within reach if he needed it. The days of storing it in the gun safe long gone.

He was asleep moments later, the glass of Jameson full and on the table.

199

Chapter 26

Monday

Andy smelled bacon and coffee before his eyes even opened. He kept them closed for a few minutes savoring the smells and sounds of a home he was once so familiar with.

Taylor was already showered and dressed for school. Bacon was sizzling on the stove top next to a large pan of eggs.

He opened his eyes and stretched before getting up off the couch, which had been surprisingly comfortable given the motel bed he had become used to sleeping on.

"Wow, the royal treatment." Andy walked into the kitchen admiring the cheese still bubbling in the pan of eggs.

"They are for my mom."

"Nice. I stay here all night just to make sure no more psychos attack you and I don't even get breakfast in the morning."

He wasn't a hundred percent sure he could joke about recent occurrences yet, but the look on Taylor's face told him it was alright.

"I guess you can have some."

Taylor set a plate down in front of him while she was munching on a piece of bacon.

"I've got to go," she said filling her own travel mug with coffee.

"Tell Mom I said hi."

"Will do," Andy said with his mouth full. "This is great by the way."

"Remember who feeds you while you fend off the psychos," she yelled back over her shoulder as she opened the door to the garage.

Moments later Andy saw, Sarah turn on to the road just as Taylor turned out. Andy was just cleaning his plate and setting out one when Sarah came in the door.

"Is that bacon?" she asked with interest.

Andy gestured to the plate on the counter.

"That's exciting," she said.

"Taylor cooked for us both this morning."

"That girl," Sarah said in awe. "There are moments when I think her life is going to break her and then there are moments when her resilience is amazing. And the kid makes delicious eggs."

"Right." Andy exclaimed. "I don't think I've ever had scrambled eggs that were that fluffy."

They both laughed. Sarah dropped her work stuff and sat down while Andy poured her a cup of coffee and pushed the cream and sugar in front of her. Andy stared at her, imagining for just a moment what their mornings could potentially look like if she would just let them. Sarah smiled at him—an easier smile than she had given him since the two had been thrown back together again.

"I'm going to get going," he said. He rounded the island in the kitchen and went to the couch, collecting the linen in a pile and dropping it in a basket in front of the basement door.

"Thanks Andy. Really. I felt a lot better knowing that you were here last night."

"It's no problem, I'm happy to do it."

"We should have left you know. When Taylor was returned to us and we realized that there was an online presence with Jacob. We should have disappeared, but Richard refused. He said that if she started running she would run her entire life. Sometimes I wonder if we had left would he be dead right now. Would she be able to just be a senior and not worry about all this?"

"Shoulda coulda woulda's," Andy said. "Those are a waste of time. You have to admit she is doing really well this year—better than she has since it happened. All things considered I think you should be really proud of her."

"I am," Sarah insisted, "sometimes I just wonder that's all."

"I understand. I need to change before work."

"Thank you again."

"No problem," his eyes locked with hers. "Call me later."

She looked away first. "I will, maybe another Sunday dinner sometime?"

"That would be nice. I'll even help cook."

***

Layla and James were at Layla's locker when Taylor got to hers. The two had been waiting for her.

"Hey," Taylor said setting her book bag down and opening her locker.

"Hey," they both said simultaneously.

Layla hit James on the chest, "Jinx!"

Taylor smiled. "You guys good?"

James shrugged, "What about you?"

"I'm OK. The police want me to keep a low profile for the next week or so.

"Are you working?" Layla asked, concern in her voice.

"Just tonight and Friday."

"Are you sure that's a good idea?" James asked.

"I can't stay quarantined in the house. I kind of want to but I also want to show these sick fucks that I am not going to be intimidated. They are just trying to scare me and I've got to tell you I feel like I have been scared enough for a lifetime."

Layla's face looked shocked. "Uhh . . . that's great, I agree with you, I do, I just don't know that right now is the time to test things, do you?"

"I think it's exactly the right time. Anybody see Peter?"

"Nah," James said, "I haven't heard from him either since the movie."

Taylor was distracted, glancing up and down the hallway. "I'll see you guys at lunch."

The days following were uneventful with the exception that Peter remained somewhat elusive. He hadn't called either, which she thought was strange.

Chapter 27

D r. Perna had cancelled their session the week before, a scheduling conflict or something of that nature. Taylor didn't know whether or not they would work on recovering memories again. She felt like so much had happened since their last session.

"Hi Taylor," Dr. Perna met her at the door.

"Hi," Taylor said, slipping past him, wondering for a minute if Peter had been in to see him that week. She wanted to ask but thought better of it.

"So, you've had a busy week and a half. I'm sorry about our last session. How are you handling everything that's been going on?"

"It's been tough. There has to be some kind of karma for these people, right? Layla was terrified; I've never seen her like that. James was incredible and I wouldn't have gotten out of there if it wasn't for him."

"It's a lot to deal with for Layla, and James. Your life has never *directly* affected them before." Dr. Perna pointed out.

Taylor nodded. "I'm just angry. I'm angry at these assholes that are trying to ruin my life, as if I belong to *him*. As if what he did to me has to follow me for my entire life." Her voice was quiet but seethed with fury.

"It's OK for you to be angry," Dr. Perna assured her, "that's normal. Don't let it control you though, don't let it become a part of who you are."

"I want to do more hypnosis though."

"Are you sure? You have a lot going on right now. This may not be the best time to take this on."

Taylor looked at him her eyes serious. "I'm sure."

"Why do you want to do this so badly? This has never been a priority before."

"Juliana is dead. She's dead. I have been living my life thinking that no one else would get hurt and now they are. I don't want to be in the dark anymore. It's exhausting. I just want to control my life again and part of that is getting these memories back."

"You know," he cautioned again, "some of them may never come back. There may be permanent holes that your subconscious never opens for you."

"Some is better than none."

Dr. Perna sighed. "Why don't you go sit on the chair and I'll get the metronome."

Minutes later he was set up and Taylor sat comfortably on the chair, eyes closed breathing deeply focusing on the tick, tick, tick, tick.

"Try to remember another time that Jacob came to see you. He was angry with you last time, you disobeyed him." Dr. Perna guided her back to her memories.

Taylor closed her eyes, feeling her fury at recent events and using that to bring her back to how Jacob must have felt.

"He was really angry with me. I didn't want to call him Daddy. I didn't want to say that I loved him."

The memory was there, right on the edge of her mind; she just needed something to jar it loose.

"Did you ever see or hear anyone else? Besides the boy, was there another person there?"

That was it. A bubble was hovering. There was something about someone else being there. Taylor could feel herself falling back into the memory.

I hadn't seen Jacob in days. I was really cold and really hungry. I think my stomach rumbled all the time, it was like the water dripping from the hose, constant. The door opened, fast, like a crisis. A man came running down the stairs, he had a beard and long hair. His nose was huge.

"I've come to take you home. Hurry. Hurry now, he'll be back any minute."

Taylor scrambled to her feet and half ran half fell toward the man who grabbed her under the arms and let her climb the stairs. It wasn't until she got to the top stair and saw the hallway that she heard laughing.

Suddenly a hand on her ankle pulled her down the stairs, she fell hitting her chin on the top step and her knees on each step below it. She could taste the blood in her mouth.

Still more laughing as she turned over still on the stairs.

"You didn't really think you were going to escape, did you?" the man laughed at her. She looked at him more closely. Everything about him was different, except his eyes. His eyes were the same, cold, blue eyes. Jacob.

"I can be anyone I want," he hissed at her as his face came inches from hers. "You don't even know what I actually look like. Jacob is just a face I use because children seem to trust that one."

Taylor started to cry, her nose running and blood seeping out of the corner of her mouth.

"You will never escape. Say 'Yes, Daddy,'" he demanded.

The hopelessness that washed over her was so immense she didn't even have the courage for another beating.

"Yes, Daddy," she said.

He laughed again and grabbed her arm pulling her into him before he pushed her to the ground. She curled up ready for the impact but instead he started to yank on her underwear until it ripped.

She fought, kicking and hitting. She didn't scream though, she didn't say stop.

"Taylor", Dr. Perna's voice cut in, "let it go and come back to the room."

Taylor's breath was coming in rapid succession, not quite hyperventilating but close.

"Breathe."

Taylor's chest rose and fell rapidly.

"Breathe," Dr. Perna commanded.

She inhaled slowly.

"That's good. Let's come back now."

"No," Taylor said forcefully hanging onto the memory

"Taylor," Dr. Perna said, "I'm turning the metronome off."

"No!" Taylor shouted.

Dr. Perna paused his hand over the metronome.

She fell easily back into the memory, like stepping off the top of a cliff.

Jacob fell on top of her, his weight crushing the breath out of her. She didn't even see how he did it but his pants were already around his knees.

She shimmied and struggled to get away from him, but he pinned her down.

"Stop," he screamed in her face, his breath rancid.

She stopped and gasped as she felt his dick enter her. It hurt and she couldn't help but start to cry.

The memory started to dissolve, but she held on wanting to know how it ended. He hit her a few times before finally finishing. She curled up on the floor sobbing into the dirt. He didn't speak to her again. He just adjusted himself and went upstairs before she heard the lock to the basement door.

She laid there for quite a while. It hurt to move but she eventually crawled over to the hose and cleaned herself off. She was cold inside and out; she felt numb like now it didn't matter what happened to her.

Taylor could feel the despair settle into her chest and she stared at the wall in the basement for what seemed like days. Until finally her gaze settled on the shovel in the corner. The corner where the field stones were somewhat loose. She only noticed because the last time she had gone to the bathroom she had leaned on one and it moved, almost fell on her toe.

Still wearing the T-shirt but no underwear, she walked over to the shovel and started digging at the rocks in the corner, seeing how many others were a bit loose.

Taylor sat back in the chair in Dr. Perna's office feeling the dirt still on her cheek. Her hand unconsciously kept wiping at her face.

"Taylor," Dr. Perna said softly, "you need to listen to me, you are pushing too hard. This type of therapy is a lot for your psyche to take on. You need to go slow; you can't just dive in like that."

She sat silently.

"Taylor, say something."

"There were a lot of masks; he tricked me each time. I thought someone had come to save me. It took me a long time to realize that no one was coming."

"He was conditioning you to not trust anyone so that you would never try to leave."

"It worked, didn't it."

"You escaped, Taylor, remember that."

"Yeah, except he still kind of has me trapped."

Dr. Perna stood and went to his desk drawer and pulled out a bag of M&M's. "Here," he said ripping open the corner and bringing them over to her. "Have some—they'll help your blood sugar."

She popped a few into her mouth but then put the bag down on the table in front of her.

"A few more," he insisted. She poured a dozen into her hand and slowly ate them to his satisfaction. "I want to call your mother and have her come get you. I want you to take it easy tonight."

"I've got to work tonight."

He sighed, "What time?"

"I start at 4:30. I was going to go from here. Are you recording these sessions?"

"Yes. If it comes to it and you are questioned in court it will help to have backups of our recorded sessions if we need them. Things that you say will coincide with the physical evidence they discovered when you were found. Like being malnourished and what was used to bind your hands and feet."

She nodded still quiet.

"We talked about this already, don't you remember?"

"Huh?" Taylor said distracted, images flashing before her eyes.

Dr. Perna let it go for now.

"Can you do something for me?" she asked standing up as she said it.

"I will try," he said.

"Andy will still be at the office, so can you call him and let him know that you are sending over a copy of this session. He needs to hear it. I don't think I can re-tell it to him right now and I have to get to work anyway."

"I want to see you on Monday after school." He walked behind his desk and checked the calendar on his computer, 3 p.m., and Taylor," he said as she opened the door to his waiting room, "if you need anything over the weekend, I want you to call me do you understand?"

"Yeah," she said dismissively.

"Taylor," she turned toward him, "Call me."

Her eyes turned downward, "Yeah," she said softly.

He watched her exit the building and walk to her car.

She looked up at him in the window aware that he was watching her. She used her hand to gesture a phone call and he gave her the thumbs up. Grabbing the phone from his desk and holding it up to the window as if to prove that he was doing what he said he would.

"Detective Fisher please,"

Dr. Perna sat on hold while he typed up notes from their session. Not that he would need notes to remind him about what happened that day.

Taylor is becoming obsessed with turning control back to herself. She has done her second hypnosis therapy session. She went farther than what was advised. It should be re-evaluated whether or not she is ready to continue with this therapy. I have concerns that such aggressive tactics on her part will result in a setback i.e.: obsessive-

compulsive behavior or disassociations.

"Hello." Andy's voice finally came through on the phone.

"Detective, it's Dr. Perna, I have an audio file I'm sending to your email. It's from my session with Taylor today. She asked me to send it to you. She remembered quite a few important details that may help you in your investigation."

Andy thanked him on the phone, somewhat surprised to be hearing from Taylor's shrink.

Dr. Perna stopped before hanging up, torn between his professionalism and his desire to make sure that Taylor was OK.

"Hello?" Andy said into the phone eager to get to the audio file.

Dr. Perna wanted to say, *I'm worried about her, keep her safe,* but instead he said, "Have a good weekend."

"You too," Andy said, hanging up the phone hitting refresh on his email eager to see what Taylor had wanted him to hear.

Twenty minutes, a cup of coffee and three laps around his desk later he still wanted to shout from the rooftops. Knight poked his head in the office on his way out, coat in hand.

"What's with you," he said.

Andy shut his laptop. "Nothing, just catching up on some emails."

Knight's eyes narrowed, not believing Andy for a minute.

"I want you off this case," Andy said.

"Well that's too damn bad, you are stuck with me. So help me get this done so we can go our separate ways."

Andy knew Knight was trouble, had known if from the start. Andy circled back around to his desk and opened his email. He hoped if he sent an email to Gonzalez he would be discrete.

Chapter 28

S*aturday*

Sarah let her car warm for a few minutes before heading home. The sun was beginning to rise over the tops of the trees, casting a warm glow despite the cold. Her shift had been busy but she couldn't keep her mind from what was going on at home. She was worried about Taylor. She had even gone as far as calling Kristen's parents hoping for some guidance.

Pulling into the driveway her phone dinged alerting her to a text message. Andy, her screen read. "Need to see you today. Let me know when."

She turned her car off before answering. "Need to see me or Taylor?" she texted back.

"Both," was his response.

"Of course," she said to herself.

Taylor was still sleeping and Sarah didn't want to wake her. She put her stuff away from work and went to bed, falling into a fitful sleep.

She stood at the edge of a building, looking down staring at the people below wondering what they were staring at. When she looked above her Taylor was floating high in the sky. Sarah wasn't scared though because Taylor could fly. Someone was tapping though, knocking really, on the building and when she looked down, people had sledge hammers and they were hitting the building. Sarah woke up with a sharp intake of breath, eyes wide, looking around for a floating teenager.

"What the hell," she murmured. She could still hear the knocking sound. It took her brain a few moments to realize that the knocking was real. Still in her scrubs she stumbled downstairs checking the time on the oven: 10 a.m.

Andy stood at the door with coffee and donuts.

Sarah wiped the side of her mouth where she felt certain she had drooled all over her pillow. "I was sleeping."

Andy laughed, "I can see that."

"You're laughing at me."

Andy did his best to look earnest. "I'm not, I promise."

"You are. What do you want?" she moaned, which was the grownup version of whining.

"I need to talk to you."

"You mean Taylor."

"Well, yes, but I did bring *you* coffee and donuts."

"Oh, good," she said back, "so you brought me something that will keep me up so I can be more tired later and something else that will make me fat. Well, aren't you just the sweetest guy in the whole world."

"You're not fat," Andy said his eyes leaving her face and tracing her outline. He looked just long enough for Sarah to feel that little tingle of appreciation.

"You both suck," came a voice from upstairs.

"Don't say 'suck,'" Sarah called back.

"Taylor," Andy called out.

"Hey, you're here about the thing?"

"Yeah, I'm here about 'the thing.'"

213

"What's 'the thing'?" Sarah asked, very much in the dark.

"I had a session with Dr. Perna yesterday," Taylor said emerging from the staircase, looking just as disheveled as Sarah.

Sarah frowned. "I thought you told me you were going to do one of these every other session, not every session."

"I was but we missed last week because of his scheduling conflict and he let me do another one."

"I need to talk to him," Sarah said looking around.

"What are you looking for?"

"My phone," Sarah answered.

"No, Mom. Listen, you don't even know what happened."

"I know he needs to be responsible while he is treating you. You don't get to drive the ship."

"It's my ship," Taylor shot back.

"Well, I still want to talk to him."

"You can't."

"Excuse me?" Sarah said indignant.

"I'm eighteen. You can't talk to him if I don't want you to."

Sarah took a deep breath preparing for battle.

"Mom," Taylor said trying to disarm her mother. "Listen to me, I know you are worried and I know you don't like this whole hypnosis thing. But you have to trust me. I gave Andy real information yesterday. Something he could investigate. Something that could lead to figuring out who Jacob is." Taylor's face was genuine and Sarah could see the pleading in her eyes. "You have to let me keep going with this. I need to."

Sarah closed her eyes praying for strength, something she did very rarely. "OK," she relented.

Andy had sat quietly during this exchange. Once both calmed down, he talked to Taylor for a while. Taylor had offered to play the audio file for her mom, but she had for the moment declined.

She knew if she listened to it she would hate what Taylor was doing even more. She needed more time.

"Are you staying for dinner?" Taylor asked.

"It's like noon," Andy reminded her.

"So?"

"Stay," Sarah said from the kitchen, "I owe you a meal anyway for staying with Taylor the other night."

"Great," Taylor said, "I'm going to Layla's."

"Whoa," Andy said from the couch, "you invite me over and then just leave—some hostess you are."

"I'll be back for dinner," Taylor said innocently.

"Yeah, yeah, have fun, kid."

Taylor went upstairs to change and to call Layla and let her know she was on her way up to her house. With Taylor out of the house everything between Andy and Sarah seemed harder, more forced. Like they were wading through quicksand.

"I can go," he offered, "and come back before dinner. I don't have to sit here all afternoon."

Sarah considered what he said. "Stay. You can help me cook. I was going to try and make a decent meal tonight. Plus, if you stay, it will keep me up and I'll be certain to sleep tonight."

"So, we'll be eating by four so you can be in bed by seven?" Andy asked with a laugh.

"Yeah," Sarah said smiling, "pretty much."

Sarah pulled a roast from the fridge and handed Andy the five-pound lump of meat. "You remember how to trim these right?"

Sarah was referencing when Andy would come over for Sunday dinner years ago. Richard would usually take Taylor outside and play with her, which would leave Andy in the kitchen with Sarah. The two of them had gotten quite good at cooking together.

Andy grabbed a paring knife and sharpened it. Sarah meanwhile gathered the spices together that she was going to use on the meat. They worked silently but together, giving each other their space, though occasionally Andy would step into where Sarah had just stood and he could feel the warmth of her hand on the counter or graze her shirt as she moved around him.

"Can you open this?" she asked handing Andy a container of oregano.

"Sure," he said putting the knife down and reaching over to her. His hand enveloped hers as he grabbed the spice from hers, but he didn't let go.

"Andy," she whispered gesturing to her hand.

"Yeah," Andy said staring at their hands.

She had pulled away at first but now her hand hung there in the open.

He took the spice from her hand with his other one and opened her palm to the sky, tracing the lines on her hand. Again, she let him.

"Andy," she whispered again, her voice raw with emotion.

He turned her hand and put it on his heart. Stepping closer to her invading her space, he was so close he could smell her shampoo.

"Close your eyes," he said.

She was breathing fast, her eyes darting between their hands and his face. He could feel her fear, but he could feel her desire too.

"Sarah," he whispered pulling her eyes back to his, "trust me," he begged. "Close your eyes."

Slowly her eyes closed.

"Do you feel my heart?"

She nodded.

"I will love you until my heart stops beating."

216

She nodded, silent still.

He bent his head so that his nose grazed her cheek willing her to pick up her head. Feeling his head next to hers, she responded and their mouths met, tentative at first but desperation came quickly and the kiss turned hard and fast like opening a spigot in the desert.

She pulled from him, pushing him back, panting, but needing there to be physical space between the two of them.

Her nipples had hardened—he could see them through her thin shirt. Her mouth was red from the stubble on his face. He could feel himself getting hard just looking at her. She had her back to the island and she could feel the cold granite against the small of her back. Andy's hair had fallen down across his forehead and his chest heaved as he breathed. The wave of desire coursed through her body. That kiss had unlocked something, something that wasn't going to be contained now that it was out of its cage.

He stepped toward her cautiously but with purpose and wrapped one arm around her waist pulling her close while his other hand cradled her face.

"Kiss me," he said.

She did, giving into the wave coursing through her body. She felt his stubble on her lips and his chest flex as he pulled her into him.

His hands under her buttocks, he lifted her easily, carrying her upstairs.

The things that would have ripped through her mind were gone. All she could feel was him. His hands, his mouth, his body.

Their clothes were thrown to the floor in a pile as they discovered one another for the first time, and when they climaxed

217

after what felt like hours they did it together.

Sarah fell asleep curled into Andy's body. Preferring to enjoy the sore mess of sex in sleep than trying to get up and make sense of it all.

Andy felt her body slacken as she drifted off. She was the most amazing woman he had ever laid his eyes upon. He lay there enjoying the moment before finally getting up and sorting out his clothes from hers.

He quietly went downstairs and finished making dinner.

Sarah woke alone under her warm comforter still naked. She lay there able to feel Andy inside her while her mind drifted back to a conversation she had a long time ago.

"Sarah," Richard said sternly, "we need to talk about this."

"No, we don't," Sarah said getting up off the couch to go do some trivial piece of house work.

"We do," he said grabbing her arm and refusing to let her abandon the conversation.

"I am not talking about what I'm going to do if you die, it's just not happening. We have a will drawn up. I know what's going on with your life insurance and all that, but I am not having this conversation."

"I want you to be happy," Richard said still holding her arm. "I don't want you to be alone for the rest of your life." Sarah stopped trying to leave and just stared at him.

"Oh, Richard," she said sinking back down onto the couch.

"What?" he said smiling. "Did you think that I expected you to become a spinster with twenty cats? We're still pretty young," he laughed. "If I live another forty years though," his tone serious, "that is exactly what I expect."

She laughed.

"Seriously though, I love you. I love you more than anything on this planet. You are my soul mate. If I die, I want you to be open to another relationship if you want to. You are too young to be alone the rest of your life and I want Taylor to have someone else in her life, too. It will make me happy to know that someone else is helping to take care of you."

Sarah sighed, "All right, do you feel better? Do we get to talk about something else?"

"What about me?" Richard said, "What if you die, don't you want me to be happy?"

"No," Sarah said seriously, "I want you to be miserable without me forever. What kind of girl do you think I am?"

Richard laughed and Sarah joined him. He pinned her down on the couch and they made love while Taylor, just two years old, napped safely in her room.

Sarah had never forgotten that conversation. She knew she had Richard's blessing, she even knew that the guys at the station would be happy for them. Whatever reasons she was tossing at Andy to keep him at bay were her own and always had been. Glancing at the clock she expected Taylor back soon. She got out of bed and hopped into the shower to clean herself up from the afternoon delight.

Andy heard the water turn on upstairs, he was nervous for Sarah to come down. He didn't know what she would think or say to him, but he knew what happened between them had been building for a long time. It wasn't going to just go away anymore.

Her bare feet padded in on the floor, almost silently, while Andy finished washing the last of the dishes. Sarah grabbed a towel and started drying.

"Let's not talk for a while," she said shutting down any attempt he may have had at discussing what just happened.

The two finished the dishes in companionable silence and took dinner out to the grill. Andy built a fire while Sarah arranged the roast on the grill and got the temperature to where she wanted it. Sarah loved to cook on the grill. Being outside was one of the joys of her life. At this time of year the days left to do this sort of thing were numbered. Once satisfied that the grill would keep its temperature she went inside and poured them each a generous glass of red wine.

Andy had just about gotten the fire lit when she got back outside.

She took a healthy drink and sat down watching Andy as he worked.

"I'll always love him."

"I know," Andy replied still working. "But could you love me too?" he said still staring at the fire not daring to meet her eyes.

"Maybe I already do."

Taylor came home as Sarah and Andy had poured themselves a second glass, thus finishing the bottle.

"Can Layla come over for dinner?"

"Of course," Sarah said.

"Good," Layla said laughing and bounced inside.

"You two seem awfully happy," Andy observed.

The two looked at each other and just giggled.

"We are going to go upstairs; call us when dinner is ready?"

"Sure," Sarah said, "there's about an hour left."

Something was weird between her mother and Andy, Taylor could tell. They were avoiding each other's eyes. Not to mention that she was pretty sure her mother was a little drunk.

The two had moved onto a second bottle of wine by dinner

time. Sarah's exhaustion coupled with the fact that she didn't drink wine often made her chatty. Andy wasn't any help either. He kept looking at her mother like everything she said was the most interesting thing ever said.

Slightly overcooked mostly because her mother forgot to set the timer, the roast was decent. Between the four of them it was devoured along with the potatoes and carrots.

"Do you want to go back out to the fire?" Sarah asked Andy.

"Yes I do," Andy said grabbing the bottle of Jameson and two fresh glasses from above the fridge.

"Don't worry," Taylor called after them, "we'll clean up."

"Oh my god! What happened? I don't think I've ever seen your mom drunk," Layla said once out of earshot of the adults.

"I've never seen my mom drunk. Did you see Andy, too? I thought he was going to fall over in his chair. He was leaning so far over in her direction listening to her. I don't even know what she was talking about."

Layla laughed, "This is awesome. Do you think they . . . you know."

"Know what?"

"Do you think they did it?"

"Did what?" Taylor asked getting frustrated and then it dawned on her. "Oh god!" she said, her eyes wide and her mouth open. "No. No. No way!"

"I don't know," Layla said. "I know what it looks like afterwards. Those two did something. Maybe not all of it but definitely some of it."

Taylor couldn't wrap her mind around that concept. She loved Andy and she knew the two of them were close but she didn't know how she felt about it if they were all of a sudden sleeping together.

221

Layla packed away the food while Taylor worked on the dishes.

They both turned when they heard a knock on the door. Taylor checked the window before opening it, Peter stood outside.

"It's Peter," she whispered to Layla.

"Open the door," Layla whispered back.

"Hi Peter," Taylor said as she opened the door. "Come on in."

The alarm gave its familiar tone as she shut the door and the system re-armed itself.

"Hi Peter," Layla called out from the kitchen.

"Hey," Peter said to both of them. "Can I, uh, talk to you?"

"Sure," Taylor said sitting down on the couch.

"I'm going to go upstairs," Layla said.

Peter nodded towards her and joined Taylor on the couch.

"I want to apologize."

"For what?" Taylor asked.

"I've been ignoring you all week. And for what happened at the movie theater. I wasn't very much help. James jumped in and took care of you. I was jealous and embarrassed which is why I avoided you."

Taylor had assumed most of this, she also assumed Peter wouldn't ask her out again. Her first and last dating experience probably until college.

"I told you, dating me is different."

"I guess. I wasn't really expecting that though."

"Neither was I," Taylor said softly.

"It really was a dick move of James to just jump in like that. I mean, I could have handled it."

"I don't think it was a dick move," Taylor said, surprised at Peter's tone. "He got us out of there, at least he did something."

"What, and I didn't?" Peter's volume had gone up.

Taylor immediately reacted, standing up and backing away.

222

"I think you should go," she said, keeping her voice steady.

"Maybe we can try going out again another time," he said.

"Maybe," Taylor said not wanting to upset him further. Something was bothering her though. Something about his mannerisms. The way his eyes kept dodging around, his restlessness. Her mind was distracted by something on the edge of her consciousness trying to push through.

Taylor stared past Peter out the bay window to the fire on the patio.

"Do you know the kid's song 'You are My Sunshine'?"

"What?" Peter said, confused by the change in topic.

"Do you know the song?" Taylor hummed the melody for him. Peter swallowed hard, "I do," he said slowly.

"I hum it," she said, in her mind's eye she could see the dodging eyes, bubbles floated everywhere above her head and she willed one of them to come down so she could explore it. Instead though she saw Peter, who had changed, almost on a dime.

He was engaged by what she was saying, no longer restless and dodgy.

"When I'm stressed or trying to figure something out."

The melody hung between them as she finished the song, "I don't even know I'm doing it."

"Why do you sing it?"

"Someone I used to know would sing it to me, when I was sad. I had forgotten about him because of what happened to me but I've started to remember."

The memory started to dissolve, floating away. She could feel it going and her eyes came back into focus.

Peter watched her carefully, not moving, his face pale. "I've got to go," he said suddenly standing up and moving toward the door.

Peter practically ran out the door. Taylor just stood and watched him.

"What did you do?" Layla asked as she came back downstairs. "I just watched Peter basically sprint to his car."

"Nothing," Taylor said innocently. "He was being weird about James and the movie theater, and then he wanted to go out with me again. Something was wrong with him, he was acting so weird."

Something was still bothering her about Peter, but she couldn't figure out what it was.

"What?" she said momentarily distracted again.

"I said, you are obsessed with that song."

"Was I humming again?"

Layla nodded, yes.

"I like it." Taylor said defensively.

"You know who you should like? Taylor Swift."

"Oh god," Taylor said rolling her eyes. While best friends the two thought very differently about Taylor Swift.

"Don't even start. That's what I'm getting you for a graduation present. We are going to a Taylor Swift concert. I'm going to convert you."

"No," Taylor said laughing, "I beg you no."

"Be nice to me this year or I'll get us back stage—you know my father can make that happen."

"All right, all right, I relent," Taylor laughed, her hands in the air, "anything you want, I'm your slave."

Layla laughed back at her. "Should we check on your mom?"

"Nah, let's leave them there. My mother never has any fun, drunk or otherwise. One night won't kill her."

"Oh my god, I might die," Sarah said from her bed the next

224

morning. Despite preemptively taking three Advils and drinking two glasses of water the night before, her head still felt like a freight train was running through it.

"I'm never drinking again," she muttered to herself. The end of the night was a complete blank she had no idea how she got into her bed. Her stomach felt wretched.

"How are you doing?" Taylor asked from the hallway.

"Softly," Sarah pleaded, "softly."

Taylor smiled, "That bad, huh?"

"Could you not talk to me, please?"

"Advil?" Taylor offered, holding the sweet red pills with one hand and a glass of water with the other.

"Yes," her mother said making a futile attempt to get out of bed.

"Stay there," Taylor said. "I'm working the brunch shift so I'm outta here, sleep it off, I'll be back this afternoon."

It was steady all morning and Taylor made pretty good money, at one point Shauna and Emily came in with their parents, leaving Taylor a pretty sizable tip.

At the end of her shift Jan handed her the schedule for the following week.

"No Friday?"

"I didn't think you would want to work on this Friday," Jan said confused. Taylor looked at the calendar. Friday would be five years since she had been abducted. Typically on that day she didn't do much of anything.

"I'd like to work if you could use me," she said. "I don't want to sit at home and stare at a wall. It'll be better if I'm here."

"OK," Jan said hesitantly. "Are you sure you'll be able to handle it? I think it's going to be busy—there's a home football game that night."

Taylor smiled. "I promise you will have my full attention."

"All right. Get home and enjoy the rest of your Sunday. I'll see you later this week."

Sarah had managed to keep down a bit of toast and some Gatorade. When Taylor got home she was watching re-runs of Gilmore Girls. A show that the two had watched when Taylor was a little girl.

Taylor plopped down on the couch and joined her. It was, all things considered, a really good day.

"I'm going to take a nap before work," Sarah announced around eight.

"I'm going to go to bed, too."

"I'll see you in the morning, sweetheart."

"Love you." Taylor stopped at the stairs while Sarah turned lights off downstairs.

"Mom?"

Sarah stopped, turning toward her daughter. "Can I ask you something?"

The thought that something had happened between her mom and Andy had taken root in her brain. Taylor had been thinking about it since Layla had brought it up the night before. She still wasn't a hundred percent on board, but the more she thought about it the more she thought her father would be OK with it. Her dad loved Andy and Taylor already knew that Andy loved her mom. The three of them were kind of like Arthur, Guinevere and Lancelot.

"Did something happen between you and Andy?" Sarah's face told Taylor what she wanted to know but Sarah couldn't find the words.

"It's OK, you know, if something happened. I mean I'm OK with it."

"I'm not sure what happened," Sarah said finding some words. "You know that no one will ever replace your dad, right—that I *will* always love him?"

"I know," Taylor said confidently. "Andy loves you too."

Taylor turned and walked upstairs. Leaving her mother to her confusion.

Chapter 29

Monday

"What's up with Peter?" Layla asked again, unsatisfied with Taylor's responses on the subject thus far. It was the middle of the week and Peter continued to avoid Taylor as if she had the plague.

"I don't know," Taylor said exasperated. "Honestly though, I care less and less. I think he's got some serious issues; at this point he just keeps ducking into classrooms when I walk by."

"No. He doesn't?" Layla said suppressing a giggle. "Seriously?"

"Yep, I'm done." Taylor said, her head shaking.

"I thought he was weird anyway," James said chiming in. He had draped his arm over Layla's shoulder as Taylor had turned to collect her books from her locker.

"You should have seen his face when those freak shows were at the theater. He looked like he'd seen a ghost."

Layla stuck out her tongue, preferring to pretend that the theater didn't happen.

"Let's talk about something else," she offered. "Like homecoming."

"When's homecoming?" Taylor asked, mostly uninterested.

"It's this week. I swear, it's like you don't even go to school with us."

James laughed. "Homecoming isn't the most important thing in the world," he said, siding with Taylor.

Since the movies James and Taylor had been getting along really well, almost like brother and sister. It was nice, and Taylor was sometimes happy to have an ally when it came to Layla.

"Don't you start," Layla said hitting James's chest. "It's our last homecoming. Be excited. Everything about this year is our last one—it is a big deal." Layla's voice had turned slightly whiny but her point was well taken.

"She's right," James said jumping back into Layla's camp.

"I don't think I've ever been to homecoming."

"You haven't, and you are coming this year. No excuses."

Taylor paused for a moment. "I'm working," she said.

"You aren't," Layla said her mouth open. "You have to get it off."

"I can't," Taylor said almost regretful, "I actually asked to work. I didn't know what day homecoming was and Friday is . . ." she paused trying to find the right word.

"Friday is the anniversary of when you went missing," James said softly.

"Yeah, I didn't want to be home all night just doing nothing and thinking about it."

"Well, now you won't be, you'll be at the dance with us. Jan will give you the day off if you ask her, I know she will. Come on," Layla begged, grabbing her friend's arm. "What better way to stick it to that day than to go to Homecoming and have a wonderful time?"

It did sound appealing. James was smiling behind Layla's back.

"Come," he said, "there's a whole group of us—it'll be fun."

229

The bell rang and Taylor agreed to think about it.

She had a session with Dr. Perna that afternoon, she was excited. She wanted to tell him about the feeling she had the other night when Peter was at the house. She had almost remembered something she was sure of it. Selfishly she wished Peter wasn't being so weird, maybe another moment or two with him would help her remember.

"So," Dr. Perna said, "we need to do some housekeeping."

"What does that mean?" Taylor said.

"I need to evaluate your mental state to see how you are handling the returning memories. It will help me determine at what pace we should keep going . . . and if we *should* keep going."

"If," Taylor said surprised, "what do you mean 'if'?"

"Let's just do this first and then we can talk about where you are."

He then proceeded to grill her on all sorts of things: how she was sleeping, what her dreams were like, how she was eating, how she had been dealing with stress, had she gotten into any disagreements lately, did she feel out of control or like she might hurt herself or others, were there moments when she realized she didn't remember how she got there.

On and on it went, until finally, "That's it," he said.

"That was a lot," Taylor said feeling very tired.

"I need to make sure that you are handling returning memories. It would be irresponsible for me to not keep track of the rest of your life. Just because this is new and exciting and something you're interested in doesn't mean we neglect the rest of what's going on with you. It's why we can't do hypnosis therapy every session. You need time to reflect and adjust."

"OK," Taylor said. Even though she knew she wouldn't be

able to undergo hypnosis this week, she hadn't been prepared for the barrage of questions. Usually their conversations were more free flowing. He would ask questions in between but it was not usually like this.

"My conference is next week," Dr. Perna said. "It's why I moved our session to today. I will be gone for the week so it'll be two weeks until I see you again. You have my number though if something happens. You call me no matter what, understood?"

"Understood."

"How was your night on Friday after our last session?"

"Distracted," Taylor admitted. "I had a hard time concentrating at work I let another woman take over half my tables."

"That's unlike you," Dr. Perna observed.

"Yeah," she admitted, "I just couldn't stop thinking about it."

"And since then?"

"It's been better. I haven't been obsessed with it like I was on Friday. On Saturday I think I almost remembered something else. It just kind of came to me. Peter came over to apologize, which kind of turned into him yelling. I don't know what happened but there was just something that he said or . . . I'm not really sure but something. I could tell that there was a memory there but I couldn't get to it. It's still there, like if just one more piece fell into the puzzle it would jog the whole thing loose."

Dr. Perna nodded. "Now that you are starting to remember some things, other memories may start to come back organically. It's important that you let them, but control them. They could be scary or disorienting."

Taylor nodded. Dr. Perna glanced at the clock and they were fifteen minutes over their allotted time.

"All right," he said standing up indicating the end of the

session, "if you need me, call, otherwise have a good couple of weeks. Let's setup an appointment when I get back."

"OK," she said making a mental note to call his office.

Chapter 30

Wednesday

W "I think it's great that you're going to homecoming. You are really taking control this year, I'm really proud of you. For once I agree with Layla—I think it's poignant that you are going to go out and have fun on this day. Instead of holing yourself up in the house."

For a couple years Sarah had tried to get Taylor out of the habit of retreating from the world, but Taylor had been having none of it. She was relieved this year would be different.

"I've got to work on Friday night," Sarah said, "I'll be able to see you off."

Even though she didn't think she needed to say it, an errant thought ran through her mind. "No parties," she warned with her finger waving in the air and her face stern.

Taylor was so taken aback by the comment she actually laughed out loud.

Sarah joined her. "I don't think I've ever had to say something like that to you. That was great." She laughed again. "Is this is a semi-formal type of thing or just jeans?"

"Semi-formal."

Sarah inhaled, "Well then, we are going to have to go get you a dress."

"No, we don't, I'm sure I can find something to wear."

"You've never gone to any of the school dances and the last time I wore a dress was at least eight years ago. We have to go buy something. Come on, it's not too late to get to the mall and see what's left."

Sarah grabbed her purse and headed toward the door.

"Grab your keys, you're driving."

The mall wasn't crowded but there was a steady stream of people. Sarah and Taylor wound their way through five stores trying on dresses and asking other people for their opinion. Finally, Taylor settled on a black lace dress that came down to her knee with a full skirt. The top was nude and black lace with a high neck and no sleeves. The back though was her favorite part. It wound around the back of her shoulders and then opened up to almost no back at all. With her short hair and her muscle tone, it was stunning.

Her mother picked out a pair of nude heels that went with it perfectly and brought both items to the register to pay.

"Credit or debit?" the clerk asked her.

"Credit," Sarah replied searching in her purse for her card.

"Mom," Taylor stopped her, the total between the two items was close to $300. "Maybe we should think about getting something else."

Taylor rarely asked her mother for anything, she knew that money was tight so anything that she needed she would typically pay for herself.

"Ahh, here it is," Sarah said her hand having retrieved the card from the very bottom of her purse. "I don't want you to worry about it, with Thanksgiving and Christmas coming up, I'll make plenty in holiday pay to cover this. It's a big deal that you are going. I want you to have a great time."

Taylor smiled despite feeling guilty that the items were so expensive.

They got home late and each searched for a snack since they had missed dinner.

"I've got to get going, hunny. Have a bowl of cereal or something and take those upstairs. I should be back before you head off to school."

Without a nap Sarah was tired and she made herself a coffee in a to-go mug before she left. Beneath her characteristic cool demeanor, Sarah could tell that Taylor was excited. She hadn't seen her this excited for a social function since she and Richard had allowed her to have a boy-girl party for her thirteenth birthday.

Chapter 31

F riday

"I am so excited!" Layla exclaimed at lunch the day of homecoming.

Taylor had successfully asked Jan if she could have the night off. Jan had actually hugged her and said of course. She hadn't even cared that it would leave her short for the night, she was just happy Taylor was going to go and do some "regular kid stuff."

Layla, Shauna, Taylor and Jessica were all going together along with James and a few of his friends.

"So what's the plan?" Jessica asked. "What time do we need to be at your house?"

"The limo is coming to bring us to the game at six," Layla instructed. "So you should all be there by four so we have time to get ready. Boys," Layla shouted down the table getting their attention, "be at my house at 5:30. Do not be late, I'm not waiting for you. If you aren't there when the limo leaves, you're walking."

"Yes ma'am," they all joked in unison.

"That was pretty awesome of your mother to get us a limo," Shauna admired. Shauna's number one goal in life was to basically be Layla's mom. A well-kept woman with too much money and not enough to do.

"I think we do our hair and makeup and then obviously just bring our dresses to school and get changed in the bathrooms. I will freeze in my dress at the game," Layla suggested.

The girls all agreed.

Taylor remained silent during their exchanges, happy to be a part of the group. She felt more comfortable letting the girls plan their hair and makeup. She didn't really plan on doing much on either front but was happy to listen to them.

After school, Taylor drove home. Her mother had just gotten up and had made her some strawberry rhubarb pie which was Taylor's favorite. She ate a healthy size slice while her mother had one a bit smaller. "You have to promise to take lots of pictures once you girls get into your dresses—I want to see all of you together."

"I will, I promise."

"Tell Layla I want her to text them to me so I can see them straight away."

"OK," Taylor laughed. Her happiness infectious, Sarah smiled back at her.

"Let's get upstairs and get all your stuff together."

Her mother insisted that she take along some of Sarah's makeup. Sarah didn't have occasion to wear it much anymore and most of it was pretty old, but she did have some nice lip gloss and a few fun eye-shadow colors.

All packed up with her dress in a large plastic bag, Sarah dropped Taylor off in front of Layla's house.

She gave her a hug in the driveway. "Have fun."

"I will," Taylor said as her mother gave her one more hug and held her close for a few moments. "Mom," Sarah's arms didn't leave her daughter. "Mom," Taylor started to squirm, "you have to let me go."

"Sorry," Sarah said as she backed away from her. "You have your phone right?"

"I do."

"It's charged?"

"Yes, I'm good. I'll call you when I get back to the house."

"Not past twelve; no parties."

They both smiled and Taylor half skipped inside Layla's open door without a backward glance.

Sarah breathed for the first time that day. "The best version of this day in five years," she said quietly to herself.

Glancing at her phone, she thought of Andy and decided to give him a call. "Hello?" he said hopefully.

"Hey Andy, are you still working?"

Andy sighed, "I actually haven't stopped working since yesterday. Ended up pulling a double, well, actually, a triple I guess now. Is it really 4:30?"

"I was going to see if you wanted to get a coffee or something but—"

"Coffee is good," Andy said before Sarah could retract her offer.

"Are you sure? It sounds like maybe you shouldn't have anymore."

"I don't think another cup will be what kills me," he joked.

"Meet me at The Barn in twenty minutes?"

"See you there."

Sarah hadn't worked out anything when it came to Andy. Her head and her heart were still a mess of mixed-up thoughts that ranged between severe guilt and strong desire. It was like sitting on the weight that swings inside a grandfather clock. Back and forth she went.

Andy beat Sarah to The Barn and grabbed a seat just inside the door. The waitstaff there all knew him, and Deb came over as soon as he sat down.

"What's the good word, Andy?" she smiled

"Not too much, Deb. You all ready for tonight?"

Andy knew it was homecoming down at the high school. They had most of the guys called in adding extra officers to the 3 p.m.–11 p.m. and 11 p.m.–7 a.m. shifts.

"Oh yeah, can I get you something to eat before it gets crazy?"

"Just a coffee," Andy said glancing at the door.

"Two coffees?" Deb asked intuitively.

Andy smiled, "hopefully . . ."

Deb clucked her tongue and headed off to the back room to get a couple of mugs. Jan's coffee was genuinely some of the best in town. Andy wasn't at all sad to be having such a cup as opposed to the sludge he had been drinking at the station.

A few minutes later Deb came back with two mugs, a half carafe of coffee to keep it warm for him and a piece of chocolate pie.

"Pie's on the house," she said when he gave her a questioning look.

A second later the bell on the door rang as Sarah stepped through the threshold. Andy watched her as her eyes adjusted to the light and she spotted him.

"Hi Deb," Sarah said, taking a seat opposite Andy.

"Hi Sarah, it's good to see you."

"Good to see you, too."

"I'll leave you two to it," Deb said turning to another table.

"What is Taylor's plan tonight?" Andy asked, he had already noticed that she didn't appear to be working.

"She's actually going to homecoming," Sarah said happily.

"Really?" Andy said a bit shocked, "That's great."

Andy knew what today was. He knew where he had been standing almost exactly five years ago at this exact moment. The memory still took his breath away.

Andy hadn't yet left the station when he got the phone call from Rich.

"I missed you too, buddy," he said jokingly as soon as he answered the phone.

"Taylor's gone," Rich said loudly.

"What do you mean she's gone?"

"She's gone, like not here. She should have come home right after school. Her book bag is on the porch, the door is still closed and locked. She's not here."

Andy could hear the panic rising in his friend's voice.

"OK," he said, "stay calm I'm going to tell Chief and we'll go from there. Rich, I need you to focus, you are her father, not a cop. You need to stay there. Maybe she went down the street or something; you have to stay there in case she comes home."

"Yeah," Rich said his voice now had the edge of despondency. "I need you to send someone to get Sarah at the hospital. Someone has to bring her home."

Andy knew there was no way Rich was going to stay at the house.

"OK, I'll call you back. Seriously, stay there."

"Chief, Chief!"

Chief Naughton had his coat on and his keys in his hand seconds from pushing the door open.

"Goddammit Fisher. What?"

"Cormier's daughter may be missing. He just got home, his daughter was supposed to go there after school, but her book bag is on the porch and the door is still locked. He's worried about her,

sir."

"It's too early to sound the alarms," the chief said, his attention now grabbed. "She's what twelve?"

"Thiteen sir."

"Get a few cars over there; get Rich in the house, keep him from blowing his lid. Get on the phone with the friends. Call me every hour. It's 5:15, I want a call at 6 p.m."

"Yes sir."

"Find the girl, Fisher."

"Yes sir."

Rich was standing on his neighbor's porch when he heard the siren. He knew it was coming and felt relieved and terrified at the same time. His neighbor hadn't seen Taylor. The woman had three young children who didn't go to school yet; she'd noticed the bus but didn't pay attention to the kids getting off.

She was just about to close her door when two squad cars, one with Andy in it, pulled up.

"Kill the lights," Andy said to the officer driving the car. "I don't want the entire neighborhood thinking there's a crisis before we know what's going on."

The officer did as he was told and the following car did the same. Andy could see Rich on the porch still dressed in his uniform.

The rain had been falling for a few hours and didn't seem to be showing any signs of letting up.

"Lieutenant, I want you to walk through the yard, look at the back pack, see if you can figure anything else. You two, up and down the street, talk to the neighbors, see what you can come up with. I want constant updates."

Three flashlights clicked on, and off they went.

"Rich, come inside," Andy yelled.

Still on the neighbor's porch, he hesitantly started down the stairs.

Unwilling to give up the position he felt he had. The rain poured down on his head, covering his face, his eyes and his mouth. His breath could be seen in short spurts as he lumbered towards Andy.

"You need to come inside," Andy said again, more softly this time. Rich's resolve was crumbling, the final wrecking ball was the third police car pulling into the driveway with Sarah inside it.

The two ran to one another and embraced. Andy almost couldn't see Sarah once Rich wrapped his arms around her. She had been sobbing.

"Come inside," Andy said as he gently guided the two toward the front porch.

"Are you sure she's not here?" Sarah asked Rich. Her eyes pleading.

"I went through the house already, she isn't here."

It was 5:45.

"I want both of you to get on the phones with every friend Taylor has. Make sure that she isn't sitting in someone's living room drinking hot chocolate."

Andy's radio crackled to life, he went into the kitchen. Rich followed. All three officers checked in, no sign of Taylor.

"She's gone," Rich said.

"You don't know that," Andy insisted. "I need you on the phone, buddy. You have to let me do my job right now and you have to do yours. Call her friends. Do what I can't, and I'll do what you can't. Please."

Andy's voice was tight, holding back emotion as he looked at his best friend's face and thought of Taylor.

Sarah was on the phone, each mother voiced their concern as she repeated the same lines over and over.

"Yes, I'll let you know . . . Yes, thank you . . . Of course, yes, as soon as we hear something . . . I'm sure she's fine too . . . Thank

you."

Click.

Because she was a mother, she began flipping on lights and picking up the kitchen as she dialed every friend she could think of, speaking to them first and then their parents.

With each recitation, however, her voice became more and more worn. Rich left Andy and went to his wife.

Click.

"Who can I call?" Rich asked.

"I'm up to F in my phone book; you start at the back of the alphabet."

Seeing them both occupied, Andy took the opportunity to slip on to the porch and make a call.

"Hello sir, no, we are not having a lot of luck finding her. I think there is something wrong here. I think we need an amber alert and more help. Yes, sir, I will call dispatch with the girl's stats. Sir . . . we need the dogs."

Click.

Sarah and Rich paced the living room each with the phone glued to their ear.

Andy was about to set up a command center in their kitchen. He prayed it was for nothing.

It was 6:32 p.m., an amber alert had been issued for Taylor Cormier: Taylor is thirteen years old, five-feet tall with long sandy blond hair and blue eyes. She was last seen getting off the bus on Elmwood Street in Templeton, MA. She was wearing blue shorts and an orange tank top with gold sandals. She is not believed to be with any known relatives. She is believed to be in immediate danger. Please call the Templeton police department or 911 if seen.

"I'm sorry, what?" Andy asked embarrassed to have not heard

what Sarah just said.

"I asked how your week had been."

"It's been busy, just trying to make sure that I don't miss anything. This Samuel Bishop thing is turning into a disaster. The press are crucifying the Newport News Police for what they claim was gross negligence that allowed Bishop to hang himself. We are still trying to track down how this group is communicating with Jacob himself."

Sarah wanted more information but she didn't press him. Technically he shouldn't say anything to her at all so the little bits of information he did give her were more than she expected. She was happy that Andy was working on the case. It made her feel better.

"You'll figure it out, just keep working on it. The important thing is that Taylor is safe. That's all I care about."

Andy smiled, "I had a good time the other day," he said feeling self-conscious.

Sarah's face turned red thinking of their extra-curricular activities.

"Not just that," he said, embarrassing himself. "I enjoyed just being at the house, having dinner with you both. It felt nice. Normal, like what a regular Saturday could look like."

"I liked it, too," Sarah admitted. She could feel the undertow pulling her heart toward his. It was like the gravitational field of a planet. She wanted to push against the table to keep herself from leaning toward him.

"I know you feel something for me," Andy said turning bold, "I could tell when you let yourself go." The memory of her surrender to him had him half hard already.

"It's not that simple."

"It could be. You and Rich had something incredible, but

he's been gone for three years now. We could have something—something real and true. You have to let us. You have to give us a chance."

Her hand was wrapped around her coffee mug, sucking the warmth from it into her wrists and up her arms.

His hands reached across the table and pulled hers from the warm mug, covering them just like he had a few days ago.

"Sarah, look at me, I wasn't kidding. I do love you. I have loved you for quite a while and I can take care of you and Taylor. Let me, please."

Tears welled in her eyes. His complete resolve for them to try to be together she couldn't ignore any more. She nodded. "Slowly," she said her breath hitching. "It goes slowly. No more sex."

"No more sex," half his mouth turned into a coy smile.

She squeezed his hands.

"Do you want some pie?" He offered her one of the forks on the plate.

"Yes, please," she said, happy to have an excuse to let go of his hands. Touching him even a little made her want to touch him more, and she needed to breathe and remember she just said they were taking it slow.

They finished the pie and had one more cup of coffee before Sarah had to say goodbye.

"I have to go take a nap," she said, yawning despite the jolt of caffeine.

She had gotten a couple of pictures from Layla while her and Andy talked. She took this opportunity to glance down at them.

"Everything OK?" he asked, interested in what had grabbed her attention so fully.

Sarah turned the phone so he could see it. There was Taylor, make-up done, her hair lightly curled smiling with girlfriends, the boys making silly faces in the background.

"That's awesome."

Sarah smiled back, "I gotta go," she excused herself, trying to throw down a couple bucks for the coffees.

"You take that money back. This was our first date."

She laughed and put her $1's back in her purse.

"I'll call you tomorrow," he promised watching her walk out the door.

His head was in the clouds knowing that she had just agreed to at least try. He felt like he could do anything.

Chapter 32

I t certainly helped to have a best friend who had a lot of money. The group of them rolled up to the football game in a stretch limo much to the envy of the rest of the senior class. The girls had stashed their dresses in the trunk, the driver promised to leave the car over at the side door so they could get to them later. The game kicked off at seven and the entire school was there cheering the football team on, despite their losing record.

Taylor was on cloud nine bouncing around from conversation to conversation, yelling at the refs for obvious fouls not called and heckling the other team at half-time. She was almost delirious with happiness. Even a downtrodden Peter, who had tried to pull her away from her friends to "explain himself," had failed to upset her. She had politely said no thank you and wished him the best of luck before returning to the fold. Layla gave her a wink and James wrapped his arm protectively around her shoulders. For the first time in a long time, she didn't shrink away from a touch like that.

During the fourth quarter—with the team losing 21-3—the girls made their way into the bathrooms and got dressed, trading in their jeans and jackets for dresses with sequins and lace.

The music had already started in the gym. Teachers were stationed at each exit. Once you were in the dance you couldn't leave and come back in again.

The boys had less primping to do but they had grabbed a packet of gum to hide the fifth of rum they managed to sneak into their locker that morning and waited patiently for the girls to finish.

Jessica, Shauna, Layla and Taylor looked at themselves in the mirror. "We are one fierce group of bitches," Shauna said, each girl laughing at her ridiculous comment, but in truth all agreeing with her.

Taylor, unused to walking in heels, felt a little unsteady but she was determined to be as normal as anyone so she took a deep breath and hoped she didn't trip.

Cat calls came from the hallway.

"Damn girls, you four are easily the best looking girls in this entire school," Mike said happily. The group was conveniently broken into four girls and four boys, each with some sort of attachment to one another. All except Taylor and, of course, Mike. He did though hold out his arm for her to take and she did, thankful to have him to lean on with the slippery hallway floors.

The music thudded from the gym, Taylor could feel her heart vibrate with the base. The lights were low and strobes went off in a corner, making it look better than it usually did. There were cookies on a table in the corner—Taylor was starving. They hadn't eaten at Layla's because they ran out of time and she'd been too distracted at the game to get a hot dog. Now her stomach tightened and she excused herself to grab at least a cookie . . . if not five.

A tap on the shoulder made her turn, her face full of cookie. Peter was standing there. He looked horrible, sunken, smaller than he had just a few weeks ago. At the game she hadn't paid attention to him. Now, in close proximity, she could see how bad he looked.

She choked down the cookie.

"Peter, listen—" she was about to make some excuse when he interrupted her.

"No," he said harshly though his voice barely above a whisper. "You listen, you have to listen. You don't know—"

"Know what?"

"Anything," he hissed. "I just wanted to keep you safe. Now it's too late, for him, it's too late. Peter likes you, and you like Peter too, but Peter lies."

Taylor backed away while he spoke, he didn't even seem to notice.

"I don't know what you are talking about, Peter. I think you need to get some help. I can call Dr. Perna for you."

Peter started to laugh, slow at first but he got louder and more maniacal.

James had been keeping an eye on her and saw the exchange from near the table.

"Taylor?" he called out, his voice loud and strong even over the music.

Her eyes met his. "You OK?"

"Am I OK, Peter?"

Peter's eyes had gone dark. "For now," he spat out as he turned and brushed past her, knocking into her shoulder and making her stumble.

Her cookies hitting the ground, she caught a whiff of something, a smell she hadn't noticed before. Her nostrils widened and just like that it was gone, replaced with the overwhelming smell of James's cologne.

"What was that all about?"

249

"I have no idea, he wasn't making any sense."

James led Taylor back to the group.

"The kid's a freak show," Mike half yelled so everyone within ear shot could hear him.

Taylor looked back at the door. "Maybe."

While the encounter had been strange, the sugar rush from the cookies and the music all worked their magic to bring Taylor's mind to the present. Whenever her mind started to wander in a dark direction she forcibly pushed the thoughts away. She wanted to have a nice, normal, fun night. They danced until their legs ached and their feet begged to be released from their heels. Mike's hands had more than once touched the bare skin on Taylors back giving her goosebumps. They had danced together at least half a dozen times and she was surprised at how thoughtful and nice he seemed to be.

By eleven the dance was over and the crowds were thinning out. Most were going to a few different people's houses. Layla, who didn't have a curfew, planned on hitting them all. Taylor though wanted to go home. It had been an amazing day but she was exhausted. Plus there were at least three blisters on her feet and if she had to stand for another minute she was sure she would start to cry.

While eight seniors had come to homecoming together, the group leaving had ballooned to thirteen. The driver had to turn away a handful of them claiming it was illegal for him to put any more people in the limo.

The first party was near Taylor's house, so Layla had reluctantly agreed to drop her off at home.

"Want me to come in with you?" Mike offered quietly in her ear while they drove into Taylor's neighborhood.

Taylor's muscles tensed having someone so close to her. "No,

I'm just going to go to bed, I'm so tired."

"All right," he said disappointedly.

The car door flung open at her house and she crawled over bodies to get to the opening. She sucked in the fresh air, kicked off her shoes and swung them over her shoulder.

James got out of the car with her.

"Where do you think you are going?" Layla yelled after them.

"I'm walking her in her house. I'll be right back, the parties aren't starting until we get there anyway."

Cheers erupted from the limo.

Taylor laughed. "You don't have to." Her hot feet relished in the cool night air.

"Yeah, yeah," he said, "let's go."

Taylor went in through the garage, opening it via the key pad on the side of the door. James followed her into the house.

"Mike's a good guy," he said to her after she had thrown her heels next to the door and deposited her purse on the island in the kitchen. The room smelled like vanilla—her mother must have made some tea before she left.

"Just keep an eye on him; he might want things to go quicker than you would be comfortable with."

Taylor opened her mouth to respond when she noticed rose petals and tea lights on the ground. Dozens of them like a trail leading to the stairs.

"What's up with that?"

"I don't know," Taylor said confused.

She looked around but nothing seemed out of place. Some-thing was wrong, though, she could feel it. Her house felt alien. Her heart started beating faster but she followed the path, petals sticking to her bare feet, James trailing behind her.

The rose petals led up the stairs to her bedroom door.

"James," she said her heart now pounding in her ears.

"This is fucking weird, Taylor. What is this?"

"I don't know," she said again, her hand stumbled in the hallway to find the lights, switching everything on. There was no one there, just the rose petals.

She could feel the invasion, even if nothing looked wrong, she knew that someone had been there. She couldn't stop her hand as she pushed the door to her room open and flipped on the light. She stepped back into the hallway like someone was going to jump out and attack her.

The first thing she noticed was the smell: latex mixed with dirt. It hit her like a wave when the door opened. Her desk was in perfect order but she could tell that things had been touched, moved, ever so slightly. Her pillows that in the morning had been thrown on to the bed were now arranged carefully. Five red roses lay splayed out on her bed with a note that looked like it was written in blood.

For our anniversary.

I will see you soon.

~Jacob

"Oh my god," Taylor whispered, "he's here."

James once again leapt into action grabbing her around the waist and pulling her out of the house. His phone in his other hand already dialing 911.

James blew out the front door, Taylor in tow, pulling her on to the lawn. The music from the limo was still blaring, at least until the alarm went off. The floodlights kicked on and the house phone started ringing.

All the kids were now piling out of the limo and standing on Taylor's front lawn—some yelling, others taking steps back into the road—all wondering what was going on.

Neighbors came out of their houses. Between the noise of the alarm and the shouting there was total confusion. You couldn't hear the sirens at first, just see their lights bouncing off the trees as half the police force sped to Taylor's house.

Layla's arms were around her friend, Taylor's head down sucking in fresh air just trying to regain some composure.

"He was here," she kept whispering to her friend, "he was in the house."

Chapter 33

Sarah heard the phone ring just as she left the desk to begin her rounds.

"Sarah," another nurse called out to her, it's for you."

Sarah stopped and went back to the main nurses desk. "This is Sarah," she said formally into the phone.

"Sarah, it's Andy. You need to come home. Something has happened."

Her stomach went through the floor as she crumbled into the chair.

"What?" she said, her voice tight dreading some horrible news.

"Taylor's OK," were his next words and air returned to Sarah's lungs.

"Someone was in your house; you need to get home."

"Are you with her?" she demanded.

"Not yet, Morse has her—I'll be there soon."

Sarah hung up the phone and explained to the other nurses what was going on. Typically she would have to wait for someone to come in and cover her, but thankfully the ward was slow that night and they had been talking about cutting one of them anyway.

Sarah had never driven faster than she did getting home.

Parents of the seniors in the limo had already begun arriving but were being held back while the police talked to them. Taylor, Layla and James stood at the bottom of the driveway with Morse and Andy.

Sarah rushed to Taylor, grabbing hold of her so tightly she thought she would crush her.

"Are you OK?"

"It smelled like him, in my room." Taylor started to cry. "It smelled just like him."

Taylor sat down on the grass and started humming as she rocked. Refusing to stop or be comforted by any of them.

Layla folded her body over her friend trying to protect her in any way she could.

"Sarah," Andy gestured farther down the driveway. "We are going to be all over this. Knight is on his way with the FBI's local forensics team. We are going to put a rush on everything. We are going to do the best we can."

"I'm getting her out of here," Sarah said abruptly.

"What?"

"We're leaving," she said again. "This guy will keep coming. It wasn't enough that she spent years of her life tortured by what happened to her, now that she is finally starting to find some peace and step back out into the world he comes back to what, finish the job he started?

"She'll be gone in thirty minutes. You have until then to ask her the questions you need to but then you won't find her, do you understand me?"

Sarah's voice was tight and short. Her chest heaved with the effort of composure.

Andy nodded, his face a mask.

She nodded back at him and fumbled in her purse for her

255

phone, walking farther down the driveway to make a call.

"Taylor, sweetie?" her mother came and sat next to her on the first step at the front door.

"I called Kristen's parents," she explained slowly. "You're going to go stay with them for a bit."

Taylor lifted her head and stopped humming,

"In California?"

"I'm not sure where. Her parents are arranging some things. I'm going to join you in a few weeks, but I can't come with you right now."

Taylor started to balk but Sarah didn't give her the opportunity

"Listen to me, you aren't safe here. You need to go."

"I don't have any of my stuff—" Taylor started to say as if accepting this news immediately.

"You'll get new stuff. I've already spoken with them. Captain Morse is going to drive you to the airport, they've chartered a plane from Worcester. You have to go baby, right now."

Sarah put her arms around Taylor's back and helped her to her feet. Her daughter felt heavy and limp like a baby that had fallen asleep. Captain Dan Morse sat at the bottom of the driveway with the car door open. He would catch hell for this and he knew it. Jacob was a bad man. Taylor wasn't safe and her mother wanted her gone. He was going to make that happen for her, damn the consequences.

Layla was talking to another officer when she saw Sarah putting Taylor into the back of the police car.

"Taylor," she called out, but Taylor didn't look up at her. "Taylor!" she shouted as she walked toward the car.

Taylor looked up spurred by the call of her friend but Sarah slammed the door shut. "Go," she said to Dan through the back window, "go now."

Light and siren on, Dan gunned the engine and threw the car into gear.

He'd make the airport in thirty minutes.

"What did you do?" Layla yelled at Sarah, "Where is she going?"

Sarah was tired and had just sent her daughter away she couldn't care less at the moment what Layla thought.

"She had to go, Layla. She isn't safe here."

"So that's it?" Layla screamed, the stress of the night breaking down whatever politeness existed between them.

"Yes!" Sarah shouted back. "That's it."

"Where is she going?" Layla asked her voice small.

"I don't know," Sarah admitted. "It's better if I don't know."

Most of the seniors at this point had been allowed to go home with their parents. The limo driver had also just been excused. James remained on the lawn with Layla.

Sarah sat in the driver side seat of her car emotionally drained.

"Mrs. Cormier?" James said hesitantly. "I'm going to walk Layla home. The cops said they don't need anything more from us. My parents are going to pick me up there. Is there anything I can do for you?"

Sarah smiled at him. He'd always been a good kid. "No James," she sighed. "Thank you for tonight. For helping Taylor and for being there for Layla right now. You certainly are good in a crisis."

James shrugged, muttered a thank you and took Layla's hand as they walked up the road toward her house.

Sarah could see Agent Knight through her living room window instructing the forensic team to turn her life upside down. She wondered if they would find evidence of her and Andy's tryst the previous weekend. She doubted they would find anything on Jacob. She had done this before.

Halfway through the car ride Taylor desperately wanted to tell Dan to turn around and take her home. That it would be fine and she would figure it out. He didn't talk to her, he just drove and drove fast. She could hear dispatch calling him. At first he ignored it and then Andy got on the radio and told dispatch he was doing something related to the Cormier case and that he would be offline for about thirty minutes.

"He covered for you," she said to Dan.

"Yep," Dan replied back, "he's a good guy."

"He is," she whispered.

"I'm sorry about all this you know," Dan said turning his head toward the back of the car.

"It's not your fault."

"Why don't you lay down. We won't be there for another twenty minutes, at least."

The back of the cop car was not the most comfortable seat but her head was killing her, she wished she had some regular clothes instead of the dress, it was starting to itch.

She loosened the seat belt and tucked her arm up under her head, staring at the stars through the passenger side window.

Dan had shut off the siren when they got on the highway. It was well past midnight at this point, no one was on the road.

Chapter 34

The airport in Worcester was small. You'd barely know it was there if you didn't know it was there. Her father and mother had flown out of it when she'd been younger, they'd gone to Florida for a wedding. Her father had brought her inside to see the planes take off before Andy brought her home.

She could see the lights of the college closest to it, their football field still light up like a Christmas tree despite the hour.

The airport was quiet with one security guard stationed on the first floor. Besides the small plane she saw on the tarmac there didn't appear to be anyone else there.

"This is where I let you off," Dan said stopping the car at the sliding glass doors. He got out and opened the back door, helping Taylor to her bare feet.

The guard came out almost immediately, "Taylor Cormier?"

"Yes," Taylor responded back.

"I need to see your license."

Shocked for just a second, Taylor realized she didn't bring anything with her.

"I've got it," Dan said grabbing her purse from the passenger seat.

She reached for it.

"Sorry T, your mom told me to keep it, said once you got on the plane you wouldn't need it anymore."

The guard looked the license over and handed it back to Dan.

"All right," he said, "do you have anything for your feet?"

"No," Taylor said back.

"Okey dokey," he said shrugging his shoulders. "Watch where you step out there on the tarmac, all sorts of stuff gets kicked up from the planes."

Taylor waved back at Dan who watched her go through the glass doors before getting back in his car.

The plane was small, not anything like getting on a regular flight in Boston. The captain met her at the bottom of the stairs and ushered her inside. The floor was carpeted and the seats were huge chairs that looked like the most comfortable recliner you could ever sit in. The captain came in behind her and introduced himself as well as his co-captain. He also let her know that there was a stewardess at the back of the plane.

The door to the outside closed behind him and Taylor reluctantly sat down. This was the nicest plane she had ever been in. In fact, it probably rivaled most hotel rooms she'd ever been in.

Seconds later a young woman somewhere in her twenties came out of a small room toward the back of the plane. "Hello," she said in an English accent. "My name is Bridget, and our flight will be about six hours long."

"Do you know where we are going?" Taylor asked her, curiosity getting the better of her. Although six hours indicated California, or at least the west coast.

"I don't, this is the most secretive flight I've ever been on."

She dropped down so she was eye level with Taylor.

"Are you famous?" she asked studying Taylor's face and outfit.

260

Taylor smiled and almost laughed. "Almost . . . I'm prey."

"Huh?" Bridget said, not getting the joke. "Well, nevertheless, are you hungry?"

Taylor didn't think she wanted anything but sleep, but at the word "hungry" her stomach growled in response leaving little doubt that she was.

"I have sandwiches, fruit and ice cream," Bridget said. We normally have much more but we had to be air ready in fifteen minutes, which didn't give me a lot of time to put together meals. They just said that we were picking up a teenager.

"That's OK," Taylor assured her. "A sandwich sounds amazing."

"Turkey or ham?"

Taylor chose turkey and Swiss cheese with mustard, lettuce pickles and tomatoes. Bridget brought out a beautiful sandwich minutes later along with a pear and strawberries.

Taylor tore into it like she hadn't eaten in a month. The sandwich and fruit were devoured in minutes.

"That was amazing," she groaned, her stomach full.

Bridget hadn't watched her eat but had barely time to clean up in the back room.

"You're done?" she exclaimed.

Taylor smiled sheepishly. "Yeah, sorry, I haven't eaten since lunch."

Bridget didn't ask but instead brought Taylor out a cup of hot chocolate and a small dish of cookie dough ice cream.

"This is all my favorite food," Taylor said in awe, "that's crazy."

"I was told what you like and what foods to avoid," Bridget chimed in, ruining the illusion that for a moment something had just happened in Taylor's favor.

Bridget continued, "No apples, that was a big one."

"Yeah," Taylor said her mind turning to the most recent events. "No apples."

Taylor as a general rule couldn't sleep on airplanes but the seats reclined almost completely and were so comfortable she couldn't resist laying back and closing her eyes. Just for a minute.

Taylor didn't wake until Bridget touched her shoulder letting her know that they would be landing soon. She rubbed her eyes, smearing her make-up and stretching in an an attempt to liven up her limbs.

"I have slippers for you," Bridget said as the plane descended. "I'm sorry I don't have anything else, we keep these on the plane but they will be better than walking through the airport barefoot."

"Thank you," Taylor said relieved. The slippers were com-fortable and warmed her toes.

It was still dark wherever they were, city lights shone into the sky like beacons.

Landing this little plane didn't take long and the nice thing was that once they landed Taylor didn't have to wait to get off.

Bridget directed her to the side door and once they exited she showed Taylor where to get into the airport. "There's a car waiting for you. The driver will be in the pick-up area with a sign that has the name Greggor on it."

Taylor thanked Bridget and the captain for everything and followed the directions toward the front of the airport. She recognized where she was as soon as she stepped inside. It was the San Francisco International Airport. This was where Taylor flew in and out of whenever she visited Kristen.

So much for the cloak and dagger act she said to herself.

A single man stood outside a car dressed in a suit with a black hat on and a sign that said Kristen Greggor on it.

It was 4 a.m. there and the airport was silent.

"Ms. Greggor?" the man asked as Taylor approached.

"That's me," Taylor responded, assuming he wasn't going to ask for ID or anything.

The man put the sign down and opened the back door, letting Taylor slide into the black leather seats. He promptly shut the door and went around the back of the vehicle before opening his own door and pulling away from the curb.

"Would you like some music, miss?" he asked formally.

"No thank you," Taylor said. "What's your name?"

"You can call me Ben," the driver said.

"Thank you, Ben."

Taylor felt self conscious in this big vehicle with a driver who obviously thought she was someone else.

"Where are we going?"

"You're going home," Ben said simply as if it would be totally normal for someone to not know where a car was bringing them.

Two hours later just as the sun was starting to rise they drove into a gated community in Monterey. Taylor had never actually been to Kristen's house. She'd only been to the camp that was about three hours north of the airport.

Once inside the community they drove to the top of a large hill and then entered another set of gates. The lawn expanded to what could only be described as a mansion set on a cliff overlooking the ocean. It was breathtaking.

Taylor made an audible noise which Ben politely ignored.

He drove up the granite driveway and stopped the car directly in front of the main door. He hurried around the back to open the car door for Taylor who had already partially opened it herself.

Seconds later the front door swung open and Kristen all but ran out.

"Taylor, my god. I've been so worried about you. Come inside, come inside."

Kristen put her arm around Taylor and ushered her in, turning quickly to thank the driver who she called by his name. He nodded and moved the car around to the back of the property.

Kristen, so used to walking in and out of the house, didn't stop to appreciate the enormity but Taylor couldn't help herself. There were two staircases that wound around the edges of the foyer before meeting at the top, and a chandelier that looked like it was made of diamonds. The foyer opened up to the kitchen and a panoramic view of the ocean.

"Wow," she said, her eyesbrows raising toward Kristen. Kristen's wealth was a topic of constant jabbing from Taylor.

Kristen was the most down to earth person you could imagine given what she had grown up around, though she did take certain things for granted like private planes and cars with drivers. She had never flown a commercial flight but she did appreciate all that she had and that was the most important thing to Taylor.

"So," Kristen said moving on, "you've got some shit going on over there on the east coast, huh?"

Now thousands of miles away from Jacob, Taylor felt like she could breath.

"You have no idea," she said. "Tell me I can borrow some clothes. If I don't get out of this dress I might just start walking around your mansion naked."

Kristen laughed, "Come upstairs, my parents should be getting up soon. They wanted me to wake them when you got in."

"No, no, let them sleep. I owe them. I didn't even know my mother had been talking to Mrs. Greggor."

"Your mom called a few weeks ago. She was worried about something. She wanted to know if you could come stay here for a while if things got worse. My mom put our plane company on notice that they may get a phone call, so when your mom called last night it was a piece of cake getting you here."

"I'm going to have to make your mother dinner or something." Taylor said genuinely thankful.

"She'll love that. Come on, let's get you into something more comfortable. Cute dress by the way."

Kristen went up one staircase and headed left down a hallway, up one more half flight of stairs and a second left, eventually coming to rest in front of a set of double doors. Her room mirrored a suite in the fanciest hotel you had ever seen in the world . . . with the exception of the clothes on the floor and the posters on the wall.

Her closet was the size of Taylor's bedroom. It was carpeted with shelves and lights everywhere illuminating rows and rows of clothes, shoes, handbags and dresses.

"Sweats?" Kristen asked.

"Sweats," Taylor confirmed.

Kristen gave her some privacy while she changed. Taylor came out of the closet so happy to be comfortable again and sank into a chair near the bed.

"Was it Jacob?" Kristen asked.

Taylor nodded. "I really think it was. When they said that Samuel Bishop was him, I don't think I really believed it, but I wanted to. I wanted that to be what I could hold on to. So I could just have a regular senior year like anybody else. But I knew, deep down, I was just fooling myself. He was in my house, in *my* room," she said staring out the window at the vast expanse of the ocean.

"How did he even get in? You guys have a security system that rivals ours."

Down the hall Taylor heard an alarm, she sat up startled.

"It's just my parents' alarm clocks," Kristen assured her.

Taylor sunk back down into the chair.

"Are you hungry?"

The two went down to breakfast and her stomach grumbled. The kitchen was already filled with the aroma of bacon and toast.

The Greggor's chef, who Taylor knew from camping, was in the kitchen busy making a breakfast that you would see at any five-star hotel. Fresh fruit was already cut up and on the table set in front of open French doors that lead to a patio area, which lead to an infinity pool, which of course then looked out over the ocean.

"Is there anywhere you can't see the ocean from in this house?" Taylor asked sarcastically.

"The front door," Kristen answered back as if Taylor's question was a serious one.

"Hi Robbie," Taylor said smiling happy to see the chef again.

"Miss Taylor," Robbie said enthusiastically. Robbie wore a chef's uniform but with a bandana around his head. He was a flamboyantly gay man who loved to joke around with the girls. Though only when Mr. and Mrs. Greggor weren't around. He would also occasionally sneak them in non-organic, sugar laden sweets that he bought at a convenience store.

Kristen had a huge sweet tooth and had very rarely been allowed to indulge. Robbie was her sugar dealer and had been for the better part of five years at this point.

Taylor sat down at the table and popped some grapes into her mouth.

"So why aren't you at school?"

"I'm doing an internship this semester. The office I'm working out of is closer to my parents' house. I actually have been staying here during the week. I had just gotten back to the dorms when my mother called and said you were coming so I drove back late last night."

"What's the internship?" Taylor asked wanting to discuss anything except her life right now.

Robbie came over and placed a plate in front of Taylor and Kristen. Eggs over easy with bacon and whole-wheat toast.

"Real butter," he whispered, winking at Kristen.

Kristen smiled, "Thanks, Robbie."

Taking a bite of her toast, Taylor listened to Kristen explain the non-profit that she had chosen to work for. It helped kids who had been in foster care transition back to their families.

"It's actually given me an idea," Kristen said, excitement in her eyes.

"Oh yeah?" Taylor said as she shoveled eggs into her mouth.

"I want to start a camp, for kids like us"

Taylor put her fork down, "What do you mean, kids like us."

"I want to start a camp for kids who've been abducted." Kristen paused, looking at her friend.

"What?" Taylor said self consciously wiping her mouth assuming she had bacon on her cheek.

"I was hoping that you would help me get it going and help me run it."

"How would we even do that?"

"That lake that we camp at is huge. My parents don't need the entire thing. They actually said if I could get this off the ground I could build a camp for the kids on the other side."

"Hold on," Taylor said, her eggs getting cold. "Your parents own the entire lake?"

267

Kristen nodded, slightly embarrassed.

"I just thought that it was like a secluded area and that's why there were no other houses."

"My parents didn't want anyone else building around them so they bought the entire area. I think it's something like two hundred acres and it's surrounded by state forest."

"That's crazy," Taylor said as she picked up a piece of bacon and started systematically eating it and everything else within reach.

"So . . ." Kristen said staring at her friend, "what do you think?"

"I think it's great," Taylor said. "It sounds like a ton of work. What would you even do with a bunch of traumatized kids though?"

"It would be just like regular camp," Kristen insisted. "The only difference would be that we would teach stuff like self-defense and we would have psychiatrists on staff. We could still do everything else you would do at any other camp: swimming, kayaking, s'mores."

Taylor thought for a minute picturing the sereneness of the lake and how good she felt when she was there. "I'm in, it sounds great. Assuming that I live long enough to see it, I'm in."

"Don't joke like that," Kristen said. "Seriously, it's not funny. They *are* going to catch him and you're going to stay here until they do."

Taylor didn't say anything.

"Taylor, is that you?" Mrs. Greggor came into the kitchen wearing an attractive track suit, her make-up already done.

"Hi Mrs. Greggor," Taylor said standing. Mrs. Greggor's arms enfolded her in an embrace, which Taylor willingly returned.

Mr. Greggor came in behind her already dressed for work in a navy blue suit. Mr. Greggor owned a movie studio along with half a dozen other businesses. Taylor had at one point known what they all were but she had lost track a couple of years ago.

"Are you OK?" Mr. Greggor asked her putting this hand on her shoulder.

She shuddered but just barely, he registered her reaction though and gently moved his hand away, smiling, sadly.

"It's OK," he said to her in a low voice. "Kristen had a hard time with me touching her for a long time too."

"Sorry," she said, red with embarrassment from her face down.

"Don't you dare apologize," Mrs. Greggor said. "You've just been through hell. It's fine, isn't it, dear?"

"It is," Mr. Greggor said changing the topic. "I have something for both of you."

"Rodney, could you come in here please?"

Rodney was the lead person on Kristen's security detail. Whenever she left the house he was with her and had been since she had been abducted. He stood just over 6'3" and must have weighed close to 250lbs. He was muscular with tattoos all over his arms. He always wore glasses—Taylor wasn't actually sure if she had ever seen his eyes.

Rodney came into the kitchen carrying a small bag. Emptying the contents over the middle of the table. Inside it were a dozen phones as well as a new computer.

"These are burner phones," he said in a thick Irish accent. "You only use these phones," he said to Taylor. "You will keep it for one day and at the end of each day you throw it away."

He handed a phone to everyone in the family.

"I will have fresh ones for you each morning in a bag in the foyer. This is a computer that's been updated with all the latest security. I have setup an email account for you that will change every three days. Let the computer choose your passwords—do not use any password that you have ever used on anything else.

"I've asked a trusted colleague to head up your security detail. His name is Patrick. His team will work in groups of three on eight-hour shifts rotating in and out every 3 days."

Taylor was astounded.

"You are going to be safe here," Mr. Greggor said to Taylor.

"For now, we would prefer that you not be anywhere in public until the media dies down a little." Rodney continued. "We've secured the Eisenhower building. It's ready for the girls, if you would like I can have them there tonight.

"Yes, Rodney, thank you, please make those arrangements." Mr. Greggor said, pleased with the level of thoroughness.

"How bad is the media?" Taylor asked. She hadn't even thought to ask until now.

Mrs. Greggor looked at her husband. He just nodded to her like he was giving permission.

"The local media is reporting but it was also picked up nationally as well. The FBI confirmed that the blood on the letter left in your house was from Jacob."

Taylor sucked in her breath. So that was it, he really was back.

"Can I call my mom?"

"I have a connection on the east coast; he's going to see your mother today and make sure she has a set of phones. Your mother's phone number as well as the Greggor's and Kristen's are in the memory of each phone.

Until this moment Kristen had sat quietly letting her friend absorb the enormity of the situation.

Taylor's head spun with all the information.

"What's the Eisenhower building?" Taylor asked, unsure of

whom to direct the question to?

"It's an apartment building my parents bought and were going to renovate," Kristen answered. "They're about halfway through it. It's still empty and it is its own gated community."

"We don't think he will follow you here," Rodney stepped in, "but we would prefer to not make it easy for him. Having you stay here would make it very easy for him to find you. Your friendship with Kristen is well known. The Eisenhower building was purchased through one of Mr. Greggor's businesses as employee housing options. It would take considerable effort and time to track that place to him and, then, in turn to you. In the meantime, renovations will continue while you're staying there so it will appear as if nothing is amiss."

Taylor nodded. They really had thought of everything. But her stomach was in knots and her head was starting to hurt.

"Do you want to lie down?" Mrs. Greggor asked intuitively.

"Yes, please, if you don't mind," she said her eyes scanning all three adults in the room.

"Of course," Mr. Greggor said. "Kristen, why don't you show Taylor the spare room, she must be exhausted."

"Come on," Kristen said grabbing a muffin and a piece of fruit before leading the way back through the foyer.

The guest room was nautically themed with light blues, greens and grays. The colors were soothing and the king bed begged for her to lay in it.

"When you get up I've got someone coming to the house with clothes for you. I guessed on most of your sizes but they will bring a few different sizes of everything."

Taylor hugged her friend; Kristen hugged her in return, patting her back.

"It's going to be OK. Get some sleep."

271

The bed was luxuriously soft, she sank into the comforter, drifting off to an uneasy sleep.

Hours later she got up and explored the room a bit more, admiring the furniture and the attached bathroom. There was even a small balcony with two sofa chairs and a small end table. The ocean crashed below and she could smell the salt in the air. She left the door open enjoying the sunshine and the sounds of the waves.

A gentle knock interrupted her thoughts.

"Hey, are you hungry?"

"A bit," Taylor admitted.

"Robbie made some sandwiches and left them out here for you."

"This is better than a hotel," Taylor said still in awe.

"One of these days you and I are going to stay in a hotel and I'll show you all the reasons that's not true."

Taylor smiled as Kristen brought in a tray of sandwiches and dehydrated pea sticks.

"Rodney is finalizing plans. He said that you would meet Patrick at the apartments. My friend came and dropped off a bunch of clothes too so we can go through those once you eat. Whatever you don't want we'll just leave here and he'll pick them up tomorrow. If there is anything else you need too, just make a list," Kristen gestured toward the desk in the room, "and Patrick will arrange for you to get them."

"Sounds good," Taylor said in between bites. The roast beef was covered in a horseradish cheese sauce. It was so delicious she wanted there to be a bowl of it she could just spoon into her mouth. Once satiated she abandoned her plate and grabbed that day's phone, eager to check in with her mom.

"Taylor?" Her mother's voice came on the line, "Is that you?"

"Mom, it's me."

"Are you OK?"

"I am. Mr. and Mrs. Greggor are taking really good care of me."

"Thank God."

"How are things there?"

"It's hectic. I slept for a few hours in the car while the FBI finished up at the house—"

"I don't want you staying there," Taylor interrupted.

"I'm not," Sarah assured her. "Listen to me, I need about three weeks to get things settled here before I can come to you. The Greggor's are putting me in touch with someone who can help. You and I are going to disappear."

Taylor started to protest.

"Stop," Sarah said. "I know this is a lot, but we can't stay here, it's not safe. This way we can start a new life."

"Where?" Taylor croaked out.

"I don't know yet, I'm still working that out. But for now, I need you to lay low. Don't let anyone figure out where you are. We'll go to Hawaii if that's what you want, just somewhere no one knows us."

Tears welled once again in Taylor's eyes and she nodded her head as if her mother could see her.

Kristen held out her hand, motioning for the phone. Taylor gave it to her walking to the other side of the room choking down her emotions.

"Hi, Mrs. Cormier," Taylor heard her say.

The two talked for a few minutes. Kristen filled Sarah in on the security details. She didn't mention the apartment complex and Sarah didn't ask.

Kristen hung up the phone without asking Taylor if she wanted to say goodbye.

"She wants us to go into, like, witness protection. Change our names and disappear."

"What do you want?" Kristen asked.

Taylor sighed, her shoulders sagged. "I want this to be over."

"Maybe this way it could be."

"This way it will be permanent. The running, the fear, the constant worrying if someone figured out who we really are. I'll never see you or Layla again."

"It's not *really* witness protection; maybe it won't be so bad starting over."

"I can't, I just can't. I hate him," her voice furious. "I hate him so much I want to kill him. I want to watch him die and spit in his face."

Kristen was quiet for a moment. "I'm going to give you some time alone."

Taylor remained in her room until two black Suburbans pulled up to the house hours later.

"You don't have to stay with me, you can stay here," Taylor offered to Kristen.

Taylor wasn't entirely sure where her mood was coming from, but she was angry at just about everything and at the moment that attitude was directed at Kristen.

"Don't be ridiculous, I already talked to my professor and my internship is going to let me work from home for the next few weeks."

"I just mean you have a whole life here, you shouldn't have to change everything because my life is a hot mess."

"Your life isn't a hot mess, and I am not changing anything. I'm working from home—no big deal."

Taylor had been running scenarios in her mind all afternoon.

Jacob flying out to California to kidnap her again. Jacob kidnapping her mother. Jacob hiring someone to trek Taylor across the country in a van. Each scenario as dooming as the last.

"Fine," Taylor said, "suit yourself."

The girls were loaded into separate vehicles. Besides the driver there was a man in the passenger seat and one sitting next to Taylor. All had short hair and tattoos, they didn't speak, not even to each other.

Chapter 35

Saturday

It took hours to get to the apartment complex. As they drove an idea started to form in her head. It scared her, scared her more than even Jacob did. The farther the cars got from the life Taylor knew, the more convinced she became that this was the only way.

Even in the dark she could tell the apartments were a far cry from the opulence that Kristen was used to. She wondered what her friend would think of this type of living. Once inside the gate the cars pulled toward the center of the complex. The front doors to the apartments all faced each other creating a common area where there was a bit of grass and a decent size in-ground swimming pool. The buildings were two story apartments, like a motel back home. The second floor had a small porch area. The external gate to the parking area was high, at least ten-feet tall. There was a secondary gate that attached to the buildings that was about five-feet tall. Once stopped, the man sitting next to Taylor got out of the vehicle along with the man in the passenger seat. They scanned the area before gesturing that Taylor could slide over and climb out of the car.

A man stood in front of her, "My name is Patrick, I'm sorry we didn't get to meet at the Greggor's House. I had some last minute arrangements to make."

"That's fine, I understand."

Patrick was the most ripped person Taylor had ever seen in her life. He wore a tight black T-shirt and black cargo pants with black work boots. His hair was cut military short and there was a scar above his left eye that made him look more ominous than his Irish accent made him sound.

Seconds later the cars pulled away and Taylor could see Kristen standing next to her own set of bags.

Each man grabbed one and headed to the apartments farthest from the front gate. The men led them to apartment 11 and 12, both on the first floor. The doors swung open and Taylor walked in behind Patrick.

"You always come in second," he said to her as they were entering. "You never go into a room first or last."

She nodded, confirming that she understood. She wondered if this was how Kristen lived or if they treated her different because she was the boss's daughter.

Bags deposited, the three men stood in front of her and Patrick introduced them as Brendan, Andrew, and Shane.

"Each of them will be team leader on the shift they supervise. They will rotate so they will not work the same shift more than a few times in a row. If you need something or have questions you ask them, please do not speak to the other people on the shift, they won't talk to you anyway."

Again, Taylor nodded.

"What you need to understand is that you are under a very specific threat. We are going to protect you differently than the way Rodney's team manages Kristen. This is not a vacation."

She stood in front of four very large men, all capable, of killing her in an instant.

Taylor squared her shoulders, "I have been in danger every single day for the last five years. You don't need to tell me that this isn't a vacation. What you need to understand is that, he will find me. He will torture me, he will break me using every means he can think of and let me tell you, from experience he is very creative. If I am lucky he will kill me. But let's be honest, I'm not a lucky person. This is what I'm looking at, this is my future."

Patrick didn't give anything away, he just stared at Taylor sizing her up. "For now, get yourself unpacked and settled. You sleep in the back bedroom. The team leader will use the bedroom next to it as an office area. There is some food in the fridge if you are hungry."

She got to work dragging her bags to the back room and getting her things unpacked. All her clothes had that brand-new feel to them and she wished she could wash them before wearing them.

She heard a knock on the wall, once and then twice. She smiled, knowing it must be Kristen. She responded with her own knock.

Moments later she heard the main door open. She paused unpacking and walked out to the living room to see who it was. Rodney walked in the door first, Kristen behind him.

"I'm sorry about how I was at your house," Taylor said. "I was just angry, I shouldn't have been so short with you."

"It's already forgotten," Kristen said.

Taylor directed her next comment at Rodney and Patrick, "I need to be able to take care of myself. This will never be over, even if I do run, he will find me one day and if I have to choose between me and him, I want it to be me."

Kristen smiled, "Are you serious about wanting to learn to defend yourself?"

Patrick eyed both girls. "This won't be easy, we aren't going to be nice to you because you are a girl or because bad things happened to you."

"Good, I'm tired of everyone treating me like I'm going to break."

"One other thing, we train to kill."

Taylor swallowed hard nodding her head.

"Be ready at 6 a.m. The first time you complain or cry will be the last time I work with you."

Patrick turned on his heel and left, Rodney followed him. Moments later two other men came in and Kristen and Taylor were left with only Shane to talk to.

Kristen motioned toward the back room and Taylor followed her.

"Are you sure this is what you want?" Kristen asked Taylor once the door had closed.

"Yeah, I'm sure."

"It's hard. They aren't going to go easy on you."

"I know, I want to do it." Taylor's face was set with firm resolve.

Kristen nodded, "I only have two guys with me normally and I know all of them. I've had the same team for years now. It's a pretty great gig for them. My parents pay them well and there are no real threats against me so they just keep an eye on me. I've never met Patrick, but if Rodney trusts him then he's OK."

Taylor stifled a yawn, the day catching up with her quickly.

"Get to bed," Kristen said, "I'll see you in the morning, say 5:45?"

"Yeah," Taylor said.

Taylor could hear Kristen leave and the door open at the other unit. The walls were thin. Hungry, she wandered into the kitchen and nodded at the guys who were playing cards and watching TV, the lights low and shades drawn. She glanced at the door, locked in all three places.

Shane saw her eyes glance at the door, "We've got this."

She turned to him and shrugged, "Habit."

She opened the fridge and grabbed a yogurt as well as a bottle of water. She also grabbed a pear off the counter before retreating to her room.

She rummaged through both suitcases and couldn't find any pajamas so she decided to get dressed for her morning run and sleep in that. The clothes that had been dropped off at the house had precious few workout clothes and no sneakers. Kristen had already asked for those items to be brought to them but it looked like for tomorrow she would be borrowing a pair.

Her snack consumed, she fell asleep quickly to the sound of the guys' conversation a few feet from her.

She heard knocking, it felt like it was right above her head. Her eyes opened roaming as they tried to find the source of the sound. Knock knock again right above her head. "Kristen?" she moaned.

Rolling over and looking at the clock, it wad 5:40 a.m. She pushed herself upright, grabbing the bottle of water next to her bed and taking a few sips before she knocked back on the wall letting her know that she was up.

She didn't have her running stick here, which she knew she would miss. She liked the weight of it in her hand while she ran. She pulled a long sleeve shirt over her head and padded barefoot into the living room.

"I need to go next door," she said to the group of guys as they hovered around the coffee pot.

Each of them noticed her bare feet.

"I need to borrow sneakers from Kristen."

"And socks apparently," Shane commented. "Come on."

The pair of shoes from Kristen were a size too large, for now it was all she had. She laced them as tight as they would go before heading out into the common area.

Both Rodney and Patrick were already outside, their breath misting in the cool air.

"You ready?"

Kristen would routinely run with Taylor during their three-week retreat in the summer. Taylor thought she was the one driving that but now she realized that Kristen had been doing much more, for much longer.

"It's ironic that we are here training together, isn't it?" Taylor said.

Kristen stopped and turned.

"I didn't listen to you about learning to take care of myself or taking control. I ignored you. I don't know why either. Like if I started to learn how to fight back it would be admitting that—"

"You might need to one day?" Kristen suggested.

"Yeah," Taylor said.

"It's OK, I didn't hold it against you. I understood why you didn't want to know how to defend yourself. It was the same reason you never wanted to know the parts of your abduction you couldn't remember on your own."

"And look how that turned out."

"You two done?" Rodney shouted into the morning air, breaking their tête-à-tête.

He started off at a brisk pace through the complex. Kristen followed him, Taylor behind Kristen while Patrick brought up the rear. Without anything to hold Taylor didn't know what to do with her hands. She tried to settle her breath to the beat of her feet but nothing felt right. The too-big shoes started to rub on her heels towards the end of the first mile. She was struggling.

"What's up?" Kristen asked dropping back to her friend.

"I don't know, I can't settle." her words struggling as she sucked in shallow breaths.

Taylor's eyes scanned the ground as she searched to find something that would help. It was unlike her to struggle this way, after all, running was her "thing".

"Finally," she thought to herself. Taylor veered out of formation and grabbed a fairly size-able rock, the weight in her hand felt good. Swooping down she snatched up another before rejoining the brigade.

One in each hand seemed to even out Taylor's stride, her breathing slowed down and her feet found their rhythm. She could feel her heel rubbing against the shoe and knew there would be a blister there but for now she pushed through it.

The quartet wound through the complex never leaving it. They circled the parking lot and the pool going up the stairs to the second-floor apartments and back down again over and over again. Taylor never knew what mile they were in, but it had been the fifth time they ran the stairs when Rodney finally put his hand up signaling that they were stopping.

Their breath came fast and short as each tried to fill their lungs. "Kristen," Rodney circled around, facing the girls, "let's show Taylor some catch and release moves."

Kristen nodded walking over to the grass area in the center of the complex. The other men on the details came out of the apartments—some had coffees, others munched on toast while they watched.

Kristen stood in the middle of the grassy area as Rodney came up behind her and grabbed her around the middle lifting her in the air. She reacted, throwing an elbow which he dodged. She twisted the other way, though, forcing him to put her back on the ground which was when she used his own body weight, now off balance, to put him on his back.

The guys whistled in admiration. Kristen smiled and held out a hand for Rodney.

The two demonstrated a few more moves, all of which ended in Kristen putting Rodney on his back.

"You ready?" Rodney said to Taylor.

Her spine stiffened. This had sounded like a great idea in her head but now the thought of someone coming up behind her and . . . her breath suddenly flew out of her lungs as a body crashed into her. Arms wrapped around her middle, lifting her off the ground moving her to a car. She screamed and squirmed but there was little she could do. Her stomach muscles clenched and she kicked her legs as hard as she could, to no avail. Her assailant opened his legs as he walked, she felt her heel ricochet off his shin once. Her head swung wildly, he was much taller than her and her head just kept bouncing off his chest.

Panic overwhelmed her, her screams came again, unable to control them she was still flailing wildly when she realized that he no longer held her.

Her hair, wet with sweat from the run, stuck to her face making it hard to see. She pushed it out of her eyes with her forearm, panting at Patrick standing in front of her. His face cool but haunted, he hadn't enjoyed what just happened. The square was quiet. The guys on the porch didn't move. No one moved.

Taylor looked around at all their faces and she saw pity. They weren't even disappointed. They never thought she would be able to do this.

"Again," she called out to Patrick.

Kristen stepped towards her friend, "maybe you should take a break."

"Again," she commanded.

Patrick's eyes narrowed as he charged her once more.

Chapter 36

Tuesday

Taylor's body ached, her mind exhausted. For seventy-two hour they had trained, eaten, trained and slept. Her arms ached so badly it hurt to hold a bottle of water to her mouth.

"You have to control your emotions," Patrick told her for the twelfth time that hour.

"I know."

"Then do it."

"I'm worried about her," Kristen said to Rodney as she watched Andrew and Taylor spar. The sun was hot and they were all working without a lot of sleep.

"She's tougher than she looks, I'll give her that. I didn't think too much of her when she said she wanted to train. Figured she'd quit before the end of the first day. But she's been pushing us as much as we've been pushing her."

Kristen's eyes never left her friend, "It feels like she's training for more than just defending herself."

Rodney shrugged his shoulders, watching Taylor's every move.

Finally he intervened, directing his comments toward Taylor, "You need to find a way to control your panic. If you start to panic you can't think, if you stop thinking you are dead, understand?"

Taylor nodded.

"You aren't bigger than him, you aren't stronger than him. You have to use what you have."

"Patrick," Rodney said to him, "charge Kristen."

Patrick took off at a dead run towards Kristen who was not prepared for him at all. She turned her body to the side and bent her knees with her hands in front of her chest.

"Watch her," Rodney barked at Taylor, who's eyes were trained on Patrick.

Patrick grabbed at Kristen's shoulders, which she ducked under putting her hands just under his ribcage. His own momentum helped her lift his body into the air as she pushed him off balance.

He landed hard on one leg and stumbled to the left, giving Kristen time to re-set herself. He charged again. This time she rolled out of the way. A third charge and he managed to get his arm around her waist. Instead of fighting him though she went with his strength and again rolled out of his grasp. The most interesting thing though was at the end of the third charge. Patrick was panting and Kristen was barely breathing heavily.

"Do you see?" Rodney asked Taylor, who stood in awe of her friend. They had drilled a lot over the past few days but she hadn't seen any actual sparring since their first day.

Taylor nodded.

They drilled and sparred for the rest of the day on stances and techniques until the sun went down and Taylor thought that she might pass out from exhaustion.

"Again at 6 a.m.," Rodney barked as the girls headed back to their apartments. "Twelve miles."

Taylor dragged herself through the doors of the apartment.

Brendan had just come on duty. "You look like arse," he said to her.

The other two guys gaffed at his joke at her expense.

She smiled back, "Yeah, I feel like it too."

"There's Gatorade in the fridge. Drink it and eat a banana—the potassium is good for sore muscles."

Taylor thanked him, grabbed the drink and fruit from the kitchen and went directly to her bedroom in the back, falling easily into a dreamless sleep.

Chapter 37

Andy could see Knight sitting at a desk in the middle of the precinct, though he couldn't tell if he was sleeping or just closing his eyes.

Andy's eyes returned to his computer screen. Taylor's image stared back at him, she looked every bit the young woman in her homecoming dress and high heels. Sometime just before Homecoming on Friday night a picture of Taylor set the message boards on fire. Fearful that Jacob's serial kidnapping would continue the FBI agreed to help track down where it had originated from.

Andy had a theory and was looking right at him. He knew Knight would do whatever it took to get Jacob—he'd developed some kind of personal vendetta.

"Morse," Andy said as Dan walked by his door.

Dan abandoned wherever he was originally headed for and ducked inside.

"I'm about to do something, something that could get me into some trouble. Sarah is staying at my motel, it's Motel 6, room 202. Tell no one where she is but help her if she needs it."

"Jesus, Andy what the hell—"

"Knight," Andy shouted from inside his office door.

Knight's head bobbed off his arm and he caught himself, looking up bleary eyed. *Sleeping*, Andy thought to himself.

"I just got the call; the tech team knows who posted the picture of Taylor."

Knight swallowed, not saying anything.

Andy kept going, "How could you do it? What did you do, follow her and take her picture while she was trying on dresses? Maybe you're the pervert we all need to be worried about."

Knight looked around, surprised he was being addressed like this in front of everyone. "Fisher, what the hell are you talking about? I'm going to bust your ass down to a traffic cop. Are you actually accusing me of something?"

"I've got the proof; I've got an IP address."

Knight smiled, "You mean, you've got your IP address and now you are trying to blame me."

Andy stopped, "What?"

"The picture came from your computer."

"You son of a bitch!" Andy yelled before he charged Knight.

The two were pulled apart by the officers after only a punch or two. The chief almost blew an artery when he walked into his precinct to find the two of them flailing around on the ground.

"You two get your asses in my office right now," he screamed.

The two sat down, clothes rumpled, hair a mess. Andy saw a thin line of blood on Knight's chin and smiled.

"Wipe that fucking smile off your face, Fisher, or I'll throw you in a cell to cool off. This is Agent Gonzalez, one of you smart-asses want to tell me what this is all about?"

The room erupted in chaos as both Andy and Knight tried to speak at once which resulted in both of them yelling.

"Enough! Fisher, you first."

"Sir, I have reason to believe that Knight has been following

Taylor and her mother without permission. I also have reason to believe that he posted the photo of Taylor on the message boards in an effort to draw Jacob out. When I confronted him he admitted to using my computer, I assume to incriminate me.

Agent Gonzalez turned to Knight.

"Is any of this true, Agent?"

Knight's lips pursed, he was actually mildly impressed that Andy figured out it was him rather than spend time spinning his wheels, which is what Detective Fisher usually did in Knight's opinion.

"It is sir, except the part about using Fisher's computer. I just wanted to get under his skin with that part."

Gonzalez took a deep breath. "You have embarrassed the FBI with this stunt. You are being placed on administrative leave pending further review. You aren't to have anything to do with this case, do you understand?" Gonzalez warned.

Knight started to argue.

"Don't," The chief yelled. "You are an idiot, I've never seen an FBI agent act more recklessly putting a girl at risk, and for what? A couple of fingerprints that we can't identify? Get out of my sight, I don't want to see you back in this precinct ever again, am I clear?"

"Crystal," Knight said as he stood and walked out the front doors.

The chief sat down and closed his eyes, rubbing his temples with his fingers.

"Fisher, I would kill you if I could. The only reason I'm not going to is because I can't lose both of my investigators on the hottest case we have had in thirty years."

"Chief, I—"

"Stop talking," the chief interrupted him. "Figure out how

we are going to catch this guy or pray for a miracle. I don't want to speak to you until you have one of those two things for me. Gonzalez thankfully will be sticking around to help out now that we are short handed."

Andy hung his head, feeling ashamed for brawling and for the fact that he still had not much as far as leads to go on.

Gonzalez left, following Knight as he gathered what few things he had in the precinct.

The Chief paced back and forth in front of his desk, rubbing his hands over his face. Andy was unsure if he should dare to leave or just stay there for more reprimand.

"What is going on with the masked men showing up around town."

Andy picked up his head. "We haven't caught one yet, although I have officers in plain clothes stationed at the three town parks just in case. They're scouting is the best word I could use. I think they are trying to find her."

"Taylor, you mean."

"Yeah."

"Have you told Sarah?"

"No."

"You know you can't keep things from her if you want her to trust you. Richard kept too much from her. You'll never keep her with more secrets."

Andy's head hung once more, "I know."

Chapter 38

Wednesday
Taylor groggily came through the fog of sleep to the now familiar knocking sound on her wall, she groaned.

Knock, Knock.

She reached her arm up and gave it a wack so Kristen would know she was up.

In between training and sleep Taylor mentally finalized her plan to finally be free of Jacob. She was happy her mother was liquidating their life there. She was working on figuring out a way to get her mother out of Massachusetts. She would never understand what Taylor had to do.

She dressed quickly, wanting to have a few moments alone with Patrick before their run. Once outside she spotted him a few yards from the building and closed the gap.

"I assume that the person Mr. Greggor sent to my mother was going to get us new IDs? New names, addresses?"

Patrick turned and nodded, he had heard her coming.

"I need it before my mother gets here."

His eyes narrowed. "Why?"

"I'm going back," she said. "I don't want anyone to know, until I decide they need to know."

"Ok, you'll have it."

She nodded, the two had developed a quiet understanding over the last few days. Taylor knew he wouldn't tell anyone what her plan was until she was already gone.

"Patrick,"

He turned.

"Thanks."

He nodded back to her.

Perhaps it was the fact that she had told Patrick of her plan. Perhaps she was just getting used to the rigorous schedule, all day during training, she felt good, strong, ready. An hour or so after dinner, Taylor could tell something was happening. Shane kept looking at her sideways. Through the curtains she could see Patrick and Rodney by the pool. They looked like they were arguing.

Rodney was upset as he stepped into the living area, followed by Kristen and then Patrick.

"You need to see this," Rodney said as he unlocked the iPad that he had tucked under his arm.

The local news network in Boston immediately sprang to life.

'Breaking news out of Templeton, MA where a high school senior appears to have been kidnapped from her home.'

Layla's house flashed on to the screen colored by red and blue lights. An ambulance was in the driveway and the front door was open. Her mother covered in a blanket.

"Oh no," Taylor exclaimed. "Layla."

The local reporter stepped into the frame. "This is the scene at Layla Baker's house. Her mother says that she came home early this evening to the front door open, her daughter's car in the driveway and an apparent struggle in the living room. Her daughter, Layla Baker, is believed to have been kidnapped."

"A member of the police force has told ABC exclusively that he believes the kidnapping is related to the vandalism of Taylor Cormier's home last night, which is about a mile away."

A shot of her house filled the screen with 'WHERE IS SHE' painted on the door of her garage.

"I have learned from Layla Baker's boyfriend that Layla and Taylor Cormier are close friends. No one has seen Taylor since her home was broken into some six days ago."

The report went on to fill in a few more details but Taylor's head was spinning.

"He took her," she said over and over again. "He took her because I left."

Rodney's lips pursed together. He obviously agreed with Taylor, she could tell just by the way he was looking at her.

"I have to go."

"You aren't going anywhere," Kristen intervened. "You can't just go hightailing it off to Massachusetts. Call your mother, find out what happened." Kristen said as she offered Taylor her phone.

Taylor took it and dialed her mother's number. Sarah picked up on the second ring. "Taylor?"

"Mom, are you OK?"

"I am, hunny. I wasn't home when it happened, I'm staying with Andy."

Taylor was a bit thrown envisioning her mother suddenly sleeping in the same room as Andy. Her mind began to envision the next step in that equation when she forcibly stopped herself.

"What happened to Layla?"

"I've just seen the news, sweetheart. I don't know. I tried to call the station but no one has called me back. You have to stay there," Sarah pleaded into the phone like she could read

Taylor's mind. "You can't come back here. I was going to wait until next week to head your way but I'm just going to leave now. I don't want you to be alone."

Taylor's mind reeled. This would ruin her plan. She had counted on at least one more week of training and figuring out a way to keep her mother occupied for a couple of days while she went home.

"I'm not alone, Mom. I don't want you to come here yet." Taylor rambled in an attempt to buy more time until an idea dawned. "I want you to find somewhere for us to start over."

Taylor made eye contact with Patrick as she continued on the phone with her mother, her words a lie that she hoped Rodney could make true.

"Mr. Greggor told me he was going to overnight your new identity to a PO box in . . ." Taylor paused, panicking on where to send her mother.

Patrick whispered, "Utah."

"Utah," Taylor said loudly.

"Why Utah?" Sarah said confused.

"I don't know, but that's what he said. A small town in Utah. He wrote the address down for me—I can text it to you. He said it would be a good place to start and see if you liked it there."

"I can stay here for now until you figure out what we are going to do. You're going to need time to find us a place to live, aren't you?"

Her mother paused thinking things through. "Yeah," she said distracted. "I'll need a couple weeks, I guess. The house still hasn't sold. I don't know if it ever will to be honest. We may have to look at renting it. I don't know how we'll start over without that money."

Taylor could hear the stress in her mother's voice. The guilt she felt was overwhelming, so much so that she almost broke. It was the look in Patrick's eye that stopped her. She took a deep breath, "I'll text you the address. We'll figure the rest out once you get there."

Her mother agreed and the two hung up.

"I'm going to need an address," Taylor said as soon as she shut the phone.

"What the hell is going on? Why did you just send your mother to Utah?" Kristen asked looking back and forth between Taylor and Patrick. "Say something, the both of you."

"I need to go home." Taylor said. Turning, she faced her friend and looked her right in the eye. "I'm going to let Jacob take me."

Her words hung in the air before they disintegrated.

"The hell you are," Kristen screamed, her voice shocked looking back and forth between Patrick and Taylor. "Rodney, help me, this is crazy. Tell them."

Patrick remained silent. "You're not ready," he warned Taylor.

"I'll never be ready."

"True enough."

"You have all lost your mind. You are not doing this," Kristen said. "If he took Layla—"

"This has nothing to do with Layla. I was planning on doing this before she went missing. But now that he has her I have no choice. I can't run anymore. I don't want to defend my life, I want to live it. This is the only way, the only way to make it stop. You know I'm right. I have to do this."

Tears had started to fall down Kristen's face. She said nothing but pulled Taylor into a bear hug.

Patrick took a passport and birth certificate and an Arizona license out of his back pocket.

"We'll drive you to the airport and get you on the first flight to either Boston or Nashua. Memorize your name and birth date. You should change your hair; it'll make it harder for him to pick you out, at least initially."

"It's already short, what else could I do to it?"

Kristen smiled with a hint of sadness in it. "This is California, hunny, we can make you look like anyone you want."

Fifteen minutes later a slightly confused stylist was ushered into the apartment complex, her tools in a small suitcase carried in by Shane. The main team that had brought Taylor to the apartment complex a week ago had been re-assembled. Shane, Andrew and Brendan all stood in the apartment discussing plans with Rodney while the stylist, whose name was Brittany, got to work.

It was surreal for Taylor, but Brittany asked no questions as if it was totally normal for her to be called late at night and whisked away in a blacked-out SUV to an abandoned apartment complex to make a girl look as different as possible.

"We could die her hair," she said to Rodney, not addressing Taylor at all. "I can give her bangs too, that will help. How completely do you want her appearance to be changed?"

"I don't want her mother to know her," he said matter of factly.

"What about extensions?" Brittany asked fingering the ends of Taylor's hair.

"No," Rodney said, "it needs to be short—shorter than it is now."

"How about a wig?" Kristen offered.

Brittany got to work. She dyed Taylor's hair first a dark brown, and expertly cut her bangs so that they hung low in her eyes.

297

"Shorter bangs. She needs to be able to see."

Finally done with Taylor's hair, Brittany rummaged in her suitcase and found a number of wigs. Most of them were brown. The hair hung down Taylor's back and made it itch. She wasn't used to feeling hair on her shoulders.

Brittany gave her instruction on how to put the wig on so that it looked as natural as possible. The group finally settled on a medium brown one that had some bounce to it and hung just below Taylor's shoulder blades. Between the wig and a large pair of sunglasses that Kristen let her borrow, Taylor had a hard time recognizing herself.

"Good," Rodney said finally giving his approval.

Shane ushered Brittany from the room, shoving some money in her hand as he put her into the back of a car, Brendan drove away.

Andrew had been looking for flights and finally let the group know that there was a direct flight leaving in three hours that went into Nashua, NH.

Taylor nodded and moved to take off the wig,

"Don't," said Rodney, "you need to get used to wearing it. Go get your things packed up, one backpack."

Back in her room she looked at herself again in the mirror. She looked pretty. She stood sideways admiring her new wig. She had loved her long hair, before. Jacob would grab it and pull her around the basement by it. When she got home she cut it all off and had kept it short ever since.

"I used to have long hair, too, you know, before." Kristen leaned in the doorway watching Taylor look at herself in the mirror.

"It's like we all have the same types of scars; we just got them a little differently."

"Yeah," Taylor admitted, forcing her eyes away from the mirror and to the task at hand. She packed two pairs of jeans, her sneakers, underwear, bras and socks plus four long-sleeve shirts.

Besides allowing herself to be abducted, which now sounded completely bat-shit crazy, she didn't have a plan. Kristen must have known this, she went to the bathroom and got together Taylor's toiletries before asking, "do you have any idea what you are doing?"

"He just needs to know that I'm back. He'll find me."

"Yes, I know that," Kristen said exasperated. "How are you going to do that, though? How do you know he won't just kill you outright?"

Taylor paused, "he was always about control. He lost control of me, now he'll fight to get it back. He might want to kill me eventually, but I don't think he'll kill me right away."

"I want to come with you."

"No," Taylor said turning to her, "you are not coming with me."

"I can help," Kristen said seriously.

"You could die. He isn't going to keep you alive for sentimental reasons. I can't live with that. I have two friends and one of them is already gone. I can't lose you, too." Taylor broke down but held her friend at bay with her hand. "I can't lose you, too," she whispered again. "You have to make this camp for us, for people *like* us. You have to do something with your life. And if I make it through this, I'll be right there with you."

The two didn't say anything while Taylor recomposed herself.

Kristen's heart swelled in admiration for her very best friend. "You have to be smart. He is smart and cunning and has been planning this for a long time. You can't just go in there with a weeks' worth of self-defense training and think that you are some badass."

"Yeah," Taylor said somewhat crestfallen.

Kristen sat down on the bed and put her toiletries in her backpack. "Let's go through it step by step."

The two did, step by step from the moment Taylor got on the plane until the moment Jacob came for her. They talked through scenario after scenario.

Rodney knocked at the door some time later. "It's time to go," he said grimly.

Taylor nodded, giving her friend a hug. Kristen squeezed back.

"Thank you," Taylor whispered into her ear, "for everything. You are a true friend and I love you."

The words screamed goodbye. Kristen said nothing, she just held her friend for a moment more. Rodney cleared his throat. Kristen released her and watched as Taylor picked up the backpack and took one last look in the mirror before walking out the door without looking back.

On the ride to the airport Patrick drilled her on her name, address and birth information until she could answer any question he threw at her without hesitating.

"Don't use your old name for any reason to anyone. You have to be Shannon Moore who lives in Arizona and is visiting a cousin."

She nodded. The airport lights were bright against the night and made her eyes squint. The glasses Kristen had let her have were in her backpack and she was tempted to put them on but decided that would seem strange to people. She had spent her life trying to blend in, now was not the time to stand out.

Patrick got out, opened the door, and helped Taylor from the vehicle.

"He will try to get into your head. That is his power. Don't let him. He will hurt you but he won't want to kill you, at least not right away. The first chance you get, you kill him, just like we practiced. Don't hesitate."

Taylor nodded.

Patrick wrapped her in a hug. Taylor had grown incredibly fond of him and he of her.

"Go," he said gruffly and she did without a backward glance.

Chapter 39

hursday

T It was mid-morning when her plane touched down in Nashua. With just her backpack she was one of the first ones off. The airport was busy and she fought through crowds to get to the exit. It was cold outside. Taylor missed the California weather already. She looked quickly at her flimsy long-sleeve shirt and knew she would need to stop and get other clothes otherwise she would freeze to death.

While she had been on the plane she dug into her bag for a toothbrush and her hand came up with a small wad of cash. She didn't know how much was there but the bills were hundreds, she guessed a fair amount. Assuming she survived this she was going to have to write a pretty lengthy thank you note to Kristen for thinking ahead for her. That money would make what she planned to do over the next couple of days a bit easier, and it would keep her out of the bank, which was important.

There were cabs waiting for passengers outside the airport so she hopped in the back of one and gave them an address in Baldwinville, which was the town over from Templeton. Her wig itched her scalp now that it had been on for twelve hours straight. She desperately wanted to take it off and scratch at her now too-short hair. She didn't, partly because she didn't want to scare the cab driver and partly because she knew that she couldn't trust anyone.

The drive took just over an hour. It gave Taylor time to think about Layla. She knew her friend was tougher than she pretended to be, she hoped she could hang in there long enough.

The streets were quiet as the car drove past Otter River Forest, a large state park.

"Can you let me out here?"

He pulled the cab over and she gave him a $100 bill out of the wad, which covered the cost of the ride and left a decent tip. She got out and started walking along the street.

"Hey," the cab driver shouted with his window down. "You sure you don't want me to drop you at a house or something?" Baldwinville was almost entirely woods.

"I'll be fine," Taylor tried to smile reassuringly, although obviously not well.

"Yeah?" the driver said. "Really, if it's the money I can just bring you down the road a couple of miles—there must be somewhere you're going."

Taylor stopped and turned towards the driver, her face serious. "I'm fine, please leave me alone."

The guy shrugged his shoulders and pulled back on to the road, looking at her from his rearview.

Taylor took a deep breath. She could have had the guy drive her into Templeton but she wanted to walk. She only had a handful of people she could go to and ask for help. She wasn't going to go driving around town in a cab. That would have attracted a fair amount of attention. A girl walking though wouldn't attract any at all.

James was first on her list. She spent an hour moving around the edges of his property, making sure there were no extra police patrols or other people keeping an eye on the house. Finally she went to the side door and rang the bell.

James came to the door looking disheveled. His confusion mounting at seeing a stranger on his doorstep.

"Can I help you?" he asked looking beyond the girl standing in his doorway wondering if someone was with her.

"I need your help; can I come in?"

James hesitated

"It's about Layla," she insisted.

Her voice sounded familiar but she wore large dark glasses.

He shook his head, "Yeah, sure . . ."

Once inside Taylor looked around and took off her glasses.

Recognition dawned on James's face. "Taylor? Where the hell have you been? What happened to your hair?"

"It's a wig so no one can recognize me.." She wanted to be blasé about it but with James she was struggling. "I've been in California. I didn't find out about Layla until last night. I came straight home."

"Where are your parents?" she asked looking around.

"They went down to the town hall. They are organizing a search like they did when you went missing. I told them I would meet them in a few hours. I was up all night with the police."

"You look rough," Taylor observed. "I need your help."

"I don't understand. He has Layla, right now he has her. You have to go to the police, you need to help. I don't know, you need to do something."

"I am doing something, but I need your help first and no one can know that I'm here."

James paced, only half listening to Taylor.

"I can't tell you what I'm planning. You wouldn't let me do it if I did. You have to trust me. I love Layla, I'm not going to let anything happen to her."

"Unless he killed her already," James said softly to himself.

"He didn't."

James continued to pace and shake his head.

"Listen to me." She positioned her face so that he had no choice but to look at her. "Jacob is not impulsive. He was mad when he took her but he isn't going to kill her. He's going to use her as leverage against me. That's what he wants," Taylor said her voice getting softer. "It's what he's always wanted, my submission."

Taylor could see the basement in her mind's eye, imagined Layla down there. She smelled the dirt and heard the water running. Except it wasn't Layla, it was her chained to the floor with nothing but a T-shirt on and his boots on the stairs.

She sat. Not moving. Not breathing.

"Would you like me to clean your face and hands?"

She nodded, still not speaking.

He acknowledged her and she stood, walking slowly to him the chain extending and clinking, her head down.

"What do you say?" he said to her sternly.

"I love you, Daddy."

"Good girl," he cooed. Brushing her hair from her face and taking a warm wash cloth to the dirt that was caked on it. He gently cleaned her face and then worked on each of her hands, cleaning each individual finger.

"Would you like something to eat?"

She hesitated, his impatience resonated from him.

"Yes please, Daddy."

From his pocket he produced a few crackers. Taylor resisted the urge to stuff them in her face, but instead held out her hand like she was receiving communion. Allowing him to place them in her hand as she carefully and slowly ate each one.

"You have been good. I have been proud to hear that you're quiet during the day."

"I have a present for you.

I am going to let you feel the sunshine on your face. Would you like that?"

Taylor's breath caught in her throat. Was he going to take her outside?

Taylor nodded.

"You say nothing, do you understand?"

His words were simple and concise and were without threat. They both knew what he would do to her if she disobeyed him again.

From a hook halfway up the stairs he took a bandana and covered her eyes. She stood still and silent. Her stomach ached as it digested the crackers, unused to food at this point.

She cleared her throat.

"Would you like to say something?"

She nodded.

"Go ahead, quietly," he warned.

Her voice struggled. She couldn't remember the last time she spoke more than a few words. She tried again but no words came out, again she cleared her throat.

"How long?" her voice croaked.

He looked confused at her question.

"Since you came home?" he asked.

She nodded.

"Twenty-five days."

She took a sharp breath. She had lost count at some point as the days and nights blurred together amidst the beatings and the two failed attempts to flee. She could feel herself slipping away, living only for his occasional visit and the food he allowed her to have. She would do anything for those crackers. She was breaking and he knew it.

Blindfolded, he led her up the stairs. The air here was different—fresh. His grip on her wrist was strong and unrelenting. She heard a scuffle behind her assuming it was the boy. While she couldn't see anything except the blue of the bandana she could feel the sun on her arms and then her face, warming them. She hadn't been warm in what felt like forever. She never wanted to leave its embrace. He allowed her to stand there for a few minutes more, then roughly tugged her back toward the door. She wanted to stay and thought to protest but didn't. She allowed herself to be brought back down to the hole. Again, the air changed and she could smell piss and shit mixed with dirt. The ever-trickling water flowed in the corner.

"Now," he said to her, "that was your reward for being a good girl. The more behavior I see like that the more things I will allow you to do. Say thank you."

"Thank you, Daddy," she replied, the words sounding like someone else's.

"Come over here and sit on daddy's lap."

She complied, knowing what would happen if she didn't. His penetrations of her were less violent now that she stopped fighting. She let him shove her into the stairs as he unbuckled his pants. His dick pinched her every time he entered her but she grit her teeth and made no noise. Rocking back and forth as he emptied into her. She wondered what would happen if she became pregnant. She hadn't gotten her period yet but some of her friends had. Would he kill her and the baby? She hoped so, for both of their sakes. He grunted and pulled out of her, his juice running down her legs and onto the stairs. He grabbed her arm and led her back to the chains. Re-attaching

her leg and shoving his penis back into his pants. He looked at her
expectantly.

"I love you, Daddy."

The scene stayed in her mind but her eyes slid back into focus.
James stood in front of her waving his hand in front of her face.

"I need somewhere to sleep."

"There's a room above the garage my parents never go into."

"Show me."

Inside the garage there were a set of stairs that led up a loft-
type area. The room was small but there was an electric heater in
the corner and James had found a sleeping bag from somewhere.

"What am I supposed to do?" he asked. "I want to help."

"You are going to. Right now though I need you to get some
sleep and go help your parents just like you were supposed to.
You and I can talk more tonight. I've got some errands I need to
run."

James nodded, turned, and started down the stairs.

"James," Taylor called, he stopped.

"How did he take her?" she asked.

His face twisted in pain. "We got in a fight—we broke up
actually. She was mad at me, said that I wasn't paying enough
attention to her, considering everything that was going on. I
don't know. She had just gotten home and was yelling at me
and then I just heard her start to scream before it went silent. I
heard a big thud and then scuffling and then nothing. She was
just gone. I called 911 but it was too late."

Taylor knew exactly what happened. He had waited for her
outside her house. She was distracted and she probably didn't
even hear him come into the house right behind her. She could
feel him grab Layla just like he had done to Taylor.

"Thanks," she said, her thoughts on Layla and what she was going through.

James turned, leaving abruptly.

In the garage Taylor found a pencil and an old piece of cardboard in the trash. She made a list of supplies that she needed. It was a short list and almost everything she needed she should be able to get at the local fish and game store.

She checked her wig, grabbed her backpack and started walking.

Chapter 40

Hours later she returned to James's house, her backpack heavier than when she had left. She did a few laps around the neighborhood, just in case, before heading up his driveway. It was dark now and she didn't need anyone seeing her and calling the police. Once inside she sat down on the sleeping bag and started to unpack, organizing her supplies into different piles. She had eaten while she was out but that had been hours ago and her stomach rumbled, hungry again. She had walked the length of town and no one paid attention to her—no one knew who she was. It was a liberating feeling, almost like being a ghost. She hadn't been so unnoticed in forever.

The room had no windows which was nice only because it meant she could turn a flashlight on and at least have some light while she unwrapped a grinder she bought at the grocery store. She devoured the entire Italian sub, along with a bag of Doritos and a coke. Her stomach was deliciously full. She tried to burn the feeling into her memory, just in case it was a long while before she felt that way again.

Seconds later she heard a car pull into the driveway. She quickly turned off the flashlight and crept down the stairs, thankful that James's garage wasn't attached to his house.

Through the windows she saw him and his parents head toward their front door. All looked exhausted, only James noticed the head bob in the window. Taylor expected James to find a way to sneak away, she was surprised when James opened the garage door almost immediately.

"Taylor," he whispered, "where are you?"

"I'm right here. What are you doing? Shouldn't you go inside?"

"Go upstairs," he said still speaking quietly.

Once upstairs he continued. "I come in here all the time and work on my dirt bike. I just told them I needed some time alone, they understood."

"How was the search?"

"You know how it was," he said defeated. "We didn't find anything, or anything close to anything, or anyone, or anything that belonged to anyone. She's just gone."

They sat silently for a minute.

"Did you get all the stuff you needed?"

"I got everything. I do still need your help though. I don't want anyone to know I'm here until I'm ready. Tomorrow I need you to tell a few people that you thought you saw me. Shauna, Mike, those types of people."

James was exhausted and it rolled off him in waves. "What does that mean? What are 'those types of people'?"

Taylor looked back at him. "The type that will tell anyone and everyone they see that I'm back."

James nodded in response.

"I've got my own things to do tomorrow but I would like one more thing from you." Taylor said.

"What?"

It broke Taylor's heart to see him like this and she hoped her next statement wouldn't upset him

"Go out to dinner with me."

"What?" Why? I'm not going out dinner while Layla is missing."

Taylor sighed. "Please, I know it sounds weird, but I promise I am trying to help Layla."

"By asking me out to dinner?" his face twisted.

"James," Taylor hissed, "do not turn this into something it isn't."

James stood and walked to the other side of the very small room.

"Look at me," Taylor said.

He turned.

"Please, just come to dinner with me. Make sure people think I'm in town and make sure you tell them that we are going out to get some food. Put it on Snapchat and Facebook, whatever. I need people to know where I am."

Realization dawned in his eyes. Not fully because he didn't really understand what she was doing, but he had suspicions.

"OK," he said slowly, "OK."

Taylor nodded, "It's getting late, why don't you head inside. Last thing I need is your parents coming out here to find you."

He nodded and headed down the stairs. "Goodnight Taylor," he said halfway down the stairs.

"Goodnight James," she called back from inside the room.

She listened to him close the door and waited a few minutes before she went down and looked out the window of the garage into his living room, watching his parents through the windows in their home. So many people didn't realize how much a person could see when your lights were on and it was dark outside.

Taylor glanced at her newly acquired watch—it was just after nine. The garage was cold. She had purchased, among other things, a sweatshirt and leggings and changed into them and huddled in the sleeping bag trying to warm her toes. Exhaustion overtook her and she was quickly asleep.

She woke from a dreamless unconsciousness with a start. It was still dark out and her watch said 3 a.m. The heater in the corner had been pulled out and was on. She looked around her panicked, but saw no one. That was when she realized that a pillow and additional blanket were with her. James she thought to herself.

She tried to fall back asleep but her mind wouldn't quiet. Looked like six hours' worth of sleep would have to be enough. The small room was warm and she relished the heat. She guessed it would be quite awhile before she woke up warm and cozy again. Taylor had been raised a Catholic. She'd been baptized and even had her first communion. After her abduction though she stopped going to church. She struggled to make peace with a God that would allow such an evil force to walk the earth. It had occurred to her over the past few days, this could be the end of her life. So, she folded her hands and took the time to pray, quietly accepting her death if that was her fate.

Once her bag was packed she neatly placed the blanket, pillow and sleeping bag together in the corner. She also made sure to turn the heater off, taking one last look around before she descended the stairs and slipped out into the night.

Her breath came out in puffs signaling it was certainly below freezing. She walked quickly trying to hold onto the warmth she had been enjoying just moments ago.

It wasn't long before she longed to be back in that little room. James's house was on the outskirts of town. She guessed it was about five miles to The Barn. That would be her first stop of the morning. She looked to the sky. The stars were bright and the moon full. That was good, it would make it easier for her to see at night, at least for the next few days.

Two hours later she stood in front of The Barn, teeth chattering. She checked the back door which was locked. Thankfully she knew where Jan kept the key hidden. Once inside she made herself a pot of coffee and a large breakfast, being careful to put Mario's pans back exactly as he had left them the night before.

Her plate was high with eggs, toast and corned beef hash. She had just torn into it when a light clicked on. She jumped from her seat startled and ready for a fight.

"Who the hell?" Jan started to yell until she saw Taylor's face.

"Taylor? Is that you?"

"It's me."

"Jesus, you nearly gave me a heart attack. What did you do to your hair?"

"It's a wig, how did you know I was here?"

"I didn't. I volunteered to feed the volunteers they'll be here getting ready to go back out in about fifteen minutes. I just wanted to get the coffee going and the grill fired up."

Taylor checked the time. It was 5:30 a.m.

"Have they found anything?"

Jan grimaced, "No. It's not safe for you here, I don't know where you went but wherever you were, you need to go back."

Jan paused, Taylor could see the pieces coming together in her head.

"Your mother left yesterday," she said, not really speaking to Taylor but to the air around her. "She said goodbye, like I would never see her again."

Jan's eyes locked onto Taylor's. "You got her to leave. She said a few days ago that she would be here for another week or so but you talked her into leaving now."

Taylor's eyes went down.

"She doesn't know you're here, does she? She thinks you're still wherever you were."

"California, she thinks I'm in California."

"What are you doing here?" Jan's voice was quiet, hauntingly so.

"I can't tell you."

"I can help you. We can get Andy over here. Do you know something? Did Jacob contact you?"

Jan's questions barraged the morning quiet.

Taylor nodded, "He did; he took Layla. There's only one way we are going to get her back."

"No," Jan said, finally understanding. "No," her head shook vigorously. "I won't let you do it. I'll tell everyone I see that you're here. I'll lock you in the walk-in if I have to."

Taylor smiled. She loved Jan. Her forgetfulness and her fierce loyalty to those she loved. It's why everyone who worked for her felt like a family.

"Did you know that I dug my way out of the basement?" Taylor asked. "Years ago. I saw a crack in the foundation and I used a toy shovel and just kept digging. Figuring eventually I would be able to squeeze through. I did too, squeezed through a tiny little hole. Scraped my whole body up. The doctors, I remember, told me that I must have been dragged over rocks or something. It didn't sound right at the time but I couldn't remember what happened. The last time I had any control over my life was when I escaped. Since then I've been afraid and just waiting for something—or someone—to come after me. I don't feel that way anymore. I need to do this. I need to know that my life means something and I need your help."

315

Taylor's eyes welled, threatening tears almost always worked with Jan, but this wasn't an act. Taylor truly did need someone's help to keep her going, to tell her it was OK. She wished her mother was there, but in her absence, Jan was the next best thing.

Jan took a deep breath. "What do you need?"

The two had some time to talk, but it wasn't long before Taylor heard the door open. The volunteers had started to arrive. Jan held up a finger motioning Taylor to wait a minute. Taylor could hear her greet people in the front and told them coffee would be out in a few minutes. .

As Jan walked back into the kitchen she expertly retrieved a to go container from under the counter and filled it with Taylor's mountain of food.

"Get yourself a large cup of coffee and scoot, I'll see you tonight."

Taylor took the long way around the building being careful to avoid the cars that all seemed to be converging on The Barn.

The food, hot in her hands, was starting to cool and she wanted to get something warm in her belly. The gazebo was in front of her so she sat on the bench and ate everything in the box along with the coffee. The sun was just starting to make an appearance, the sky turning the lightest shade of pink as the stars disappeared in that section of the sky.

For the rest of the morning Taylor walked through town. She felt strong, undaunted by the task in front of her. In the afternoon she bought a movie ticket and sat in a dark theater alone letting her mind be consumed with someone else's drama for just a couple of hours.

The movie ended, it was time. She knew she had to make some noise to make sure that he paid attention. She took the wig off scratching her head. Her hair was now pixie short with a set of bangs. It felt foreign to her fingers.

She let the wig fall onto the floor of the theater.

As she walked to the bathroom she made eye contact with each person working the concession stand. One was a junior she recognized, the others she assumed were freshman. She had barely turned to go into the bathroom when she saw their phones come out.

Inside the bathroom she opened her backpack.

At the moment she was wearing jeans and a sweatshirt but she wanted to have as much mobility as she could and didn't need bulky clothing getting in her way. She changed into a pair of yoga pants. She pulled an underarm shirt over her head and studied herself in the mirror. Her shoulders were more muscular and she could see the definition in her arms. She put the boots back on that she had been wearing during the day but with a fresh pair of socks. Next she took out her newly acquired hunting knife and harnesses. She tried a few different locations on her body but in the end she settled on the only place she didn't think Jacob would see right away. She tucked the three-inch blade with its cover on into her bra and adjusted her shirt. Barely noticeable.

Next she unpacked fishing line, putting a line in each side of her bra, each about three-feet long. Now dressed she wrapped her wrists with ACE bandages.

Lastly she took off her charm bracelet and her necklace and dropped them into the bag. She knew she would be cold without her sweatshirt but she didn't need one more piece of clothing he could use to grab her.

She glanced at her watch—it was just after four. She called James.

"It's me, will you pick me up? I'm at the movie theater."

317

Emerging from the bathroom, the junior said nothing but her fingers moved incessantly across the screen of her phone. Taylor walked, head up and shoulders back, to the door. Few people were coming to the movies given the missing girl and the manhunt that was going on. There was a couple, though, who stopped as she walked by, not believing that it was actually her.

James pulled into the parking lot minutes later. He must have been close by.

"Where were you? I've been out looking for you all day."

James leaned in over the console. She could feel the lump in her throat and the heat on her neck. She looked across the car at this boy she used to like and, for a moment, she remembered the girl she used to be. James stared back at her, as though seeing her for the first time in years.

"Taylor . . ." his voice was husky.

She could feel herself leaning forward. The voices that would have normally told her to stop, uncommonly silent.

His forehead leaned against hers, his scent enveloped her nose. All she could see was him. Her face tilted toward his ever so slightly and his lips gently brushed hers in a kiss that brought tears to her eyes. His lips were smooth, gentle and fleeting. As he sat back in his seat she took a moment to compose herself. She could still feel him, smell him. It took her a few minutes but she came back to her truth.

"I need you to hold on to my backpack. My charm bracelet is in there, I don't want to lose it."

James nodded, "You ready?"

"Yes," she said and she meant it.

Chapter 41

F*riday*

Going to dinner with James felt normal, like something a girl her age would be doing on a weekend night. For a moment Taylor just wanted to pretend that this was her life. That Layla was planning on meeting them and the three of them were just going to have a regular night.

Regular though was for other people, not for Taylor.

"Did you tell people about dinner?"

"Yeah, I did what you wanted." His voice was sad.

The parking lot at The Barn was almost full. Deb gave Taylor a forced smile as she came in and led her and James over to a booth in the back corner of the restaurant. It looked as if half the school was already there. Shauna, Jessica, Mike and Sean were already seated across the restaurant, looking disapprovingly at James. There were at least a dozen other upperclassmen there as well, most of whom Taylor had never spoken too.

"Great job," Taylor whispered. "Looks like I can draw a crowd all of a sudden."

James looked at the students with disgust. "I don't think I realized how much I don't like these people until this very moment."

"Don't be mad at them," Taylor pleaded with him. "They

319

shouldn't be judged on this type of thing. They shouldn't have ever had to deal with something this serious. They are just reacting, it's not their fault."

"You're more forgiving than I am."

"Maybe," she mused, "or maybe I've just been doing this a bit longer than you."

Taylor didn't know what they expected to see but it was evident that they didn't expect to see her looking like that.

Shauna and Jessica whispered to each other in the corner. James shook his head disapprovingly at his friends as Jan came over and took drink and appetizer orders from him and Taylor. She must have said something to the staff that night because no one addressed her, not Deb or Mario—they all pretended like she wasn't there.

Sipping on their sodas Taylor scanned the restaurant. It took her a moment before she realized who was there. Patrick, stood at the ice cream counter, so close to the wall she almost didn't see him. Their eyes met.

"Who's that?" James asked, turning around to get a better look.

Taylor didn't realize he had seen their brief exchange.

"You are irritatingly observant," she said to him. "He's a friend, sort of."

"They look like marines."

"They?"

Taylor's eyes scanned the room again, Brendan, Shane and Andrew were sprinkled through the restaurant, looking casual enough to almost blend in. Her heart swelled.

Taylor grabbed her phone out of her bag and brought up one of half a dozen websites that contributed to the idolization of Jacob. People were posting every few minutes. They knew where she was.

Mr. Moriarty sat in the corner. Taylor could see his irritation at the sheer number of people in his restaurant.

Jan came over and dropped off an appetizer and asked Taylor and James what they wanted for dinner. Taylor waved her off. She'd eaten enough popcorn at the movie theater to put a person to shame. James ordered a burger.

The front doors flew open and men in masks once again descended into Taylor's world.

"Taylor Cormier," they shouted in unison.

The restaurant fell silent.

"Time to go home, time to go home, time to go home," slowly they walked toward her.

From the corner of her eye she saw Jan slip into the back room and Mario came charging out of the kitchen with a bat.

Taylor stood as Mario slammed the bat on the floor stopping the advances of the men in masks. "I am going to knock your heads off if you take one more step."

Panic began to spread through the restaurant. Chairs were knocked over, people began to move toward the exits. The masked men spread out blocking people's path.

Everyone's fear was palpable, except one person. One person remained sitting, his eyes trained on Taylor.

For all of Taylor's planning she wasn't entirely sure what to do. The restaurant felt like a bomb waiting to go off. She felt eyes on her, searching desperately for their source. Then she saw it, Mr. Moriarty stood, his cane abandoned. His eyes met hers, smiling before sauntering out the door.

Jan emerged from the back room, gun in one hand and the phone pressed to her ear with the other. Taylor could hear the sirens in the distance.

The fear in the restaurant was spreading like wildfire, the masked men started to shift, the sirens scaring them.

Patrick finally made his move and shouted above the crowd, "Freeze!"

She wanted to say goodbye to James but she knew she didn't have time. In the commotion, she slipped out the back door and waited to hear the sound of footsteps come around the corner.

The previously frail looking old man stood in front of her, suddenly taller and more noticeable. She could smell the latex on him and it made her want to vomit in her mouth. She had always had somewhat of a visceral reaction to the way he smelled but she assumed it was because he was old.

"Taylor," he whispered using his real voice.

Chills swept over her body. That voice had been her nightmare for years and to hear it again was disorienting.

"Jacob," she replied back keeping her voice even.

"This was well done," he said to her. "I'm impressed. A little theatrical but I suppose you wanted to make sure I showed up. Are you surprised?"

"Nothing you do surprises me," Taylor said honestly.

"Are you ready?" he asked as if he was giving her a choice.

She nodded.

He indicated she should walk into the parking lot and she started to when the back door crashed open. James flew through the door but stopped short when he saw Taylor standing near an old man.

"James," Taylor said loudly and sternly, "go inside. Now!"

It was too late though, Jacob had already begun running at James.

Taylor screamed but Jacob was fast, too fast. He spun and grabbed James's head, covered his mouth and pulled a blade

322

across his throat faster than you could blink an eye. James crumpled to the ground.

Taylor knew he was dead. Her hands stifled her screams as Jacob grabbed her by the wrist and dragged her to a car parked next to the building.

He maneuvered her to the car. She had until this moment continued to stare at James's body unmoving in the alley, barely putting up a fight against Jacob. He threw the back door to the old sedan open and tossed her inside onto her stomach wrestling her arms behind her.

"No," she said forcefully and with a fair amount of volume.

He ignored her.

"No!" she said loud enough to call the attention of anyone within hearing distance.

He stopped.

"No ties." she said rolling onto her back and pushing herself farther into the car.

The old man nodded, "Get in the front then—you're driving."

Taylor tried to breathe evenly as Jacob slid into the back seat after she climbed into the front one.

"Where?" she asked as she started the car.

"I'll let you know," he answered back.

The engine groaned in the cold. In her rear-view mirror, just as she backed out of the parking space, she saw people filing out of the restaurant and running up to their cars. Jacob turned to look as well, stealthily she slipped the phone out of her pants and tucked it into the seat crevice. Taylor could see the lights of the police cars bounce off the trees as they approached. She turned the car in the opposite direction and pulled away.

Chapter 42

Taylor kept track of where they were going, making notes in her mind of the street names, trying to remember landmarks.

Eventually though Jacob instructed her to turn onto a dirt road. They must have traveled three miles before they came upon a house.

"Don't worry," he said as he watched her head swivel from side to side. "There's no one out here to hear you scream." He chuckled to himself at his own joke.

"Get out of the car. Don't run. I don't want to chase you. And I'll slit your friend's throat if you do, so there's that."

Taylor stepped out of the car and stood still. Jacob took long strides before standing in front of her. He grabbed the back of her neck and brought his lips down to the corner of her shirt.

"What do you have on you?" he whispered in her ear.

Taylor's heart raced as she struggled to breathe. "Nothing."

"I don't believe you," he whispered.

His hands slid over her shoulder and under her arm, all around her waist, over her crotch and down around her ankles. She was breathing so heavily she knew he would find the knife. All she could hope for was that he couldn't feel the fishing line. A sound in the woods interrupted him, Taylor's breath hitched and Jacob stopped and turned. Staring into the darkness willing something out there to challenge him. After a minute had passed he roughly pushed Taylor toward the steps of the house in front of them. Her knife still safely tucked between her breasts.

Breathe, she thought to herself, *you have to remember to breathe.*

Her hands trembled uncontrollably. She'd planned and prepared but nothing could prepare her to walk back into a house with this man. She forced her feet forward, one in front of the other until she was just over the threshold. The house was small, more like a cabin. There was one floor with a kitchen and living area on one side, and what looked like two bedrooms on the other side.

Jacob stood in front of the basement door and Taylor inhaled. He smiled at her discomfort. Mentally, she put up a wall and steeled her face, she was not going to let him enjoy this.

"Because I enjoy games, and mostly because I'm still shocked at the fact that you came back, I'm going to give you a choice. This is a one-time-only choice; once made it can never be unmade."

Taylor nodded accepting his terms.

"You can walk out the front door—I will let you. I will never come near you again, I'll shut down the websites and the trolls. You will be free in every sense of the word."

He smiled and he tilted his head, "or — you come down into this basement with me and save your friend. You accept that you belong to me and are mine. You don't try to run, you don't cause problems, you accept your fate. If you can do this, I will let your friend go home. Two doors, which one do you pick?"

Taylor glanced at the front door. Everything she had ever wanted was through *that* door. Layla, though, was through the basement one. Layla, who was like sunshine and puppy-dog tails, and who didn't deserve any of this.

"Open the basement door," She said.

Jacob smiled, bowing slightly before he strode to the door and yanked it open, motioning for her to descend into it.

The smell of stale air, moisture and dirt assaulted her senses and made her want to flee.

Patrick had told her to wait for her moment. That when it came, she had to act immediately.

She walked slowly toward the basement door giving him any opportunity to make a mistake. He stayed out of arms reach of her though as she started the descent.

Her eyes adjusted quickly to the dimness. One overhead light hung at the bottom of the stairs but that was it. When Layla saw her she started screaming through her gag. Her face covered in dirt and tears. Taylor didn't react to her friend, keeping her emotions in check. If she was screaming then she wasn't dead, and that at the moment was all Taylor cared about.

Taylor was so focused on the footsteps coming down the stairs she didn't see the movement in the corner until it was too late.

Arms grabbed her by the shoulders pulling her into a body, another body, not Jacob's.

"Hey sweetie," the voice said whirling her around to face him. Peter stared back at her, the warmth of his eyes gone. Replaced with pools of nothingness. His face registered delight at seeing her shock.

"No," she whispered.

"Oh yes," Jacob replied. "You remember my little pet, don't you? He used to sing to you, if I'm not mistaken."

Taylor couldn't get past the shock. The little boy. He seemed so little through the cracks of the basement door she thought he'd been younger than her but here Peter stood looking every bit an 18-year-old.

"How?" she asked looking from Peter to Jacob.

"Peter caught my eye in New York. His name back then was dreadful. Do you remember?" Jacob asked him.

A test.

"No, father," Peter responded, well trained.

"It was something silly. Chase or Warren, who can remember? I had to have him, though. He was a scrawny thing, short and skinny but he was the most beautiful child on that playground. He was my first boy, too. I never really paid attention to them before but turns out there is something about little boys. So much more engaging than little girls. He took everything I threw at him and he didn't dissolve into a pool of tears like the girls did before him."

Jacob paced the basement. "They are so irritating after a point. Killing them was really more a matter of wanting some peace and quiet. The others weren't like you two. Jacob's eyes settled on Peter who was still holding Taylor in his grip. You two would have been my magnum opus. I knew Peter was special before I took you, did you know that?" Jacob asked.

Taylor's head nodded as her mind whirled trying to figure a way out of this.

"He had promise . . . to be more than just my toy." Jacob starred longingly at Peter.

"And you," he said as his blue eyes trained on Taylor.

"You, my dear, did you know that you were really too old for me. I had my eyes on another girl—one much younger—but you, sweetheart, you came to me and all but begged me to take you."

Taylor bit her lip. This was what she had known all along. That

327

she had done this to herself. All of it.

"Fate is interesting, isn't it? Putting people together when they need to be."

Peter continued to hold Taylor in a death grip.

Layla had stopped screaming and was sobbing quietly.

Taylor had an idea.

"What's your point?" she asked, an edge in her voice. "So you bred another psychopath? He probably would have become one anyway."

Jacob's eyes narrowed staring her down. "You think you're a clever girl now, don't you? I own you!" he screamed at her. "Everything you are, everything you have done, is because of me. You belong to me."

His outburst scared Taylor but she saw an angle and decided to go for it.

"Belong to you?" she yelled back. "I don't belong to anyone, least of all you. You're an old sick fuck of a man. I came here to save Layla, isn't that what you wanted? Me to come home to call you Daddy again?"

Jacob laughed and Peter joined in.

Taylor was confused.

Peter gripped her shoulders and whirled her around to face him.

"He doesn't want you, father likes children. Your tits, that ass—he doesn't want you *now*. I wanted you," Peter studied Taylor's face, taking glee as this information sunk in. "Father made us leave when you escaped but I wanted you back."

"It's true," Jacob said admiring his son. "He was relentless. At first I thought he just wanted a little friend. But then it became clear that there was something else there. I decided he deserved to have you if that was what he really wanted. He used my name, of course, to rile up the internet trolls, get them to do things in my name. He was running the show though. Even the good old doctor turned out to be useful."

Jacob covered half of his mouth as if he was telling Taylor a secret, "I told him to just kill him."

"No," Taylors face fell, "not Dr. Perna?"

"Did you know," Peter continued his father's diatribe, "that when I first started seeing Dr. Perna he really thought I was just some kid with social anxiety. It took him a little while but he figured out that I was lying, most people can't do that."

Peter smiled, "I liked him actually, but you, you had to try and be a hero. Had to try and save Juliana. How did that work out for you?" She's still ended up dead and you are here, with me."

Taylor started to cry, her resolve crumbling.

"I didn't remember. I wouldn't have left you with him if I had."

"Well, you did," Peter said his eyes empty. "You did leave me. Father wasn't kind when you escaped," Peter's tone was far away.

Peter's entire demeanor changed, like a light switch was turned on. One second his eyes were hollow the next second they were writhing in pain.

"Taylor? Is that you? We have to escape, we have to run."

Peter let go of Taylor, his eyes darted around the room trying to find the exit.

"Fuck," Jacob swore and grabbed a piece of wood that was leaning up against the corner of the basement and, like a baseball player, swung it at Peter's ribs, knocking the wind out of him.

Peter screamed like a wounded animal and hit the floor. Jacob turned to Taylor.

"Peter suffers from a slight personality disorder. That little

329

shit of a kid that I took from New York shows up sometimes. A good beating though and Peter comes right back. Don't worry, he's never gone for very long."

Peter started laughing from the floor, spitting out blood.

"He knew you would come, if we had something you cared enough about."

Peter, now standing, grabbed Taylor's shoulders and used one hand to push her bangs back with his finger.

"We'll have to let your hair grow out, you look like a boy."

Taylor was too astounded to speak, what she just saw was insane. It made sense though why Peter had been so charming at times but then so weird at the homecoming dance. She just couldn't believe that all this time he had been a part of it.

"Do you remember the song I used to sing to you?" he asked her, his breath on her cheek.

Taylor nodded.

"You used to sit at the top of the stairs, you didn't say anything but I knew you were there."

His lips brushed her cheek, just like they had that night in the theater when he leaned in to check on her.

He whispered in her ear, "Do you still like our song? Does it make you feel safe?" His face had twisted into something unrecognizable. Excitement mixed with hatred and crazy.

She didn't respond to him, turning her face away from his.

He gritted his teeth. "Say yes," he said she turned to face him.

"Yes," she said, her eyes lowering.

Peter whooped with glee like a child at Christmas. "You are so beautiful," he said to her, his hands trailing down her shoulder, her heart raced as his hands crossed her stomach and grabbed between her legs. "I can't wait to taste you," he whispered in her ear.

She could feel the vomit rise in her throat.

He released her in a flash giving her free rein to walk around the basement. Jacob stood by the stairs looking old, still in the mask and make-up of Mr. Moriarty.

Taylor breathed heavily, fighting down the panic that threatened to consume her. This was not the plan, this whole time she thought that Jacob wouldn't let her go. Everyone told her pedophiles don't come after grown woman but she wouldn't believe them.

Peter's head turned on a dime, "Wonderful. You will stay here and in return I will kill Layla now and not let her suffer anymore."

"Wait, what?" Taylor said startled. Her head pivoting between Peter and Jacob. "No, this wasn't the deal."

"I lied, I don't need the two of you, she was just bait. Peter wanted you," Jacob sneered at her, "I'm just sticking around in case you have children."

Taylor took a sharp breath. "Peter, please, I'll do anything."

Peter stopped his advances toward Layla.

"I want her to live, that's all. She'll never tell anyone, will you, Layla?" Taylor looked past Peter to Layla. Her face panicked but she nodded no.

"I'll stay with you, I'll do what you want, I'll be what you want, just don't kill her," Taylor begged.

"You are going to do that anyway," Peter said, his eyes cold. He turned back towards her.

Taylor saw no window, no mistake to take advantage of, it was now or never.

She screamed and charged running full tilt into Peter's back using her shoulder as a battering ram. She hit him hard throwing him off balance and they both went careening into

Layla knocking her chair over, breaking the legs on one side.

Jacob stood by the stairs not moving.

Taylor reached inside her shirt and pulled out the hunting knife. It was a three-inch blade and would do enough damage, she hoped.

She started to stab wildly at Peter, but he scrambled up and got on his feet more quickly than she did. He tried to kick her but Taylor rolled out of the way, stepping backward, putting space between the two of them.

Peter wailed like a child whose toy had just been destroyed.

"No! No! No! No!" he screamed. His face menacing as he stalked toward her. "I took care of you. I defied father's orders, brought you food, I sang to you."

Taylor's eyes filled, remembering those acts of kindness.

"And for that," she whispered, "I will kill you now and not let you suffer anymore."

Peter lunged at her. She dropped down into a defensive stance and used his body weight to throw him to the ground. Simultaneously, she swung her arm down with so much force she was sure her shoulder would come out of its socket. The blade sunk deep into his stomach more easily than she thought it would have. She could feel the warmness of his blood seeping out from under the handle.

The knife was slippery and difficult to hold, so she abandoned it. Spinning she grabbed the board Jacob has used to beat Peter.

Jacob had climbed half the stairs during the fight and now stood staring down at Taylor. The stairs were too narrow to swing the weapon she held, so she threw it aside and charged him.

He brought his foot up to kick her and she let him, circling his leg with her arms and using his own momentum and a pull from her to bring them both down the narrow steps. Fumbling through legs and arms she climbed on top of his back and pulled the fishing line out of her bra. His hands reached behind her grabbing on to her shirt to try and pull her off of him. She managed to get the line around his throat and pulled using all her body weight as his fingers struggled to get between the line and his own neck.

He threw himself back against the foundation. Rocks slammed into Taylor's back and head, she saw stars and began to lose her grip.

She heard him gasp. The line cut into her hands and the blood was making it too slippery to hold. She let go of the wire and wrapped her legs around his middle and locked them together in the front. She pulled on her sleeve and wrapped it around his neck pulling again, feeling the skin on her hands tear in protest.

Again he slammed her into the wall she could feel blood oozing down her neck. But she held on.

"I'm going to kill you, you son of a bitch," she whispered in his ear.

He fell to his knees and still she held on.

He sunk to the floor and still she held on.

It took minutes for her to come to her senses again. She released her shirt sleeve, it unwound from his neck with blood stained on it.

She was panting and looked around for Peter but he wasn't there.

Layla lay on the floor unconscious. Taylor ran to her, feeling for a pulse.

Her fingers found a strong steady rhythm in her neck she heard the sirens first and saw the lights second. She crawled over to the pool of blood on the ground and grabbed the knife she had used on Peter.

She stabbed Jacob in the heart. The blood eased out slowly, without a pulse there was no expediency to its exit.

Taylor slumped back against the wall. The adrenaline was still taking the edge off but she could feel blood dripping down her back. She was tempted to reach around and feel her head but thought better of it.

She stared at Jacob's face, now slack. That face that haunted her dreams and her nightmares. Her fingers itched to touch it. She leaned forward, his cheek was still warm. She ran her fingers along the jaw line until she felt a seam and she peeled. First a chin, then a forehead next. His ears were fake like his cheekbones. She took away all the masks until she was able to see him for who he was. His skin was red and irritated. It must have been from being under all that glue and plastic all the time. There were scars on his neck and cheeks and what looked like a burn mark on his forehead. This face was a face that a person would remember.

Seconds later flashlights blinded her as boots stormed down the basement stairs.

"Taylor, are you OK?" Andy stood in front of her a bullet proof vest over his suit.

"I'm OK."

"Thank God," Andy said.

"It worked. The GPS on the phone?."

"Yeah it worked. The signal was a little spotty all the way out here but we were close the entire time. I'm just glad you weren't hurt."

Layla was just starting to regain consciousness. An EMT came in behind the police when they realized that the immediate threat was over.

They worked to unbind her from the chair and assessed her condition.

"Taylor?" she called out once they removed the gag from her mouth. The EMT wouldn't let her move her neck.

"I'm OK," Taylor called out to her, "you OK?"

"I'm OK," she said. "My head hurts."

Taylor snorted, "Mine too."

Two separate ambulances waited for the girls.

A hearse was called as well.

Epilogue

Taylor looked around the room. She couldn't believe that all this was happening.

In the last six months she had finished her high school work, mostly online preferring to not return to the school itself. Instead she had flown out to California and worked with Kristen to establish Camp Taken. Where children from eight to eighteen could attend free of charge if they had been kidnapped for any length of time regardless of the circumstances. The non-profit had taken off. Originally they planned to begin with two weeks of camp but had expanded it to four. Registrations were already full and they were looking into next year. The camp was fully funded as well. Not from Kristen's father but from businesses that Taylor had courted.

The door opened and a kid who looked about twenty years old poked his head into the room.

"They're ready for you."

Taylor and Kristen followed him down a hallway and on to the set. The two were making their rounds on the morning shows. Taylor hadn't known the first thing about business when they began but she was learning quickly. Part of what she had learned was you need a brand and she and Kristen were the perfect spokespeople. The press loved them, loved their story and loved their plan to give back.

As she walked down the hall, Patrick followed close behind

her, he and his team were now her protection full time and were always within arms distance from her.

"Remember don't look at the cameras when you answer the questions," the boy reminded them before gesturing they should take their seats on set.

Taylor could see her mother and Andy in the front row of the audience, sitting next to Mr. and Mrs. Greggor. Andy's hand entwined with Sarah's as they waved hello.

It was only a few moments before they heard their introduction and the lights in front of them turned on.

***

The television in his hotel room was small, but the only bar in town didn't open for another two hours. It was a shame, at least they had a high-definition.

He listened to the introduction and then saw her face.

The wound in his abdomen still pained him. The cut had nearly killed him on its own. Add to it the fact that his bowels had emptied into his stomach causing a massive infection. It was a miracle he was still alive.

Her hair had grown out some but was still very short.

Her face, though, was angelic. Light and happy, she was happy.

He smiled and began to sing.

About the Author

MJ lives in New England with her husband and three children. It wasn't until her third child was born that she decided to leave her career as an event manager and begin her journey towards becoming an author. MJ independently publishes, blogs and offers help to those on their own writing journey. Please like and share her website and tell your friends.

Please, please, please review the book on Amazon. Your feedback is what will help other people see the book when looking for something to read. Without your help no one else will get to experience Taylor's journey as you have.

Part 2 is in the works!! Follow my website to see special unpublished excerpts and get details on when the new book will be released.

You can connect with me on:
- http://www.mjflemingbooks.com
- https://twitter.com/m_flemingagent
- https://www.facebook.com/MJFlemingbooks

Made in the USA
San Bernardino, CA
08 June 2019